Acclaim for
Postcards
from Heartthrob T

"Gerard Wozek's *Postcards* is a fascinating collection of stories that capture the excitement, sensuality, longing, and melancholy of travel—and of life and love as well. His prose is evocative and his descriptions have the clarity and romance one feels when seeing a fabled, foreign city for the first time."

—Jim Tushinski
Author, *Van Allen's Ecstasy*

"In *Postcards from Heartthrob Town: A Gay Man's Travel Tales,* Gerard Wozek crosses continents in a journey of discovery. Poetically detailed and strikingly personal, each story offers a unique setting, and an array of enchanting men encountered and seduced along his journeys; a casual Southern charm of a model-turned radical faerie, a sultry German violinist, an alluring healer of Oaxaca.

Whether winding through trails in Sitges, cruising parks in Berlin, or sipping a perfect borscht in a Krakow cafe, Wozek's adventures carry a sense of longing that any experienced traveler will recognize. But his tales also offer a warning; while the loss of one's wallet or sense of direction may be a common problem, a greater threat is that of heartache that knows no borders."

—Jim Provenzano
Author, *PINS* and *Monkey Suits*

"Gerard Wozek's work glows with a tenderness and understanding for human relationships that's made a life-long fan out of me."

—Aldo Alvarez
Author, *Interesting Monsters*

More Acclaim . . .

"By weaving fictional stories with true ones, Wozek aptly highlights the mythological nature of place itself—how the silent backdrops of our lives act as stages that endure longer than we do. With a clear-cut voice and vision, he paints with watercolors the isolation travelers invariably encounter on their journey, and the sweet alienation which gay protagonists have always known. Perhaps the path of accepting ourselves as queer is parallel, after all, to the path of accepting the world as a whole."

—Matthew Link
Travel Editor and Journalist

"Gerard Wozek poignantly captures the ache of wanderlust in a gay man's heart. His genuine characters explore the geography of men and the landscapes they inhabit. He delivers vivid snapshots illustrating the erotic lure of travel and our own evolving Eros, showing how these transitory experiences can influence and shape our lives. Gerard takes you through the thrill of pursuit, the climax of capture, and the introspection of potential loves lost."

—Sean Meriwether
Editor, *Velvet Mafia*

"*Postcards From Heartthrob Town* journeys to the spirit and soul of homoerotic experience. Wozek writes with a poet's lyrical flair, taking his readers to places both evocative and erotic. Truly one of the most compelling and original voices working in gay literature and travel memoir today."

—Mitzi Szereto
Editor, "Erotic Travel Tales" series

More Acclaim . . .

"The narratives in Gerard Wozek's *Postcards from Heartthrob Town* concern aliens in alien land. Even those stories set within the family home disclose a pervasive alienation: a child from parents, a son from a father, a young man from his family history or from his religious tradition. The theme is universal, and will appeal to a wide audience, but Wozek's tales remind us of its particular significance to queer writers and readers in a tradition stretching back to Aristophanes' myth recounted in Plato's *Symposium* (in which we seek our separated other half) all the way ahead to E. M. Forster's aphorism, 'Only connect.' We are alienated from each other because we are alienated from ourselves. Like the pithy, sometimes cryptic, missives one finds in stacks at a flea market, these 'postcards' convey an ironic message: This place is here, wish you were beautiful."

—Thomas Lawrence Long, PhD
Professor of English and Chancellor's Commonwealth Professor
Thomas Nelson Community College

"Wozek's snippets from a restless writer's memory, and the effortless short stories he spins with such grace from those memories, span the generous possibilities of a fine gay imagination. Some of these tales tingle with erotic potential and sexual satisfaction. Some are essential queer travelogues, fusing personality and place with an assured imagination. Some shout out the glory and the wonder of an innate gay spirituality. Each of them offers the reader the seductive opportunity of joining with the author on the journey, as universal as it is personal, into a questing queer man's uncharted emotions and emerging character."

—Richard Labonte
Editor, *Books to Watch Out For*

NOTES FOR PROFESSIONAL LIBRARIANS AND LIBRARY USERS

This is an original book title published by Southern Tier Editions™, Harrington Park Press®, the trade division of The Haworth Press, Inc. Unless otherwise noted in specific chapters with attribution, materials in this book have not been previously published elsewhere in any format or language.

CONSERVATION AND PRESERVATION NOTES

All books published by The Haworth Press, Inc., and its imprints are printed on certified pH neutral, acid-free book grade paper. This paper meets the minimum requirements of American National Standard for Information Sciences-Permanence of Paper for Printed Material, ANSI Z39.48-1984.

DIGITAL OBJECT IDENTIFIER (DOI) LINKING

The Haworth Press is participating in reference linking for elements of our original books. (For more information on reference linking initiatives, please consult the CrossRef Web site at www.crossref.org.) When citing an element of this book such as a chapter, include the element's Digital Object Identifier (DOI) as the last item of the reference. A Digital Object Identifier is a persistent, authoritative, and unique identifier that a publisher assigns to each element of a book. Because of its persistence, DOIs will enable The Haworth Press and other publishers to link to the element referenced, and the link will not break over time. This will be a great resource in scholarly research.

Postcards
from Heartthrob Town
A Gay Man's Travel Tales

HARRINGTON PARK PRESS®
Southern Tier Editions™
Out in the World
Edited by Michael T. Luongo

Postcards from Heartthrob Town: A Gay Man's Travel Tales by Gerard Wozek

Other Titles of Related Interest

Elf Child by David M. Pierce
Huddle by Dan Boyle
The Man Pilot by James W. Ridout IV
Shadows of the Night: Queer Tales of the Uncanny and Unusual edited by Greg Herren
Van Allen's Ecstasy by Jim Tushinski
Beyond the Wind by Rob N. Hood
The Handsomest Man in the World by David Leddick
The Song of a Manchild by Durrell Owens
The Ice Sculptures: A Novel of Hollywood by Michael D. Craig
Between the Palms: A Collection of Gay Travel Erotica edited by Michael T. Luongo
Aura by Gary Glickman
Love Under Foot: An Erotic Celebration of Feet edited by Greg Wharton and M. Christian
The Tenth Man by E. William Podojil
Upon a Midnight Clear: Queer Christmas Tales edited by Greg Herren
Dryland's End by Felice Picano
Whose Eye Is on Which Sparrow? by Robert Taylor
Deep Water: A Sailor's Passage by E. M. Kahn
The Boys in the Brownstone by Kevin Scott
The Best of Both Worlds: Bisexual Erotica edited by Sage Vivant and M. Christian
Tales from the Levee by Martha Miller
Some Dance to Remember: A Memoir-Novel of San Francisco, 1970-1982 by Jack Fritscher
Confessions of a Male Nurse by Richard S. Ferri
The Millionaire of Love by David Leddick
Skip Macalester by J. E. Robinson
Chemistry by Lewis DeSimone
Going Down in La-La Land by Andy Zeffer
Friends, Lovers, and Roses by V. B. Clay
Beyond Machu by William Maltese
Seventy Times Seven by Salvatore Sapienza
Virginia Bedfellows by Gavin Morris
Planting Eli by Jeff Black
Looking for Love in Faraway Places: Tales of Gay Men's Romance Overseas edited
  by Michael T. Luongo

Postcards
from Heartthrob Town
A Gay Man's Travel Tales

Gerard Wozek

Southern Tier Editions™
Harrington Park Press®
The Trade Division of The Haworth Press, Inc.
New York • London • Oxford

For more information on this book or to order, visit
http://www.haworthpress.com/store/product.asp?sku=5732

or call 1-800-HAWORTH (800-429-6784) in the United States and Canada
or (607) 722-5857 outside the United States and Canada

or contact orders@HaworthPress.com

Published by

Southern Tier Editions™, Harrington Park Press®, the trade division of The Haworth Press, Inc., 10 Alice Street, Binghamton, NY 13904-1580.

PUBLISHER'S NOTE
The development, preparation, and publication of this work has been undertaken with great care. However, the Publisher, employees, editors, and agents of The Haworth Press are not responsible for any errors contained herein or for consequences that may ensue from use of materials or information contained in this work. The Haworth Press is committed to the dissemination of ideas and information according to the highest standards of intellectual freedom and the free exchange of ideas. Statements made and opinions expressed in this publication do not necessarily reflect the views of the Publisher, Directors, management, or staff of The Haworth Press, Inc., or an endorsement by them.

This is a work of fiction. Names, characters, places, and incidents either are the products of the author's imagination or are used fictitiously, and any resemblance to actual persons, living or dead, business establishments, events, or locales is entirely coincidental.

Cover design by Jennifer M. Gaska.

Library of Congress Cataloging-in-Publication Data

Wozek, Gerard.
Postcards from heartthrob town : a gay man's travel tales / Gerard Wozek.
    p. cm.
    ISBN-13: 978-1-56023-623-8 (pbk. : alk. paper)
    ISBN-10: 1-56023-623-X (pbk. : alk. paper)
    1. Gay men—Fiction. I. Title.

PS3623.O95P67 2006
811'.6—dc22
                                                                2006016531

I am on a lonely road and I am traveling
Looking for the key to set me free.

Joni Mitchell

CONTENTS

Foreword:
A Note from "Out in the World"

I have a certain philosophy when I travel. Having visited nearly one hundred countries and all seven continents, I know that each of them is vastly different. Every encounter and experience within each country, whether simply asking for directions, taking a job, or especially, those late-night adventures that make life worth living, will be just as varied and distinctive as those places where I happen to find myself. My first Haworth book, *Between the Palms,* an edited collection of gay travel erotica, was reflective of this philosophy, with each story shared by the various authors tinged with its foreign setting, each erotic encounter from all six inhabited continents as diverse as the languages spoken across the world. And yet these detailed encounters were deeper connections, not merely the chafing of flesh against flesh—the stories were about the powerful unions of souls from dissimilar cultures. The experiences had changed both parties, a piece of each person remaining in the psyche of the other, in much the same way that the broader experience of travel to a locale stayed within each writer's imagination and character forever. From this book was born the series, "Out in the World," Haworth's new collection of gay and lesbian travel themed literature.

I only got to know Gerard Wozek after I had edited *Between the Palms,* but I feel his work shares much in common with the philosophy behind the reasons why I travel and write about my own experiences. Wozek's project here is to divine the elusive spark that brings men together, or in some cases, to locate what causes a rift between them, within these foreign settings. His writing delves into that ignition point created between souls who come from two distinct cultures and in doing so he takes his readers on a passionate journey through both physical and emotional landscapes. It is for these reasons that

Postcards from Heartthrob Town: A Gay Man's Travel Tales
Published by The Haworth Press, Inc., 2006. All rights reserved.
doi:10.1300/5732_a

this collection, *Postcards from Heartthrob Town,* is the first book in the "Out in the World" series. Wozek's themes of shifting identity and wanderlust aptly reveal the connections fused between men from one part of the world with those of another. How those idiosyncratic places and people impact the traveler's sense of self is well detailed in each of Wozek's stories in this book.

Wozek's storytelling is as skillful and emotional as good poetry, with particulars in each story your heart will choose to linger on. In the first story, "Tenderness Among Wolves," a tale which reveals his emerging homoerotic feelings as a child playing with G.I. Joes in his secret clubhouse as neighbor boys played football on an adjoining field, readers are escorted back to childhood, to stirrings barely intuited or understood. There is one line especially in reading this account that absolutely halted me, which had nothing to do with the wonderment of budding sexuality. The author describes how in winter he would wander alone and "step on the thin layer of ice that forms over spring dandelion heads and watch my boot make white veins over the frozen surfaces." He was in awe of the weather and how its physical influences become a new way to play when one is a lonely, misunderstood child lost in naive thoughts. I did the same as an introverted child, but never thought about it again until reading Wozek's description of the act. It is these remarkable details, these acute memories of geographical and emotional points within the book, that envelop and inspire the reader throughout this collection. The reader derives a powerful satisfaction following Wozek through these travel travels as he expresses his intimate motivations to set out on flirtatious encounters both with location and other men.

In conversations about the book during its development, Wozek explained what he was hoping to convey throughout these short stories. Our exchanges focused on how a gay man defines his impulse to trek to foreign locales, how setting off far from home heightens one's desire to merge on many levels with others in an unfamiliar terrain, and how memory and childhood inform an urge to journey out as an adult. Through it all, Wozek's lyrical prose uncovers how his own sensuality is reflected in his travels, how he uses it to create connections with men, and what he calls, the "spirit of place" he keeps encountering again and again throughout the world. I believe he achieves everything he hopes for and more within the pages of this book.

Delving into this intense and well-crafted work is to embark on a memorable and sensuous journey. Turn the page and begin your own passage into this author's heart and mind, and let this ardent experience inspire you on your own travels.

Michael Luongo
Senior Editor,
Haworth's Out in the World series
on GLBT travel literature

Tenderness Among Wolves

I invent the world from inside my playhouse. My G.I. Joes have never left home or been to war. I have buried their jeep ranger in a gopher hole along with their tiny plastic bayonets, combat helmets, and grenades. They wear long skirts fashioned from wheat stalks and field grass. They dangle on wires when I want them to fly. They practice the Kama Sutra on one another in secret. Inside my playhouse, they embrace, they kiss, and they writhe under the weight of one another's bodies. They live out their deepest passions in private.

My playhouse is made from cast-off railroad planks and a tangle of willow reeds that have fallen from the trees behind my parents' home. It leans against my grandfather's chinchilla house, a small concrete hovel covered with a roof thatched from Irish grass and putty. I have been told that a long time ago, the pelts of these tiny rodents were skinned off here, tanned and sewn into winter coats. No one comes near the old workshop with its active wasp hives built into the corners, and the untrained eye could easily miss the barricaded lean-to I've constructed next to the back wall of my grandfather's corroding workstation.

I live with my brother and my parents in an unincorporated rural subdivision in southern Illinois. There are development signs everywhere on empty lots that are waiting to be dug up and turned into hot real estate properties. We moved here three years ago when my father's factory relocated. Most of the time, he labors at double shifts making deodorant soaps and dandruff shampoos for Armor Dial. I can always tell when it's four-thirty in the afternoon because that's

This chapter appeared originally under the same title in the *Blithe House Quarterly* (http://www.blithe.com/) 2(2). Copyright 1998 Gerard Wozek. Reprinted with permission of the author.

Postcards from Heartthrob Town: A Gay Man's Travel Tales
Published by The Haworth Press, Inc., 2006. All rights reserved.
doi:10.1300/5732_01

when the smokestacks unleash their burning tallow oils. The air is always thick and pasty and smells like the rotting corpse of a run-over skunk.

I don't always feel like I'm home when I'm inside my family's house, so I go wandering to see where I belong. I spend most of my time playing in my lean-to or wandering the leftover cornfields and empty lots behind our suburban ranch, walking through the sod fields, singing to the red and purple maple trees. Once I made up an entire operetta about an enchanted forest with Viking-helmeted grasshoppers and lovelorn field mice.

Inside the play hut, my Joes sleep together inside neatly stacked Buster Brown shoeboxes. On the low ceiling above, I have pressed on cracked appliqués of cherries and tangelos and a galaxy of glow-in-the-dark stickers shaped like shooting comets and stars. There is a tangle of sleeping bags and Indian blankets tossed over the painting tarp that covers the wet, rotting smell of meadow grass underneath. I've strung puka shells across the low entrance and set up my tape recorder on a bamboo breakfast-in-bed tray. There are half-melted beeswax candles set inside glass mason jars, surrounding piles of cassettes and album covers that open up to liner notes and photographs of Karen Carpenter and her older sibling Richard.

Sometimes I think I want to be Karen Carpenter. I think of her as the Voice of Perpetual Sorrows or Our Lady of Unrequited Love. I don't know exactly what Karen means when she says "no one in the world ever had a love as sweet as my love." But I like to lie on the ground of my playhouse, thinking of Karen falling prey to the shoddy romantic trappings painted into her lyrics. She is the overdubbed, undernourished girl drummer—willowy, slightly gawky, and stiffly posed next to Richard on the inlay of these airbrushed album sleeves. It doesn't matter that her bangs always look like they have been cut with dull pruning shears, or that her stiff hippie lace collars make her teeth look buckled. I hold up a mirror with leafy willow branches falling over my high forehead and crew cut and start to lip-synch to her remake of the Beatles' "Ticket to Ride." My mouth forms the words: "he said that living with me was bringing him down," but it is Karen's melancholic alto that seeps out.

My brother says that sometimes he jacks off to fantasies of Melanie and Olivia Newton-John. He says that Janis Joplin would "probably be a good lay when she's not super trashed on dope" and that Grace Slick from Jefferson Airplane is "kind of a fox." He says he likes to think he'll marry someone who looks like Carly Simon or even Cher. When he asks me who I like, I don't say a word. I look at the cover of the Carpenters' *We've Only Just Begun* album and I think of Karen's brother Richard. I think of sitting next to him on a deserted stretch of beach in California. I imagine the iridescent sprinkles from breaking Pacific waves behind us and the heat from Richard's hand as it grazes my own. I think of singing a song with him and touching his dishwater-blond curls. But I don't tell my brother Wayne this. He thinks I like Karen.

I have never let anyone into my playhouse. Not even and especially not Wayne. Sometimes I'll hear him playing with his jock buddies across the way in the mowed-down cornfield where they're supposed to build a church. I hear their rough voices from my lean-to and their exaggerated groaning as they shove muscle into one another, their moans as a football goes out of bounds. I imagine their rough tackles, their sweat tricking onto one another, their soiled callused hands groping and tearing at one another's clothes. I imagine myself caught somewhere in their pile-ons and crunches, tumbling and somersaulting through their heated crush. Sometimes I think I hear my name floating on the air, in between their yelps and curses, but it's just the odd way the wind whirrs through the vents in the tar boards that serve as the ceiling and walls for my sequestered play hut.

In the early fall, I like to crack open milkweed pods or step on the thin layer of ice that forms over spring dandelion heads and watch my boot make white veins over the frozen surfaces. Sometimes I see a murder of crows or a wandering turkey and on rare occasions, I spy what looks to be a scared coyote. My brother says it's just a rabid dog that lives in the wild, but when I see it I could swear that it is more like a wolf. It looks as though it is gun shy, as though it has been wounded as it stumbles and limps over the rotting gray cornstalks. From a distance it looks like it might have sharp fangs as I watch it shuddering behind rusting combines and in the recesses of the farm pastures left fallow.

"Someone ought to shoot that pathetic creature," my brother once said. But in the summer sometimes when I sleep out next to the chinchilla house, I hear it howling in the distance or choking on the chalky night air. I leave a dish of water and a bowl of Milk-Bones for it. I think I might be able to make friends with it and tame it somehow, but it stays far off, never sniffing near the backyard swing set, its tracks never loping toward the hut.

At Clinton Middle School, I walk with a boyish swagger, keeping my upper body rigid and my legs slightly extended. I dress in torn OshKosh jeans and faded flannel shirts, sometimes sporting a Cleveland Indians baseball cap for a jock effect. When the guys talk about "humping some bitch in the bathroom" or "copping a feel under the football stands" I smile and say that's cool.

I always try to imagine how those boys think. How they walk around in their football jerseys and pinch the rear ends of cheerleaders. How they hunger for jacked-up racing cars spinning out of control on drag strips or watching oiled-up wrestlers on Saturday television beating on someone's craggy nose. I never think of skateboarding in the school parking lot or lighting firecrackers inside of people's mailboxes. I never conspire to douse cats with lighter fluid and set them on fire—swinging them by their tails. I think of Karen Carpenter. I think of squashed desire. I think of being rescued from a world where I sing and nothing comes out.

My mother has informed me that my cousin Leigh will be staying with us for a weekend while my aunt and uncle make arrangements to move into our subdivision. When I think of Leigh I think of smoke rings. The summer I turned nine, Leigh and his parents came to a family picnic. My Uncle Kenny made a huge bonfire and we ate charred pig ribs and drank warm strawberry Kool-Aid. Leigh couldn't have been more than twelve or thirteen then when he took a large cotton blanket and demonstrated how the Shawnee Indians communicated with other tribes using a covert code of smoke signals.

"We learned this in Boy Scouts." To some it may have appeared that Leigh was boasting, but there was a kind of sincerity in the way that he spoke; a vulnerability that made him seem soft, as though he could be easily overtaken or preyed upon. I wanted him then. I thought my cousin was the bravest guy I'd ever seen, the way he'd puff up his chest and slap Wayne on his back. I wanted his masculinity and his open candor. I admired the comfortable way he could move his hard body. I'd let my eyes linger on his full lips, his thick, black eyelashes, his strong tanned neck.

I remember that Leigh and I once talked about the great magician Houdini. We talked about sustaining breath in a glass box that is plunged into deep water. I remember that Leigh and I had gone into my room once and we experimented with taking quick short breaths and exhaling out all the air from our lungs. We'd stand behind each other and press out all the oxygen until tiny prickles formed on the top of our heads. We'd take turns falling down in a dizzy stupor. I'd come out of that woozy state feeling as though I'd been walking outside of my body, still feeling Leigh's arms pressed around the cave of my ribs.

When I think of Leigh now I still become breathless. I still feel woozy. I still find prickles on my arm and a strange hollow feeling in my gut. When I think of Leigh now I see myself stranded on an island of dense fog; endless curling vapor trails and the soft, deep purr of his voice.

My cousin Leigh arrives the day my brother gets shin splints. My mother is fussing over Wayne with cartons of Epsom salts and totes a leaky hot water bottle to his bedside with mugs of steaming Ovaltine. When Leigh walks in, he seems much taller than I remembered him three or four years ago, and there is a sandy stubble of hair around his full lips and chin that gives him a soft, sylvan look.

I sit across from my handsome cousin and I feel misshapen, obtuse. I think of my mother's story of purgatory and how the embers of one's sins can burn the untarnished lining of one's soul. I think I have fallen into that silent limbo as I sit on the divan watching, then trying not to watch Leigh. When Leigh moves it is as though he is conscious of a certain warm energy that is snaking through his body and it comes out as pulses of white light through his fingertips. He doesn't fidget or jerk his head back the way I've seen Wayne or other guys at school do. His voice doesn't boom off of the walls. He lets his fingers tangle around the chestnut curls of his hair and this one rhythmic motion seems to reveal a kind of innate sensuousness.

Sitting so near to him, I think I can hear the blood beat inside of my own head. I think that I can feel my chest ribs trembling, my breath turning to vapor.

"I saw you come from behind those trees in the backyard," Leigh points to a spot beyond the clump of willows out the window. "What's out there?"

"Just some soggy marsh fields; nothing really."

"I was thinking we could go exploring back there while I'm here. You know, we don't have much farmland back in Akron." Leigh moves over and lowers his head as if he is speaking to me confidentially. "Do you smoke?" Leigh raises his thick eyebrows as if to suggest a quiet camaraderie.

"Not really."

"Don't tell your ma or anyone, okay? I got a whole carton of Camels in my jacket and I was hoping we could go out back and mainline some nicotine." He moves in close so I can almost feel his full lips on my cheek. "You know, we can shoot the shit. I just don't want anyone to know."

"Sure." I am thinking now of my grandfather's chinchilla house but that seems too close to my play hut and I'm afraid my secrets will be uncovered.

"Take me out there tomorrow." Leigh caresses his soft chin hairs with his index finger. "I want to get the lay of the land. Maybe we could even throw a tent and camp out there."

I nod as my mother brings in a plate of unwrapped Suzy Q's and some chocolate milk. She offers Leigh a set of blankets and a pillow for sleeping on the couch. I say good night to him but our soft conversation jostles in my mind.

Coiled in my bed, I think that I hear something moving outside my window. There is a tender, muffled heaving. Then a whimpering sound as if someone is crying. I think it must be the crippled coyote and I move toward my window. In the hazy moonlight, I think that I see the outline of a shadow darting, hobbling in and out of a line of bushes. I think I hear a wailing or a sobbing sound. I try to see, try to make my eyes adjust to the night. I keep scanning the dark horizon of fields, but I still can't make my eyes see anything.

By early morning, I have dismantled the interior of my playhouse. I have removed the boxes of military dolls, the strung-up shells, the candles and jars of dried honeysuckle and jonquil petals, the cassette tapes and album dust jackets. I stow everything into the chinchilla workstation under a large metal table where the tiny animals were once pinned down and flayed open. I go back to the house to get Leigh and we return to the empty playhouse I've built.

"Wow. Is this for real?" He surveys the interior of the now-vacant hut. "Can we sleep out here tonight?"

I stand on ground that seems to be caving in.

"I mean, it would be so cool to lay out here under the stars. We could build a fire, blow farts into the wind. Man!" Leigh sits Indian style on the ground next to the hut and begins to stake out the territory.

We return home and gather small items for the campout. My mother provides us with extra sheets, a quilt for the chill, a set of kerosene lanterns, and a jumbo bag of marshmallows. I'm thinking all the while of Leigh's hands, of the way my breathing changes when he stands next to me, of the gentle way he charms and makes me forget myself.

"Let's pretend we're explorers," Leigh says. "You know, like Lewis and Clark, we're setting out into unmapped territory."

"Say we're looking for that elusive water route across North America," I try to hold back the excited pitch in my voice. "Say we're going to keep a journal of everything we find there. Say we'll chart the glacier lilies and the grand fir trees. We'll be journeymen taking careful notes of our wild travels to new territory."

Leigh seems to be deeply listening to what I'm saying as I go on inventing the landscape we'll traverse.

"We'll draw pictures of the black-billed magpies and the northern bobcats. The leaves of a fernleaf desert parsley or an Engelmann's spruce. We'll survey the customs of the Blackfoot Indians or the Paw-nee or Tillamook. You ever just wanna take off like that?" I watch as Leigh begins to sketch the outline of a cumulus cloud in his mind.

"I know something is bound to find me and sweep me out of this place." Leigh closes his eyes for a moment as if the cloud is resting on his thick eyelashes, then whispers, "So let's go."

Inside the weedy hut, Leigh takes off his boots and props his pillows up against the side. "Remember, it's a secret." Leigh strikes a pack of Camels on the palm of his hand. "Sure is quiet out here. What do you do with all of this quiet?"

"I like that about the country, I guess." I feel nearly immobile, my joints stiff, like the rusted screws that hold together my soldier dolls.

"I don't know. Back in Akron there is so much going on. I never have the time to notice how soft . . ." his voice drifts off as he inhales his cigarette deeply, letting the nicotine whirl through his veins.

"You really like to smoke, don't you?" I try not to meet his eyes.

"C'mere," Leigh rolls over to where I'm sitting. "You can get a real buzz off of this." He places his hand on my head and moves his face very close to my own. "Now," he instructs, "you inhale when I exhale."

His lips seem to brush over mine as a finger of warm smoke chafes over my open mouth and face. I can't help but start to choke.

"You're just a pup," he laughs and begins to blow cigarette smoke rings into the air. "Do you remember that old Indian code?"

I watch him make loops of smoke for what seems to be a silent eternity. "Just like the Shaw-neee!" He smirks and folds his arms behind his head.

The idea of being so close to him has made me still inside. I watch the small rings dissolve in the air. Outside there are locusts eating up the damp night. I watch Leigh, and then look away when his eyes attempt to meet mine.

"Do you ever hunt out here?" Leigh snaps the awkward hush.

"I've seen pheasant roam around the county line wire fences but I don't think anyone ever shoots at them."

"My dad likes to hunt, you know." The clumsy silence descends again.

"You and Wayne went hunting once, didn't you?"

"Yeah. He really got into it, dressing up in camouflage like we were in Vietnam or some shit." Leigh has a way of making you feel as though he is always telling you a secret. "He's really got killer instincts, your brother. I mean, the way he held his breath and aimed, just bagged that poor beast. I'll never forget it."

"What happened?"

"It was just the way your brother watched that stag die. You know, that thing was alive and when we went up to it, you could see the eyes still open and the blood pouring out of its temple. It was still breathing and Wayne didn't even flinch." Leigh inhaled deeply from the filter tip of his Camel. "I mean, shit, it's like we're all untamed, just out for the kill, out for the fun of it." He blows another ring into the sticky air.

Silence invades the playhouse. Through the light coming in from the lanterns, it seems as if I have never seen this hut before. I think of my G.I. Joes sunk into their carnal embraces and remember that I once showed my collection to Leigh. They were dressed in Army fatigues and Marine uniforms then and I can't help but wonder what Leigh would think if he could see them as they are now, braided in palm leaves and wheatgrass, the little joints of their hands grasping one another's scarred faces and necks.

"So what do you do in the summer?" Leigh fumbles for another cigarette.

"I like to sing." I can't believe the words have come out.

"You sing what?"

"I mostly just make stuff up." I know my face is inflamed but in the lantern light I don't think he can tell.

Leigh begins to sing, "Whee, dee dee dee, duh dee dee dee dee, the lion sleeps tonight."

I chime in, "Hush my darling, don't fear my darling, the lion sleeps tonight."

Together we join in for a chorus of, "A weema-wep, a weema wep . . ."

The air that was once turgid and foreign now seems to be charged with a lightning energy. We begin to make up our own lyrics to songs we already know. Then, we just sing in any fashion. We sing about a pirate who has lost his treasure map but continues to search for his bounty until he dies. We sing about a lost planet that is sending out signals to other planets so that it can be recovered. We sing about swimming in a river that makes you invisible. We sing about flying in our dreams. We sing about the Shawnee Indians and their secret smoke ring code. We make up songs about a mermaid whose kisses bring dead sailors back to life and about the astronauts who cut their oxygen pipes and perpetually free float. We sing about waterfalls that gush gallons of Dr Pepper and trees that grow steaming Pop-Tarts. When we can't think of things to make up, we sing songs we remember from off the radio.

When Leigh pulls the sleeping bag over his body and turns over, I know that our serenade to the night locusts has ended. I sit up, watching Leigh's firm chest slowly move up and down. A slit of moon in the pitch of the hut makes Leigh look a little like Richard Carpenter, with his spiraling curls and soft features.

I sing a Carpenters' song to myself: "Long ago and oh so far away, I fell in love with you." Leigh stirs in his sleeping bag and the air is heavy and smells like tobacco. My skin and hair smell like stale Camel smoke.

I watch Leigh's breathing grow heavy. I watch, try not to watch. I see his mouth open and think of the gentle curve of his lips where he blew smoke rings. I think of Houdini and how he would be able to imperceptibly place his mouth over Leigh's and steal a silent kiss. How that breathing would merge and become one solitary long breath, a seal to a clandestine bond. I begin to ask myself if I have read the smoke signals correctly.

Then I see myself in that James Dean movie *Rebel Without a Cause,* and I think about that sidekick of his, Plato, and I wonder if I have become that character. I wonder what really is this obsessive fascination I have for my cousin; this fugitive boy who barely talks to me, or makes me feel I am his equal.

What makes me hungry for Leigh? Sometimes I don't think he is that smart. I suppose that he smells good. The curve of his lips compels me to think about kissing him. But he doesn't make me want to tell him my secrets. He doesn't give me back to myself. Still, I guess that there is something in that maleness. Something in that rough, sinewy exterior, that laugh, that wild breath, the way his eyes flash. I ask myself if it is Leigh or if it is just being with a boy. Just being near him. I want to absorb all of that male light. I want to take in all of that boy scent. I want to have his swagger, his confident air, the way he is included in the affairs of the world, the way he stands in place as though he belongs there.

I watch Leigh for a very long time. I keep vigil over his involuntary reflexes, watching his muscles tense and then soften. I inch my body over to the sleeping figure. I watch his nostrils flare out. I listen for the deep breathing that comes only within the dream state. I feel like a predatory animal as I position my head over his and draw back. I think for a moment of Karen Carpenter and how she is always falling for all the wrong men. Or how she sang, "time and time again the chance for love has passed me by."

I place my head directly over Leigh's. I wait. I listen for his slow heavy breath wheezing through his softly parted lips. I silently bend over. I place my mouth on his and pause. I let my lips linger on his to feel their texture. I can taste the tobacco residue mixed with burnt marshmallow. I taste Leigh. I draw back, holding my breath in. I find it impossible to breathe. I can't make myself breathe. His eyes are wide open.

I sit up. I look out the entrance to the fort. Leigh rustles in his sleeping bag, then turns over. I let the silence devour my insides, ravage the air in the playhouse. My body is burning as though I've fallen through to the coals of my mother's Catholic purgatory.

I move away from the lean-to. I look up at the sky swollen with dead stars. The stars succumb to the mercy of thin air and vanish. I walk, and then begin to run. I feel a trail of cool sweat inching down my back. I look toward the shell of the playhouse behind me and the makeshift hut has completely vanished. It has imploded into nothingness. It has been obliterated, become a huge smoke ring ascending and evaporating into the sky.

I think of my Joes with their tiny mouths clamped over one another's. I think of the airless cardboard boxes turning into little coffins and I can see the naked dolls squirming to get oxygen. I begin to sing in a low, breathy voice, "don't you remember you told me you loved me, baby, you said you'd be coming back this way again, baby?"

I stand in the center of my backyard and picture Karen Carpenter languishing on my old swing set. I think of her dowdy hair, her thin, colorless features. I think of her eyes that hold in all the collapsed hopes of all the sissy preteen boys and mawkish girls in the world. I think of her mop-headed brother and how he duped his own sister into becoming a victim in every song she sang, a vapid Pollyanna blathering about vacuous relationships. How she couldn't be Joni Mitchell or Joan Baez and sing about how men were polluting the environment and how you could miss them but live just fine without them all the same. I sing for Karen because right now I think that she's just a sad, frail voice encircled in a world of brutish men. I imagine Karen sitting here now and dropping my head on her wan shoulder and sobbing. I sing to her, "baby, baby, baby, baby oh baby, I love you, I really do."

From behind the chinchilla house, I think I hear someone shout out the word "queer." I can't be sure if it is the wind coming down the knoll or if Leigh has gathered his senses and is rabid for me. My whole body is perched to hear the night sounds.

I am not on a faraway journey. I have not left the confines of my neighborhood. In my mind I was at a campsite on the Kaskaskia River in uncharted Illinois. Or I was entering the Great Plains to list and describe unknown plants and animals. In my mind I have been on a great expedition to name the world. I was a traveler, content to wander and let myself be claimed by the soil under my feet. But I shake to discover that I am nowhere but here. I try to regain my balance by looking at the antennas sticking out from all the roofs around me; I am still on foreign terrain.

I think of the circle of men that hold up the planet. The men who carry baseball bats and hunting rifles. The men who don't flinch when they take a knife to cut open an animal. The men who dress in uniforms and set up minefields. The men who substitute slang words when referring to women's body parts. The men who, when met with a certain tenderness, turn over on their sides and pretend to go on sleeping.

In the still stark air I think I hear the wailing of the coyote. I can hear him rustling through the bushes and I begin to make out his jagged outline. I see his ratty, cocklebur-covered fur as the wolfhound hobbles through our grove of willow trees. It looks as though he is bleeding and it seems there is a whole universe of fear in his narrowing eyes.

The moon churns above like a murky, orange poultice. The light glints off of several of his long, sharp teeth. The wolf stares back at me, foam creeping up at the edges of his black lips. I sit perfectly still, my breath forming perfect vapor rings in the evening air.

Postcards from Heartthrob Town

I'm invisible. I can see my father in the front seat of our wood-paneled station wagon. I can see his stubbled jaw jutting and the outline of a pulsing vein at his right temple. I watch his eyes move from the pavement of Interstate 24 to the rearview mirror. For half a second I could swear he looks right at me. But I know better. My father doesn't see me. He sees the long highway ahead of him and the dazzling white lines that slip underneath the car wheels. He sees the roadside billboards and the blasted granite that wedges out on either side of the paved road. He sees the names of railroads and graffiti painted on the flaking overpasses. He sees the hood ornament that catches the gritty wind and the gossamer of shredded dragonfly wings. My father doesn't see me.

My mother shifts uncomfortably in the front seat. She's been fumbling with an outdated road atlas since Lexington and trying to snag a strong radio signal from country stations that meander in and out of listening range. For a moment, Loretta Lynn warbles, "I'm gonna take this chian from around my finger. And throw it just as far as I can sling 'er."

"Can't a man think?" My father flicks the dial off and for a moment we're suspended in the hushed mountain air. He looks unnerved, as though he's holding his breath underwater. Outside, the chalky fog of the Smoky Mountains enfolds the automobile and smothers us in its lacy shroud.

We're going to Florida, or as I like to think of it, Heartthrob Town, a destination that I have anticipated for months. We want to clop

This chapter originally appeared as "Postcards from Heart Throb Town" in the *Harrington Gay Men's Fiction Quarterly*, 2(4):53-64. Copyright 2001 Gerard Wozek. Reprinted with permission of the author.

Postcards from Heartthrob Town: A Gay Man's Travel Tales
Published by The Haworth Press, Inc., 2006. All rights reserved.
doi:10.1300/5732_02

around in our spongy thongs, get snagged by the amateur art galleries and the Aunt Nancy's Fudge Shops that line the gulf vista along the boardwalk. We want Donald Duck sunglasses and snow globes with plastic palm trees flecked in glitter. We want to inhale the candy orange blossom cologne and test the desk lamps fashioned from pelican beaks and driftwood. Bring on the glass-bottom boat tours and the mechanical cheetahs that swing on the Jungle Book safari ride, the tingle of sun balm on overexposed shoulders, the smell of coconut lip balm mingling with the menthol of the ice cold Solarcaine.

On the way to Heartthrob, I look over my postcard collection. I take out my old Keds shoebox and finger through these souvenir notes, most of them sent to me by friends who reside there. There are stacks of them and I keep turning them over, reading their scrawl and well wishes:

Come back soon, my good boy. It's not the same without you.

The messages on the backs of these secret cards are for my eyes only. I read them to remember where I've traveled to, where I belong. Some of them smell like lemony vervain or drugstore musk oil, some like the dollar bills folded into my father's humidor. A few have a scent like the strange bleach odor that leaks out of my dad's sock and underwear drawer, a place where I run my fingers to feel his soft oversized BVDs all neatly folded and waiting to hold my father's skin.

"Honey are you hiding something in that box there?" My mother's question mark floats over our baggage and seems to sway in the atmosphere.

"No, it's just some old shells from our last trip." I try not to let my voice waver. "Just stuff." I wedge the overstuffed box back into my Cub Scout knapsack and she turns the page of her magazine.

If I peek over the Styrofoam ice chest where my father has stowed the Orange Crush and the Polaroid film wrapped in foil, I can see the expressway lamps fade out against the brightening sky. Through the elongated windows I watch the predawn light dust the snowy tops of this Kentucky mountain range. By the time the Holiday Inns have cut off their blinking arrows, I'm propped up against our Samsonites, searching for one of those road signs painted with Rocky the mountain elf—a cartoonish fairy who offers each motorist the exact number of miles it takes to reach the Lookout Mountain Resort. I read that it is possible to view six states from the vantage point of Lookout Peak, see the prehistoric splendor of Mammoth Caves or take the funicular ride up to Ruby Falls. But somehow my father has built up enough stoic indifference to not visit the mushroom guru painted into green Peter Pan tights.

My father works with hard things, drill bits and metal screws, steel beams and cranes. My father wears a hard silver cap when he works. He walks on solid iron beams and likes to end his sentences with phrases like "stupid Polack" or "dumbass." He likes to chew spit tobacco, make songs like "Yankee Doodle" out of his extended belches. My father sports an army crew cut, has a scar on his wrist from the war, likes to talk about ships and history and guns. My father is no sissy. And now, with his right foot sewn to the gas pedal, I know better than to suggest to him that we take the detour to Lookout Mountain in order to break off faerie ice crystals or crawl through torch-lit caves. Instead, we swerve into a rest area—a cottage toilet squat sequestered behind two buggy cypress trees and a gravel path dotted with garbage cans chained to cement posts.

"We want to hit Marietta by early dusk so don't take all day," my father warns as he hastens us to the restroom before popping a can of Crush. I push away from the car and move into a circular grove of pines looming behind the wooden bathroom stalls. There are cigarette butts strewn under the boughs and I follow a footpath toward an overlook. I make my way up the side of a hill to a shoddy wire fence where there is a steep drop off into a craggy gulch. For a second I think that I must have stumbled onto Lookout Peak.

"Hey, I'm up here!" I'm waving my arms to catch my father's attention but he's drawing a line over the map of Georgia. I look back at the red dirt on the side of the gorge and the boulders that seem as though they could be set in motion with one low moan, one keening pitch, one wail set loose from my lungs.

For a moment, I want to spread my arms like moth wings and let go of the spiky wire that separates me from oblivion. I want to dive into the heap of stones at the bottom of this gouged-out hole; let the wind carry me down into the ravine where tourists will mistake my bones for tree stumps. If I could be that line of foxglove traced into the shadowy recesses of this mountain glade. If I could be a vein of ore roping its way through the crevice of this cored-out hill.

"Louis, what are you doing up there?" My mother yells up at me as she picks through her wicker satchel. "We're waiting for you! C'mon already."

I throw my arms in the air and race back down the side of the embankment toward the idling car. "I'm Rocky the elf!" I'm flailing my arms from side to side, skipping over strewn pinecones and crushed beer cans. "I'm Rocky!"

There is a look on my father's face. It's a look as if to say "What desert is this and where can I find water?"

Our eyes don't meet. My father's line of vision takes in only so much. He seems to ignore the sprig of poppy entwined in my red hair, seems indifferent to the violets and daisy heads that I've crushed in my hand. He doesn't seem to see any of this. He studies the side-view mirror and positions the glass so that it reaches the correct angle. He looks at the license plate of the car tailing behind us. He accelerates and cuts off another vehicle trying to pass us. He watches the eyes of the passengers in the other cars and smiles at their dazed expressions. He watches the long tangle of road signs tacked over the expressway. He looks at the long highways ahead of him and bores into nothingness.

My mother points out the clay stain on my linen shorts and begins to pour ginger ale into a clump of tissues. "Maybe the carbonation will loosen this." She sounds like the whizzing of a small electric blender, a familiar melancholy laced through her edgy whine. She rubs the copper spot but it seems to only get worse. "It's hopeless." She drops the soggy tissue into my lap. "We'll have to soak it at the motel."

When I think of my mother sometimes, I see her wedding picture instead of her broad, pudgy face. I see an airbrushed photograph of an ingenue, a debutante with a white veil. Anyone looking at that picture would see Jane Wyatt in *Father Knows Best* or Donna Reed. When I look at her face I think she would have been happier if she'd followed her modeling career through or if she'd kept dancing on *The Lawrence Welk Show.* But instead she traded her strap-on pumps and shoulder pads for corduroy dusters. She picked up the accordion and invented polka songs to play at first communions. She dried flowers and learned how to can Christmas yams. She invented bedtime stories about the erratic lives of the saints.

I no longer see signs pointed toward the Lookout Mountain Resort or the overlook of Enchantment. By the time we've hit the Georgia border, the Tennessee mountain dwarf has given way to another roadside character—an athletic woman in a shrink-wrapped pink strapless bathing suit. Set in midair over an advertisement for Atlanta's "world famous" Lido Motel, she prompts a sensation of chlorinated water up my nose and the rush of gravity loss in the deep end of a cement swimming pool. There are at least twelve billboards with this diving diva springing off her board, but eventually we pass the last-chance off-ramp. We never stay at the Lido. But I think of meeting her there sometimes. I think of her resigned caved-in features and her swan dive on the billboard sign. I think that for her it is better to never hit the water, to retain perfect posture and perpetually free float over the sooty Georgia expressway, while sleepy motorists imagine the jet-warmed water temperature of that Olympic-sized pool and her sensuous splash that must eventually break the surface.

My father owns that cliché "It's never like you think it will be," but I begin to think that perhaps he's on to something. I remember the first time driving down to Miami. I was nine when he told me that the mermaids at the Weeki Wachee water show zipper themselves into fake fins and use oxygen pumps to fill their lungs.

"Mermaids don't exist," he stated emphatically. "It's all just a myth."

"And mermen, they're not real either?"

My father simply rolled his eyes. Still, I want to suspend my disbelief just like the diver stretched out over the cold surface of the painted pool. I want to free float over the grasshopper air of this interstate and see into every car, into the Ruby Falls and the lantern-lit caves. I want to bounce on the pulse of the heart of the Smoky Mountains, because I know there is such a thing. I know there is.

My father has clamped down on the accelerator as he pulverizes a butterscotch candy in his mouth. My mother has made a six-o'clock reservation at the Howard Johnson Hotel in Marietta, Georgia, so the car pulls off the expressway and heads past the farmers' peach stands and tin-roofed pecan pie huts and finally into a Piggly Wiggly for groceries.

Once inside this air-conditioned dinosaur, I'm overtaken by the images on the food. I want to stand next to the delirious Contadina maiden in the tomato patch or merge with the conspiritorial hush on the bearded lips of the caped, sunken-eyed Rembrandts sulking on the Dutch Masters cigar-box lid. I want to uncover the mystery in the bodhisattva-like stare of the Land O'Lakes Hiawatha, spellbound in the dairy case, or kiss the Quaker Oats minister with his white tufts of snowy hair. Under the influence of a piped-in Neil Sedaka, it has become obvious that my mother and I haven't come for just groceries, but because we're voracious for adventure, which seems as easy to take on now as it would be to buy a package of Uncle Ben's New Orleans-style rice.

My father fills our flimsy ice chest with cans of chocolate soda, rye bread, and liverwurst. He tosses in Lava soap and shaving cream, a sample-sized package of tooth powder and a generous bag of lemon drops. My father is taking us to Heartthrob. I want to believe that I can drink the oozing sap from the coconut trees that sway there and press on toward the Cuban floor dancers and the stuffed, shellacked swordfish mounted over the juice bar. I want to feel the pulse on the wet surface of the sand, kiss the cheeks of friends I imagine will belly surf in on the curl of foamy waves.

I take out my postcards and begin to shuffle through them again. There are hardly any pictures of beaches or pineapple-shaped motels or straw-covered cabanas, mostly just photos of my friends from Heartthrob. I've carefully pasted pictures from *Teen Beat* and *TV Guide* onto large index cards. There is Bobby Sherman with his smooth tanned chest and almost a nipple showing, and Davy Jones from The Monkees with his shiny bangs. There is a photo of a grinning Elton John wearing palm-tree glasses and the Smothers Brothers with their arms around each other. I've managed to superimpose John

Travolta's head onto the body of a beautiful male underwear model, and on another, I've glued a kind of chummy close-up of Simon & Garfunkel. There are other beautiful men who I've collected from my father's old muscle magazines: Armando Vega, Steve Reeves, and even an oiled-up Jack Lalanne holding up an overworked bicep.

It's the postcards I always wanted to receive. The moonstruck young Brando from the movie, *A Streetcar Named Desire*, has written a secret wish that one day I will return to the sand dunes to be with him. He writes:

> *Now that Blanche is gone and Stella has her hands full with the baby, I'm all yours, Louis! Meet me by the bowling alley entrance tomorrow at dusk.*
> *Yours,*
> *Stanley K.*

I don't think my father would want to know about these heart-throbs. He would not want to see my secret rendezvous or know about my ongoing correspondence with the ghost of Sal Mineo or the young Tab Hunter or even Brazil '66's Sergio Mendes. My love letters get sacked away again and I keep my hand over the carryall, as though I'm protecting them from a strong wind or a predator. I try to imagine a dialogue I could have with the man who is driving the car, but he keeps staring out the windshield, never glancing back to notice me.

When we finally arrive at the motel, stiff with leg cramps from sitting too long, my parents fall asleep on vibrating fingers woven into the snaky bedsprings. I lie awake on a fold-up cot, chewing on salt-water taffy sticks and watching the patterns of light falling through the slats of half-drawn blinds. As the sounds of my father's snoring rumble through the room, I take out a postcard of Mick Jagger from my knapsack. Like a sand crab I crawl across the shag carpet to the bathroom, switch on the night-light and squeeze into the concave of the tub. I slip my shorts and T-shirt off and, as the warm water quietly fills the bath, I gently kiss the pillow lips of my favorite Rolling Stone.

My body grazes the edge of the porcelain bottom. As the water fills in around me, I begin to float on my back as though in a wide ocean womb, my face the only exposed disk on the surface of the water. I look up at the facsimile of Mick, who begins to crinkle from the steam, and I smile up at him like a mer boy, who sings a siren to make even a rock star fall in love. I drift in and out of this weightless rapture, touching myself, feeling the smooth round surface of my body turn into jets of warm currents and waves, and I fall asleep, unafraid of drowning.

Before checkout time, my father justifies packing the motel bath towels and tosses in a flyswatter and a crocodile-handled back-scratcher. But this is just a pit stop. We're bound for Heartthrob, bound to lose ourselves in the "spray-laden breezes, which will catapult the weary sightseer into drunken raptures at the tiki-torched cantina."

We stop for gas at a Gulf filling station, where the air is warm and smells like fried dough and spilt diesel fuel. I step out of the car and, in the pumpkin glow of the towering light display, I reach for the pump nozzle. "Let me do it." My voice mimics a sparrow's.

"Louis, you can't." My father pulls the hose out of my shaking hands. "There's no time to fix your mess."

I stare at him, unfixable, as he goes soft in the caramel light of the Gulf sign. His face reminds me of a photograph taken at a party to celebrate my fifth birthday. In the picture, he has his burly, tattooed arm around me, the one with the Navy anchor on it, and I'm dressed in an official Little League baseball uniform, complete with a miniature bat and pitcher's mitt. Anyone looking at that photograph would think that here is a father who will teach his son to play baseball. Here is a father who will take his son on long walks in the woods, who will teach his son to fly-fish, who will teach him how to rewire an engine rod, who will leap up when his son pitches a shutout game.

But I never played baseball. In fact, I never even threw a baseball to anyone. It was my mother who let me make up imaginary games in the backyard—the misunderstood genie searching for the lamp, for example. She praised my crayon drawings of castles and oceans on the sidewalk, let me string clover and berries and make necklaces, listened as I blew through faerie whistles fashioned from tall grass, or giggled when I wore a faux tiara to my first Halloween party.

"Louis, boys don't wear babushkas!" The softness has vanished from my father's countenance now and he takes the dry Handi Wipe used to wash windows from off my head and throws it in the trash bin. "You're going to be a man, so act like one." It's the shaking of the head with disappointment; it's the lost lingering feeling in my stomach that rattles on as we drive away.

In the time it takes to fill the tank with gasoline, we've reached our destination. We want to think that here is our *Lost Horizon,* here is our rescue, our balm. We settle into a motor lodge called the Whispering Palms because my mother likes the name.

My father and I dash into a private cabana to change into bathing suits. There seems to be no oxygen in the striped tent as I look at my father, naked in the half-light. As if some primal bleating in my veins has been acknowledged, my father looks at me for a moment, deeply, then quickly ties up his trunks. "You better hurry," he quips. "We want to get in as much sun as possible."

My father looks like the man in the travel brochure, slender and wrinkleless in his swimsuit. He ambles down an arcade-dotted fishing pier and his sprite heels lift him toward the Gulf of Mexico. I don't remember the jackhammers pulsing behind electric fences and the telephone poles that must have been airbrushed out of the slick brochure. There are ospreys diving at orange rinds and french fry cartons. The rows of motels are more of a bleached-out gray than pastel green and the sun seems more oppressive than I remember. The beach, almost airless.

My mother puts on sunglasses with flamingo edges, reclines into a foldout stool, and wades into another pulpy magazine. My father looks for conch shells along the seaweedy coast and I trail steps behind him with my mother's bathing cap in my hand. Every now and then I spot the perfect shell and stow it inside the rubber sheath. My father walks in front of me and when I call out to him he answers me with his back toward me.

I stumble and gasp out loud, "What's this?" My father seems oblivious.

"What now?" There is an agitation and a kind of weariness as he slowly turns around.

I point to an opaque gel-like substance half burrowed into the sand. There is a clear encasement around what appears to be a tiny pump and miniature vital organs; there are the lungs, the baby kidneys, the lidless eyes, and it almost seems to be breathing, but just barely. You can see the whole insides of this creature: the shells and the pale rocks that it has swallowed, the jagged sand-dollar edges and the lucky pennies that float inside of it, the barnacle grief encrusted with saltwater stains and brine. As I move nearer to the lifeless creature, it seems to jump. I take in a whirl of air and spill the bathing cap and its contents into the onrushing tide.

"It's a jellyfish, for Chrissakes." My father walks away shaking his head. Another man who has been looking on greets my father and they walk together with a similar gait, some sort of instant male club from which it seems I have been excluded.

I pick up a long stick from the beach and spear the wicked heart of the daddy sea urchin, the dreamless jelly king, the blinded despot. I skewer his limp body onto the pole and throw him into the shivery Gulf, then let out a little puppy yelp in triumph.

I take out the shells I've collected in my pockets and the bathing cap, the polished sea glass and slime-wrapped crab legs. I open my knapsack and set down the box of postcards I've brought with me and begin to half-bury them, putting together a makeshift altar of eisenglass and beer caps, madrone-like cinnamon bark and kelp bulbs. These castaway remnants mark the spot where all my postcards, my beautiful ones, will sleep now. I dig into the wet sand and bury the effigies of Mark Spitz and Robert Redford, the cutouts of Donny Osmond, David Cassidy, and all the rest.

"I'll be right back for you," I say quietly to the little burial mound. "You'll be safe here."

I stumble onto all fours in the cold slap of waves. Without thinking, I put on my mother's swim cap. It is a yellow-petaled bonnet with flouncy gold beads sewn into the centers of the rubber flowers.

The waves seem to be getting higher but from where I'm standing, I think I can see a sandbar. I jump up to miss a wave. I shout to two male figures on the beach that seem to be very far away. "Hey, Dad, are you there? Can you see me?"

There is an uncomfortable look on my father's face. I think the man next to him has asked him something like "Is that your boy?" My father looks like the withered chokeberries that used to hang on our garden trellis in autumn. He looks as if someone has taken all the air out of him, like a deflated pool porpoise. I squint and I think he sees me but he doesn't seem able to move.

There is a tug at the bottom of the sand. My toes can't quite hold onto the rushing silt and the disappearing floor. There is a sweeping tide underneath the basin that wants to drag me under it. For I moment, I want to just slip into that underwater cove. I think I've become the diver on the Lido Motel billboard and I have finally crashed onto the glassy surface of that mythical water and I'm breathing in waves, down near the mermaids and mermen—the real ones.

My head goes under and I think a whitecap has stolen the flowered hat. Saltwater stings my nose and for a moment my head bobs up and I can see that the parchment motels on shore are crumbling, their tacky neon facades are all sloshing into the sand. The lifeguards doze in the midday heat and the whole roadside town seems to tilt into the ocean.

I slip underwater again and let the wild current take me. It's as if my body surrenders, goes limp, and in that moment I imagine that it is my father beside me who is drowning, not me. With his implacable veneer scrubbed off, he is being pulled out with the riptide, and I can do nothing to carry him back onto dry land. With the spindly crab shell of his bravado loosened, he struggles to reach the air and I begin to sense how we are both fragile, both alike.

We tumble together through the rough ocean churn. Our legs kick, hands reach out to barely graze each other. Stranded from rescue, watching each other sink and rise in the haphazard roil, I ache to put my arms around him, become the buoy, the preserver, that will lift us both up to breathing.

When we finally get back to the empty shore, my father touches my head and tells me to go find my mother. He's gasping for air, sitting on the shore shaking his head over and over. He's shivering when I ask him if he wants the towel and he tells me to take it. He rubs his biceps, stares at the waves, bites down on his blue lips. He looks down at his hairy feet, looks at a stone jetty going out into the water, and gazes straight on into the horizon line.

As I make my way back to the lodge, I see that the tide has moved in and destroyed the little grave site. The ocean has toppled and unearthed the driftwood and coral marker, torn apart the cardboard casket and swallowed up my coveted postcards; all of my radiant, undying comrades have been sucked into its giant belly. Those cutout smiles, made-up words, incantory love spells scrawled on the back, won't return now, and if they did, the ink surely would have run, the messages would have blurred, shredded into fragments, and folded themselves into the peaks of benign whitecaps.

I don't go back to the Whispering Palms. I don't care if my mother worries. I don't care if anyone will wonder where I am or even think about seeing me.

I walk along the shore. I don't look for shells or lost shovels. I don't look for sand dollars or dropped watches. I don't look at the bones of dead gulls or the outlines of starfish in the silt. I stay at the beach for a long time, combing the foamy dark waters, hoping that one of my lost, inscrutable sea phantoms might smile up at me in their undying beauty, reminding me that I still exist.

Paris Angels

Angel of the veil. Angel of whirlwind and smoke. Angel of the unknowable rune. What angel did I invoke, that sends me jetting 4,000 miles from Chicago to Paris, to board a metro that clatters now through an early April drizzle, as it careens through a landscape of blinking green pharmacy crosses, twisted rain spigots, vacant market pens, Plexiglas towers, and countless billboards advertising Sade's *Love Deluxe* CD? Our pop princess of trip hop pop, our one-word diva Sade, is trapped in a pose of carnal rapture. Our goddess-elect of the underground tunnels is whispering "this is no ordinary love, no ordinary love." Sade, with her smooth golden skin glossed over in amber honey tones, is folding the quaking French capital to her naked breast.

I think of the letters that have brought me here to Paris. Your postcards of the city, dipped into ambergris. The promises of walks through the Tuilleries at dusk, the Bateau-Mouche rides at midnight, *riz au lait* at the Hotel Vendome. You write to tell me that this is where Fred Astaire stayed in 1936 after making the film *Swing Time* and my mind begins to fill with images of dancers in a plush ballroom, a Gershwin tune playing on the piano, and the tug of two bodies sparking together. I pass over the lines of your last letter, which indicate the directions to our meeting point. Though we have never actually seen each other, we have held each other through our phone calls, our instant Internet chats, our correspondences, our thoughts. I write in my journal:

Paris angels, protect me. Protect this new love that aches to soar.

This chapter appeared originally under the same title in *The Road Within: True Stories of Transformation* (San Francisco: Traveler's Tales, 2001). Copyright 1997 Gerard Wozek. Reprinted with permission of the author.

Postcards from Heartthrob Town: A Gay Man's Travel Tales
Published by The Haworth Press, Inc., 2006. All rights reserved.
doi:10.1300/5732_03

Wedged between my knapsack luggage and a train window that's held open with an old copy of *Le Figaro,* I'm suddenly thrown back to a Saturday afternoon when I'm ten years old and sunk into an old Charlie Chan movie from the '30s. Warner Oland is suited in taupe linen and Keye Luke hovers nearby as his dutiful number-one son. From the terrace of some swank deco apartment terrace, this detective duo surveys a hazy view of the Eiffel Tower—and I'm completely crushed into the lushly painted backdrops of this pot-boiler mystery: wisps of gray smoke curling around lampposts, mustached crepe venders in striped T-shirts, cafés with netted candle gloves on tables, boulevard strollers in their tilted berets—Paris dressed as a cheap Hollywood myth.

In my memory, it seems as though it is always twilight when Chan is out sleuthing Paris. Leaning my fey belief structure on the hokey plotline laced through the film *Charlie Chan in Paris,* I deduce that Parisians are nocturnal creatures who speak English with an exaggerated French accent, breathe through their Gitanes, and subsist on *croque monsieurs* and *café noisettes.* At ten I decide that I want to be just like Charlie Chan, looking for clues and solving mysteries on the Left Bank, as a gray clouded moon peers over the sullen gargoyles of Notre Dame. I want to wear crisp beige suits with a soft key light cast strategically on my face. I want to lean over the railing of a Bateau-Mouche with a fair amount of urbane nonchalance, as I observe the ancient bridges and classic spires needling the skyline.

How I ate up all those Hollywood archetypes of Paris where the city is more a cutout facsimile of its true essence: Irma LaDouce and her tame desolation in the red-light district, Gene Kelly twirling in a red bandanna over an effigy of the Arc de Triomphe, even Maurice Chevalier eyeing pubescent girls in the Tuilleries. So many cliché travelogue film clips fed my dreaming: the image of cobblestones nudged against the banks of the Seine, the whirligig jag of Montemarte's sidewalks, Edith Piaf singing "La Vie En Rose" over a café crowd, the rust of fountain water over mute and solemn statuary in the Luxembourg Gardens.

In my journal I write in the spirit of the German poet Rilke:

What angel presides over the hour when a pilgrim finally arrives at the entrance to his or her destination? Angel of doorways. Angel who hands over the key to all locks. Have I done all that was necessary before passing through the gates of this city? Angel of the promenades along the Seine. Can I walk your labyrinthine streets and become your own fleshy angel—solid and faithful to your ancient stones? Will you welcome me the way you have always welcomed lovers, poets, and exiles before me? Will I reinvent you in my diary, in my recollections of you? Can I fall in love with your skies, your arches, your revenants, the way so many others have done before? Paris, my beloved Paris, have I wished hard enough for you?

The drizzle seems to be turning into more of a fervent pulse as I emerge from the dank metro tunnel near Sainte-Chapelle. It is within the confines of this spot that you and I will finally meet. I will recognize you only by your self-description and the photographs I downloaded from the Internet.

I still remember that afternoon when I was browsing the international chat rooms and stumbled onto your poetry. I e-mailed you and through just our brief chat exchanges, I felt I had found another kindred soul. You spoke of twirling spheres of light, of celestial realms that were waiting to be explored. You spoke of angels the way Rilke does in his work, as though you were part of their sacred hierarchy. When you entreated me to come to Paris, I was cautious, but something compelled me to purchase my ticket anyway. I have always wanted to lose myself in this overwrought myth. Now I'm half-dazed thinking that I will embrace this passionate adventure with you.

I walk the bridge that leads over the Seine and find it hard to catch my breath as I scan the spires of Notre Dame. I feel like Fred Astaire as he raced to meet Audrey Hepburn in the musical *Funny Face.* From the open window of a passing car I can hear Sade's honey voice singing out, "Did somebody say that a love like that won't last?"

I make my way toward the chapel entrance, pay my fee, and enter the area where light is falling through the tall stained-glass windowpanes that depict various scenes from the Bible. The tourist brochure explains that Sainte-Chapelle, erected in 1248, is the French capital's most significant medieval monument and the place where Louis IX and his family worshipped.

I whisper a prayer under my breath. Angel of translucent hope. Angel of winged rapture. Whatever angel brought me here, let me find the romance and inhabit the travelogue that I have craved my whole life.

I smell smoking beeswax and burning cedar as I sense the arrival of my French companion. Rilke said that "every angel is terrifying." I lose my breath as he approaches. Somewhere the beating of wings, perhaps in my chest. Somewhere, a halo of light, perhaps a visible aura around his face. He bends down toward me to say in broken English: "You've found your way to Paris; you've found your way to me *mon amor*. Welcome home."

My Polka Kings

23 October 2001

Booked a train passage from Budapest to Poland today. I'm leaving for Krakow in the morning, so I thought I'd dash off this aerogram to you before I head off. I still have the old *Polish Translation Made Easy* booklet that you gave me when we lived together and so far I can manage "How are you?" and "It's cold here" in Polish without stuttering. It's not that I've grown tired of staring into the gray murk of the Danube. I like walking over the Chain Bridge and I could linger in the wet sauna and thermal pools at the Gellert Baths all day if given the chance. The waiters at the New York Café even know me by name and always bring me an extra serving of Gundel pancakes and don't seem to mind that I sit all afternoon drinking egg coffees and writing in my journal. But I'm hardly getting any sleep at the youth hostel. The raucous crowd keeps playing old Aerosmith songs at all hours of the morning and the smell of hashish and Nag Champa incense has permeated every one of my pullovers. Yesterday was the anniversary of the revolution against the old Communist regime in Hungary and I found myself with my arms linked around the shoulders of total strangers. I swayed back and forth with the crowd, trying to match the foreign syllables of Hungarian folk songs at that weepy, public commemoration. Men, mostly with unkempt mustaches and fraying wool overcoats, were passing around little bottles of apricot brandy and lighting the wicks of vigil candles. I stood in the dancing shadow of the Mary Magdalene Tower and the solemn melodies and low chanting only halted for the occasional intervals of the glockenspiel. I let the musk of my newfound comrades wash over my hair and my neck. Then I walked back to my room trying to rub off the dried

Postcards from Heartthrob Town: A Gay Man's Travel Tales
Published by The Haworth Press, Inc., 2006. All rights reserved.
doi:10.1300/5732_04

candlewax crusted on my sleeve, resolving to finally leave the damp chill of Budapest behind me.

25 October 2001

Last night a cold spell paralyzed this sleeping medieval Polish city. I was struck at how unprepared for the freeze I was. I stepped out of the compartment, strapped on my backpack, and purchased a hand-knit scarf from a woman standing just outside the Dworzec Glowny station. I gave her a few extra zloty because I noticed her chafed fingertips were poking out of her torn knit gloves. I followed the blue signs leading me into the Old Town toward my hotel room. I walked through the narrow streets, the vague smell of broiling sausages in the nippy air, and out of nowhere I was recast into a childhood memory. On Sundays, my mother would always cook a caramelized pork roast and we'd listen to the "Polka King's Dance Program" on the radio. The Six Fat Dutchmen, Frankie Yankovic, Jimmy Sturr, Little Wally, Marion Lush, and Happy Louie and his polka band (all bands you loved as well) would play tunes all afternoon while my mother would stir a pot of steaming sauerkraut or make her butter-laden potato kugel casserole. I'd listen to the singers and imagine their stout handsome bodies, laughing, playing accordions, sweating over the microphone. I think somehow I half-expected my Polka Kings to greet me when I got off the train. What is it that ultimately leads us to our destinations? I am still that drowsy little boy half-dozing under my mother's ironing board; the kid who imagined that Poland was simply a place where blonde dancers in festive red-and-white folk costumes would obligingly perform the three-step, where matronly grandmothers wearing flowered babushkas would offer trays of powdered-sugared kolacky and matronly hugs as I stepped down the fairy-tale streets of Kraków. But the anticipation has been lost to the gritty reality of my late arrival: shuttered cigarette and hamburger stalls, drunken locals in the waiting room, and streets with unpronounceable names. It's the scarf I purchased and wrapped around my mouth last night that somehow smelled vaguely familiar and offered me a compass pointing me back into my memory. The scent on the tightly knit yarn reminded me of the spray starch my mother would drench my Catholic uniform shirts in. How she would carefully press each crevice of the high collar. How the sharp edges would burn my neck every time I turned my head.

29 October 2001

I moved from my dowdy, windowless room at the Cracovia Orbis a few days ago, to a small lodge run by a retired soprano from the Polish Radio Choir named Miss Barbara. She and I were able to exchange just enough words in English for her to gather I'll be touring in Kraków for at least a few more weeks. I have a small bed and a simple writing desk with a view over the Grand Square. In the afternoon she tutors students on the harp and sometimes when they practice and I am journaling in my room, I can almost see cherub wings darting out of the windows of the Cloth Hall, circling amid the souvenir stalls and hot kielbasa stands. Right now I'm writing this letter from a pew bench inside the Basilica of the Virgin Mary, which is purportedly the most famous church in all of the country. There is something about the way the light comes through the stained-glass windows in the nave and hits the relief scenes of the Holy Family painted with warm tones and gold foil. The light then filters downward to the Gothic altarpiece, where two hundred linden wood sculptures seem to be heaving and sighing beneath the Coronation of the Madonna by the Heavenly Trinity. Outside the church, just before I entered, I was wandering down Florianska Street. I heard a bugler from the church tower and it was the startling sound of that trumpet that ultimately brought me in here, a kind of invitation to sit under the starred ceiling, among the haloed statuary of apostles and saints, and soak in the scent of the smoldering frankincense. The bugler plays at every hour because, as legend has it, a fireman in 1241 spotted Tartar invaders on the horizon. As he began to play his horn to warn of the attackers, he was struck in the neck with an arrow. Still, he played loud and long enough for the town to rouse itself, just in time to create a line of defense against the attackers. I have sat with the ghost of that watchman for the past hour or so, glancing up every now and then at the genealogical tree of Jesus Christ and the Blessed Mother. My eyes have been scanning over that ornate predella, lingering on the strained faces of Bible characters I cannot name, wondering where on earth I fit in.

1 November 2001

On All Saints' Day in Kraków, Catholics remember the dead by praying over cemetery grave sites and laying wreaths of fresh flowers over tombstones. I've never felt that private mourning ceremonies should be a spectator sport, but I wanted a chance to move beyond my normal walking routine in city central, and the holiday was merely a tourist's excuse to engage in local customs. Rakowicki, the city's best-known cemetery, lies just northwest of the old train station. Once I got to the entrance gates, I quietly followed a solemn procession into the monument-laden landscape. Family members were huddled around gravestones, setting tall white tapers on top of the granite stones and murmuring prayers with their heads bent down. I wandered among the grieving families, caught up in their rituals of remembering their dead. There were rosary beads woven from actual dried flower petals that were gently garlanded around the grave sites. Tiny wrapped gift boxes were set down near the engraved markers. A few gatherings even had picnic blankets spread out with a place setting for their remembered deceased individual. I meandered around the various sections, and then crossed the street to where casualties of the military were buried. Polish soldiers lost in both World Wars, British airmen struck down, and Red Army troops were being honored there. I looked for your great-uncle here (recall the old photographs you used to show off of the two of you at some festive occasion), but there were so many names, I finally had to give up. In a more remote area of the cemetery, I stood next to a wreath made of stone at the foot of a standing war commander. A gentleman stood below the statue, sloop shouldered and graying. He toasted the frozen official with a half-filled cordial glass. I approached slowly, and then halted as he turned around and began to speak softly to me in Polish. The tones were gentle and tender, as though he somehow recognized me as an old friend, a buddy who once served with him in the war perhaps. I was taken back when he proceeded to embrace me. We stood there for a long while, his head resting on my shoulder, while processions of quiet mourners walked on, hardly noticing two men collapsed into each other, in a field set aside for the long dead.

5 November 2001

Today I strolled the Planty Garden Ring in Krakow. Miss Barbara said to go early because evenings in the park can be dangerous. Even in the early chill of November when nearly all of the lush plants have withered, there are a good number of bundled tourists and residents wandering about. The circular gardens were built in the mid-1800s and consist of various loops around the perimeter of the oldest part of the city. The ancient buildings of Kraków take on a certain mystery, seeing them ensconced amid the charcoal November skies, tree branches, and widely flung lawns. I kept taking photographs of the decaying cupolas, ornate facades, carved religious figures, crumbling fountains layered with leaves, and the tops of church towers that seemed to surround and encroach upon the entire park. On my circuitous journey around the dying gardens, somewhere near the Slowacki Theater, I met Piotr. "Your hands are shaking cold," he said as I was fumbling with the strap of my camera. "Shall I snap you?" Four photographs later I found him offering me back my Canon and gently rubbing the chapped skin on the back of my wrists. We walked a while, then leaned against the ancient defensive walls of old Kraków. He pulled out a cigarette and spoke in slow English. There were details about his life he told me that I don't remember; I was fixated on his blue eyes. Blue in a way I wish I could describe to you here in this letter, almost aqua, almost the color of a shirt you once wore when we first met. For a moment, it seemed as if I might sink into the dense fog of those glowing orbs of his and never get out. I don't know why I'm writing this to you. I should be describing the zigzag of the cobblestone streets or the proski and cheese pierogies Miss Barbara fries up for me in the morning, or the way the scarred ocher walls of the Old Town make me feel at home somehow. I guess I can't help but still tell you everything that happens to me, even though we're no longer together. It's a bit of a compulsion and I hope you don't mind me writing this to you in such candor. But back to Piotr. Yes, I kept saying his name as he was kissing me behind a vine-covered fence. "Piotr." We were covert, secretive in a cluster of dense branches. I whispered his name into his ear and my breath came out in little puffs of fog. "Piotr, Piotr." I tried to tell him about his eyes. The way the color seemed to envelop me until I lost my bearings. It was an afterthought, that I should have taken a picture of him. Funny, but when I got back to my studio tonight, I couldn't find the scrap of paper he wrote his number on. And the photographs in my Canon, they're gone too, along with my expensive camera. I don't care somehow though. I'm not shaken. I suppose I'll buy a disposable one tomorrow and that will be that. It's that indescribable color in his eyes that I can't get seem to release, that elusive territory I want to inhabit, where the sky ends and the first stars begin to emerge.

8 November 2001

Miss Barbara's harps are still playing in my head. I've been sitting in different churches—St. Francis' Basilica, the Church of St. Adalbert's— listening to choir music for the past day just to change that dolorous melody that kept plodding through my brain. I decided this morning to take an excursion to the Wieliczka Salt Mines as a day trip away from the city. In medieval times, the Polish kings who profited from the resource's ability to preserve food, among other things, owned the salt mines. I tried to imagine the crouching miners who worked a thousand feet below the surface of the land in order to supply the ancient kingdom with this food enhancer. For two hours I found myself struck by the intricate details of the brine statues, the little salt gnomes waving back at me for luck, the tiny dining rooms carved out of hard crystalline rock, the labyrinthine tunnels and passages through the chambers and around the underground lakes, the healing center where asthmatics can take in the salt air. Imagine a world made entirely from salt, dear one. Can you? It is a world I believe we once inhabited. (Billie Holiday records and candles and goosebumps on that old pull-out sofa?) Do you remember? How we'd let our tongues carve a path over our salty skin. The damp sweat at your belly fur. The musky crevices of your body where I'd linger. I'd find salt on your eyelashes in the morning. And a brine cellar when I'd enter your mouth with my tongue. Then in your hair. Then on the nape of your neck. In your little ears and in the small of your back. Salt. All through the tour I'd imagine us in various positions as the guide showed us chapels where miners once prayed and old tracks where the salt was hauled back. I could almost see them, digging their way through the charcoal gray. Wary of the corrosive effect of the brine. The fear that water might flood the tenuous mine shaft or accumulations of methane might cause an explosion. My once-named beloved, we were like those agile miners seven hundred years ago, heading toward that transparent cathedral buried under the earth. Their feeble lanterns waving in the dark. The scraping away through hundreds of miles of tunnels, through oblivion, to bring back the precious green crystals to the king's table. Dust of water, tongues of brine, a rime of glistening salt over our bodies. The frail luster of that pearly residue resembling something like finely crushed bones, or the entrails of fallen stars.

11 November 2001

Miss Barbara insisted I listen to her version of Enya's "Orinoco Flow" before I left this morning and all day I've heard that song plunking across my synapses. I've given up on the translation book you gave me. Now I simply fumble around, pointing at inanimate objects or my own body parts, or mumbling some of the chorus I vaguely remember from Bobby Vinton's hit song "My Melody of Love." "Moya-droga-yah-shey-koh," I half-sing to the store clerks who seem at once

bemused then eventually shake their heads in bewilderment. Gener-
ally, residents of Kraków have been patient and tolerant of my sometimes oafish manner. I asked for a coddled egg for breakfast this
morning at a small deli and received a plastic container of boiled
dumplings. I accepted the pasty dough balls with a Styrofoam cup of
hot tea and moved on to the sights. I took a tourist bus up to the
Bielany Monestary atop Srebrna Gora. Camaldolese monks have surrendered their personal autonomy for the austere rules of their strict
order so that they might hear the voice of God within the secluded
walls of this archaic sanctuary. What struck me here were the seventeenth-century, four-storied crypts which contain mummified bodies.
Standing next to the decayed bones and skulls I swear I could almost
hear the vague whispers of deceased monks: "It was the sins of the
flesh I needed to repent. It was the promptings in my erotic heart I
could not vanquish." The living monks, icy in their long white robes,
seemed removed from the secular gawkers. They go about their duties
seemingly content, self-contained, and morosely prayerful as they
stroll the quiet gardens in stoic pairs. I can't help wondering what desires are veiled beneath their piousness. So far, I have resisted the impulse in my mind to indulge in some pornographic imagery of a lusty
old abbot instructing his novice monks in the secret ways of the
brotherhood, although it is a somewhat tempting, albeit clichéd fantasy. The Pope's autocratic fist is still felt throughout much of Poland
and it is challenging at best to locate any signs of openly gay life here
in the city, though my handy little Damron's guide suggests several
little cafés and bars which I've yet to locate. After surveying the mon-
astery, I wandered out on the edge of the Bielany Forest overlooking
the Vistula River and the peaks of the Tatra Mountains and imagined
that I was floating in bright colors above the waves à la Enya: "Let me
reach, let me beach far beyond the yellow sea." For a moment, I had
the conviction I was becoming a channel for the withering corpses of
those dead or dying monks. That I had become the mouthpiece that
must speak aloud those furtive promptings that have been silenced.
The mediator between what has been denied and denounced, and all
that must be finally revealed.

18 November 2001

Who would have ever guessed I'd find the best Russian red beet borscht right here in Kraków. Or be able to locate the finest Hungarian goulash outside of Budapest! Or dine on schnitzels and Viennese tortes even though there are Polish delicacies waiting for me everywhere. But today, I had an appetite for something more indigenous. I was determined to finally visit Poland's national sanctuary, the Wawel Royal Castle, home to three dynasties of Polish monarchs. In the sixteenth century, King Sigismund brought in Italian artisans to fashion a majestic Renaissance palace on top of this limestone hill. I paid my zloty to gain entrance to the royal apartments where the Wawel kings ruminated amid the Dutch paintings, handwoven tapestries, and Chinese ceramics. This was not the world I imagined to find in Kraków. It was not my childhood's recollection of Little Richie's Polka Party. It was not even our haphazardly fashioned world—the universe we both extended out from our upbringings filled with Polish foods and flowery decorations and arcane little traditions carried down through generations of your Polish family. How you insisted one day we would come to Kraków together to visit your great great grandfather's home. How we would make a pilgrimage here in order to solve the riddle of where your ancestors came from. "I came from a line of great rulers," you always insisted. Seeing the regalia and the royal reliquaries and the somber rows of coffins where the great kings of Poland are buried, I see now that it is true. But I cannot bury you. I've come here alone, though I've carried you somehow in my blood. You're still here, seeing all the sights with me. Sampling the sauerkraut and pork shanks, tasting the fresh-baked obwarzanki bread with me. (Yes, it's perfectly round, as you said it would be.) You see, I've carried you all this way from the states. All this way to where I thought we'd be standing together. Tonight, for the first time, I heard a polka song right here in Kraków. My Polka Kings from childhood were serenading me all the way back to you. And we were moving across our old apartment floor in our stocking feet. In my head I'm still gripping your broad shoulders and yielding to your imposing frame. You don't seem to mind that I keep stepping on your toes, and we go on jostling like that, song after song, until we collapse into a sweaty heap and give in to our predictable baby talk, then the usual pillow kisses, then finally, something that carries me off, something like sleep, but gentler, somehow, even softer than that.

25 November 2001

I asked Miss Barbara for a souvenir of my stay with her: a broken harp string I found on the living room floor the other night. I couldn't think of a better remembrance, though she insisted on filling my backpack with those little painted eggs you get at the Cloth Hall. "Good luck charm for making many babies," she laughed. And I even chuckled too. I sent you a turquoise one; they're known for prosperity as well as fertility, so I thought I'd share the wealth. You'll see I finally had some of my photographs developed here in Kraków from my single-use camera. I enclosed several here for you, including my view overlooking Rynek Glowny and my favorite food cart where I'd purchase barley and carrot soup for lunch. (Remember how you taught me your mother's recipe?) Also, a photo of the cave by Wawel Hill near the river Wista where, legend has it, a dragon once lived. I guess you figured out by now that I have not slayed my own dragon. You'll notice the photograph is a bit dark and blurry and the edges of the great opening to the cave are a bit smeared. You see, I wanted to enter that cavern with you, my reluctant beloved. But of course, I have realized too late what you knew all along; I needed to accomplish that feat on my own. I needed to know my own courage. I am leaving Kraków with most of my fear and grieving for you intact. I have so many stories to tell you when I get back, if you'll listen to them. And pictures that I'd love to show you of everywhere I've been. The Gothic spire with eight turrets where I imagined us dancing in twilight. Da Vinci's *Lady with an Ermine* painting where I missed your discussion of the artist's great weakness for the male visage. The Zygmunt bell, so massive, I could imagine us standing beneath it and shouting out our names just to hear the echo of those familiar syllables merging together. I bought another inexpensive one-use camera for my trip to

Prague. You mentioned, one day, how you want to go there, so I'm touring that capital to see exactly what it is you longed for. I'll see some light shows, I'm sure, and hear some popular Mozart concertos and stand on the famous Charles Bridge. There will be statues of royalty there, cast in crumbling stone along the edges of the busy viaduct. Czech kings and princes I've never heard of before. And I'll discover that city's own intrinsic music, not the pleated accordions of my laughing Polka Kings, but violins or cellos perhaps. I'll bring back pictures of all the usual tourist stuff. The Prague Castle. The Jewish cemetery. The Golden Ring House. You may not see yourself in any of those souvenir snapshots I capture but, somehow, I'm certain, I will.

Reuben Ran

Reuben liked to run with the wolf boys. He liked to walk in thick packs that inspired fear from his classmates and feel his square shoulders rub up against his two best partners Mario and Deek. He liked to slick his black hair back with wet-look gel and wear orange leather cock rings around his wrists. He liked to sneak out of his bedroom window at night to smoke Camels in the park after curfew.

He would pull up the collar of his jacket and say to his tribe, "Don't I look like Chayanne now?"

"Chayanne's a pussy-face," the wolf boys would jeer.

"You wish you could have this mug."

Reuben liked to run with danger. He liked to shoplift jelly donuts and Heath bars from the 7-Eleven around the corner. He liked to pour the Kahlua he would steal from his stepfather's liquor cabinet into the cartons of milk he would gulp down in the cafeteria at high school. He liked to play online poker at the computer terminals in the library. He liked to openly French-kiss his flashy wolf boys in the parking lot and dared anyone to call him a faggot or take him down.

The code among the wolf boys was to flirt lavishly with one another and even experiment sexually, as long as it was safe. Reuben often engaged in long smooch sessions with his fellow wolves. He even watched his two best friends make out on occasion. But there was a part of him that felt detached from the exploits of the incestuous clan, as though he were always dashing away from any kind of close intimacy or bonds that would draw him into any kind of serious relationship.

He was the first guy in his sophomore class to have his eyebrow and tongue pierced. He sported an inky tattoo of a dagger on his forearm and wore tight, black mesh shirts that displayed his oversized nipple

Postcards from Heartthrob Town: A Gay Man's Travel Tales
Published by The Haworth Press, Inc., 2006. All rights reserved.
doi:10.1300/5732_05

rings. He listened to Mudvayne and Pantera along with Gabriel Faure's "Requiem" on his walkman. He habitually skipped gym class and biology and the truant officers often found him underneath the football bleachers, smoking a rolled cigarette or drawing in his sketchbook.

Reuben liked to draw.

He drew maps. He drew pictures of places he wanted to see when he was older. His eighteenth birthday was next year but wedged in the middle of his senior year in high school, that landmark seemed aeons away to him.

He rendered detailed visions of destinations he read about when he was younger or seascapes in Puerto Rico he heard his father talk about when his dad still lived at home, before he walked out of the house for a case of Coronas one Saturday, and never came back.

Reuben drew the decaying streets and crooked ironwork of porches in the old part of Havana. He drafted the views from a mountaintop looking down over the sun-bleached houses of Santorini. He pictured the darting traffic lights at night from the frenetic Bund in Shanghai, China. He sketched the gravely beautiful ruins of Machu Picchu in Peru.

"You should frame these," Mario said one day. "I'm not saying I know anything about art, just that these drawings really make me want to get on a plane."

"I don't even know where Ephesus, Turkey, is on a globe," Deek interjected, tracing the shaded lines of a hand-sketched Greek pillar. "But I wanna go too."

"I travel all the time." Reuben was not shy with his broad, gap-toothed smiles. "I just follow my hand as it crosses over this white paper, and it's like landing in the middle of paradise."

Reuben dreamt of running down La Rambla in Barcelona. He dreamt of drinking sangria with a handsome mustached artist under a café umbrella and talking about Picasso and Cubism and negative space. He pictured himself opening bottles of beer from the top of one of the squiggly towers of Gaudi's Sagrada Familia church. Or dancing on a torch-lit float during Carnestoltes. Or weaving through the old

Barri Gotic quarter, learning common Spanish from the tavern own-
ers and street pickpockets.

Sometimes he would sketch himself inside his drawings. Kneeling
before a jade-carved Buddha in a temple in Bangkok. Snorkeling with
a sea turtle in the luminescent turquoise lagoon waters off the island
of Aitutaki. Standing before the Uluru in Australia, the largest mono-
lith in the world, as it rusted into a brilliant shade of orange-red right
before his very eyes.

"You've got the sickness known as wanderlust, *mi amigo.*" Mario
flicked a cigarette ash into the stream of wind coming through a humming box fan in the window. "You wanna roam everywhere with just
your beat-up knapsack and your sketchbook and think that you can
live off your big fat grin. You think you can blow some trollish sugar
daddy and live in Cinderella's castle. I'm telling you, homeboy, you
better think again."

Reuben looked up at the twirling globes suspended with fishing
wire from his bedroom ceiling, seven little replicas of Earth that si-
multaneously spun in the fanned air.

He thought of what it must be like to be able to jet around the
world like Ricky Martin or Donald Trump. He thought of how impossible it was for him to hold down any job, always getting fired for
having a "lack of motivation" or simply doodling in the suffocating
back room of the Payless shoe store he once sweated in for five
months.

He thought of graduating from high school and applying to a local
art school over the summer, but his grades would most likely be too
low and, besides, he wanted to traverse the variegated landscapes of
the planet first. He wanted to cross the ocean waves. He wanted to
wake up in a place where nobody spoke his language. He wanted
to mix with the natives, even sleep with the handsome ones. He
wanted to be an explorer first and then perhaps get a degree to hang
on his wall, next to his framed artwork.

"Betcha you can't draw me into one of these travelogues." Mario
shook one of Reuben's desert images in the air. "I'd like to see you put
me on top of one of these pyramids in the distance. Boy, can't you just
see that?"

As hard as Reuben tried, he could not picture his sidekick Mario in any of his drawings. He saw his companion sneaking into the seedy gay bar in the college town just down the highway, wearing blue-tinted sunglasses and flashing a fake identification card. He saw Mario smoking reefer behind the bushes at lunchtime or hanging out in the school locker room discreetly watching the football jocks undress. He saw him working for his uncle's auto repair shop after graduation.

Then, he pictured his friend getting older; losing the trademark hoop earrings and skull-and-crossbones bandanna, giving up his part-time sex obsession with Deek and maybe casually dating some young woman his strict Catholic family would pressure him into marrying one day.

He saw his friend eventually fading into a whittled-down, pre-scribed life in rural America. A kind of sterilized simpleton, hypno-tized by a stream of mindless sitcoms, renting a two-bedroom ranch house behind his hometown's Wal-Mart and the Pizza Hut. He could not see Mario anywhere near the Great Pyramids of Egypt. Nowhere in any of the far-off places that Reuben imagined for himself.

Reuben knew that he was running out of time. He had to pass all of his course work in order to graduate but if he missed any more science classes he would fail and have to take summer school. Reuben could not invent a superhighway or outline a jet plane that could carry him out of the dilemma of having to attend the monotony of his classes at school. He showed up at homeroom, was present for attendance from eight in the morning to three, but he felt a little piece of himself dry-ing up. He felt as though a part of his life was withering as he prac-ticed archery and scribbled notes down on mitochondria and the process of mitosis.

Often Reuben would sketch pictures of his missing father in far-off dreamscapes. He would try to imagine where his dad might have ended up after he walked off that day when Reuben was only seven. On a ship sailing off the coast of his hometown of San Juan? Sloop-shouldered on a nameless Jamaican beach or living out his days as a guitar maker in the Virgin Islands somewhere?

"Your father majored in daydreaming too," Reuben's mother warned him. "Be mindful you don't wander down the same careless path."

Reuben was certain he had the same desire to travel embroidered into his genes. Like his father, he wanted to leave his footsteps on the white sand beaches of Dorado. The only thing that mattered to Reuben was to ramble the world and capture its incandescence somehow in the pages of his sketchbook. He was convinced his urge to roam beyond the confines of his small town would never leave him.

"Have you ever thought of doing something with your talent?" Reuben's history professor was amazed at the graphic novel he had turned in depicting the Bolshevik Revolution that occurred in the early twentieth century in Russia. "The images you've created of the storming of the Winter Palace in Leningrad are absolutely stunning. You've rendered such detail."

"It's my way of entering the moment," Reuben spoke quietly without pretense. "I want to be able to see for myself what the actual soldiers saw as well."

"And I'd like your own peers to be able to share in your vision too. What would you say to transferring this work onto a larger scale? Say as a full mural here at school?"

Reuben looked down at the floor, then flashed his irresistible smile directly into the eyes of his teacher. "For extra credit?"

"I think we can find a prominent space somewhere here for you."

For the better part of the next semester, Reuben worked tirelessly at re-creating the Leningrad of 1917. He drew the massive structure of the palace that stretched some two hundred meters along the riverfront. He rendered the dome and gold spires and the statue of Catherine the Great. He captured the revolutionaries as they marched in and overthrew the Russian czars. The detailing was so precise, the energy captured was so palpable, that one could easily imagine walking directly into the turgid scene and getting caught up in the passion of that historical era.

"Dude, your images of Russia are awesome, but you're so out of it." Deek gently tugged on the outline of the ring jutting through Reuben's green polyester shirt. "Do you think you can pass with a D in bi-

ology when all you're doing is working on the wall painting and
scribbling in that damn sketchbook of yours?"

"I've got two more weeks of this classroom tedium to manage,"
Reuben said. "After that, I'm gone."

"Gone where? Stepping into one of your pictures like Mary Pop-
pins?" Reuben detected a thread of jealousy running through Deek's
chilly pitch as he turned away from the mural.

"Just gone."

Reuben finished his course requirements but he didn't wait to see if
he passed biology. It didn't matter to him if he stepped across some
platform to get his diploma. His mother and stepfather would be dis-
appointed about not having an opportunity to take photographs of
him in his blue cap and gown. They would feel bad about not being
able to treat him to that long-promised gathering in the basement of
their home, with relatives and wrapped gifts and even some of the familiar wolf boys sipping beer at the table.

Reuben ran. He ran from his past delinquency with schoolwork
and the slipshod moral code followed by his wolf pack. He ran from
his late-night posturing in the park at night, his dalliance with daydreaming about his absent father and the secret shots of Kahlua, and
even his acquired habit of petty shoplifting. He ran from the Reuben
who only wanted his art to remain in his private sketchbook with his
feet planted on his parents' modest front porch. He ran from those
hollow replicas of the Earth strung over his narrow bed toward a ver-
dant and living terrain.

Three weeks after his eighteenth birthday, Reuben ran away from
home. At least that's what his mother called it. "But how can you run
away from a place that was never really home to begin with?" Reuben
countered back at her from a phone booth in St. Petersburg. "I think
I'll be able to call Russia my home now."

Reuben felt kindred to the Winter Palace in St. Petersburg, having
spent so much time researching and rendering it for the prize-
winning mural. He inhaled the actual rising mist wafting over the
frozen river Neva now as though it were some kind of strange elixir.
He liked the way the sun reflected off the gold dome of the palace and

he practically lived at the Hermitage, going early nearly every day before class in order to get a seat in front of a treasured Monet or Picasso.

"The scholarship money will cover another year at the St. Petersburg State Theatre Arts Academy," he explained to his mother. "I'm learning set design and I'll be painting backdrops for world-famous theater companies. Eventually I'll get to travel around the world and pretty soon I'll be drawing myself into those exotic, faraway scenes."

Reuben kept sketching his maps to anywhere. He drew his own atlas of the world, complete with images replicated from the window of a speeding train, the pattern of streets and the diminishing jagged topography he himself would encounter from the porthole of a jet just taking off.

He still drew beaches in Rio de Janeiro and orange sunsets over the town of Zanzibar, the ocean vistas in Haiti, and a herd of reindeer scampering across the Western Lapland, but more often than not he drew himself into those sketches.

He even sent home hand-drawn postcards to his disbanded wolf pack friends, one of which portrayed himself and another striking fellow standing shoulder to shoulder with each other, looking up at the chandeliered ceiling of the Pavilion Hall Gallery in the Hermitage. On the back of the card, it read:

My mate Vladimir and I have finally found each other. We share a love of great art as well as for each other. He is helping me develop an appreciation for classical Russian paintings and I am guiding him with his own design work. He is also teaching me to speak and translate the nearly incomprehensible Russian language. The struggle for a complete social acceptance of our kind of obvious affection for each other is quite difficult here in St. Petersburg, but I am not willing to escape from the challenge. There are still many places in the world I feel I am destined to see, but I am thrilled knowing that I will be able to share my inbred wanderlust with another kindred spirit. How could I ever run away from that?
Yours always,
Reuben

Kissing the Buddha

"Get me out of this Zen garden!" Marley's remark lingered over the dry atmosphere. "I can't stand all this gray slate and white stone. It's so Nee-shee."

"You mean Nietzsche," his companion instructed gently. "You have to stress the last syllable a little differently."

Marley kicked off his orange suede Keds and seemed disinterested in the Japanese rock formations bordering the café patio. It was an afternoon tea ceremony at Hoshoan in Osaka Castle and only Marley's new beau Jinn could have possibly persuaded him to come to such an opulent setting. But it was unseasonably warm for early December in Osaka and Jinn couldn't resist taking advantage of sitting on the straw pillows thrown around the terrace of the botanical's courtyard.

"I think my ass has fallen asleep." Marley couldn't get his legs to surrender to the lotus position no matter how Jinn tried to massage his hamstrings. Even coaxing him into a sutra-inspired meditation failed, and the arcane ancient Japanese koans Jinn tried to recite seemed to evaporate into the air.

"I'm trying to teach you something about traditional Japanese culture," Jinn implored. "About growing into wisdom."

"Can't I just wait until I get there on my own?" Marley stared at the indecipherable Japanese characters on the edge of the fragile teacup.

"The story of the ancient wanderer is a story about all of us." Jinn insisted on telling the parable. "He walks without his sandals because his weathered feet have become impermeable. No thorns, not even the craggy rock bed will harm him. He keeps his eye on the distant mountaintop—steadfast, certain."

Marley examined his feet. "I could use a new pair of tennis shoes, I guess."

Postcards from Heartthrob Town: A Gay Man's Travel Tales
Published by The Haworth Press, Inc., 2006. All rights reserved.
doi:10.1300/5732_06

Jinn held the steaming brew to his lips for a long time, then breathed deeply as his heavy-lidded eyes seemed to roll to the back of his head. There were moments that seemed to become almost unbearable for Marley. In those ponderous sighs, Marley became completely eroticized; that deep inhalation reminded him so much of their lovemaking. Still, it seemed Jinn was disconnecting from the present moment and going into some kind of an impermeable trance.

Just last night, Marley was tumbling in the throes of heavy breathing himself, all instinctive Tantra-like contortions, all sweat fire and kisses: the two of them were caught in a soft womb that seemed to float perpetually in the air. He pined for the gooey yolk of that warm egg where it was just damp skin on skin and shared pulses, the slow wash of their gingery tongues, one on top of the other, the squash of bony hips thrusting onto each other, over and over.

Marley excused himself and moved to the other end of the café to light a cigarette. The smoke curled around the bowers of a freshly clipped bonsai tree sitting near the patio ledge that overlooked Osaka Bay. He used the wing of a miniature glass pagoda wedged into the potted soil as an ashtray. As he eyed the pruned dwarf boughs, Marley imagined himself as the ancient Japanese wanderer, fumbling with his cane, trying to make himself fit through the miniscule doorway of the faux porcelain house. No luck. Maybe it was bad fortune, or maybe Marley was just too "rough around the edges," as Jinn liked to tease him, to ever fit into that delicate scenario.

A soft-spoken Asian waiter in an embroidered tunic made his way over to Marley with a fresh pot of barley mint tea. Jinn had tried to fill him in on the rigors of the Japanese tea ceremony, the *cha-no-yu,* which literally meant "hot water for tea" that was used along with the flower arranging, calligraphy, and incense. However, Marley would often drift during these ponderous cultural lessons.

Marley waited on tables at a small American-style diner that opted for a 1950s Elvis meets *Happy Days* pastiche. Instead of pressed silk, Marley wore plastic apron overalls; when he wasn't serving homemade hoagie sandwiches and fried pork rinds to homesick tourists who wanted a nostalgic taste of a *Leave It to Beaver* America, he was perfecting his own cooking skills. The restaurant where he worked was a curious American outpost in the middle of downtown Osaka. The old neon jukebox and ceramic busts of Marilyn Monroe and James Dean on the diner wall stood in garish contrast to the quiet simplicity of the line drawings framed in this more traditional tea-house.

Marley had been offered a scholarship to study culinary arts at the Osaka Culinary Institute. He was training under the best iron chef in all of Japan. But he couldn't get used to the unusual seaweed dishes or the creations made from raw eel or turtle. Sometimes the city itself was overwhelming. The language barriers on the street wore him out quickly and the Japanese script in the railway station often misled him in the wrong direction.

"Where are all the kimonos?" He remarked to Jinn early on. "Why is everyone so remote? I mean, people are friendly here and whatnot, but it's as though they're living in the space within themselves."

What threw him most about Japanese culture was the youth trend known as Goth-Lili. Everyone under the age of twenty seemed to be wearing dark clothes, painting the crevices around their eyes black, and listening to masochistic rock groups like Caligari and Mook.

"You need to come with me and watch Kabuki," Jinn would plead with his companion. "You need to see some real face paint."

"I'd rather watch reruns of an old Super Bowl game, if you don't mind."

When it seemed too oppressive, Jinn would take Marley to a public *ofuro* bath. The traditional Japanese believe bathing consists of more than just scrubbing yourself clean. A hot soak up to your chin should provide a meditation on one's life, a sensual pleasure that would re-store a sense of harmony. Despite the long restorative soaks, Marley remained a perpetual awkward tourist, aloof from everything that was geographically and culturally Japan.

Still, he loved being around food. He adored the aroma of simmer-ing meats on a stovetop; the way chefs could alter the taste of some-thing just by a saki marinade or a sugary glaze. Even as a boy Marley loved to sculpt Spam into unusual forms and make smiley faces out of pancakes using bacon strips and poached eggs. Once, using toothpicks and licorice whips, he helped his mother turn a ground beef meatloaf into a detailed replica of the Golden Gate Bridge.

Over the past three months, Marley had become an expert in the diner's kitchen. No other chef could match his grated potato cakes or the taste of his grilled rib eyes. He dressed the hammered chicken patties and roasted gyro sandwiches with sumptuous dressings, taking extra time to season the onions in a bit of vegetable stock to bring out their subtle flavors. The broil marks on his marinated sirloins had to be perfectly aligned and his maple syrup Southern grits always had the right pinch of nutmeg.

"A little to warm your cup?" The waiter in the silk pleated coat seemed to wince as though he was sizing up Marley's unkempt attire.

Marley looked down at his stained drawstring pants and declined a new pour from the teahouse helper. He much preferred those testosterone microbrews he could get at the American Beauty near the Kuromon Market, or watching the televised chubby sumo wrestlers with their thick ponytails and thighs of iron, their merciless headlocks. "I love when they mow them down with their nipples," Marley would confide to his co-worker pal, Sol. "The way they use their sweat to wriggle themselves out of their opponent's fat forearms. Just amazing."

For hours Marley and Sol would shell peanuts at the bar railing and trance out on the widescreen television, until one of them would reach over and notice that their pitcher was warming up and they needed to call the bartender over for one more. It was a game to see who would disentangle first; they both were so enamored with the athletes on the screen.

"Do you ever wonder what two men in a ring would do if there were no rules in the game?" Sol would muse to his cohort. "I mean, just imagine if they were set free to be themselves?"

Marley would finger the new foam that poured down the side of his glass and keep his eyes steady on the ponytail of one of the wrestlers. "Yeah, imagine reviving the gladiators."

The New Age music that played at the teahouse brought him out of his reverie. Marley wanted to pour a pot of oolong into the speaker and wash out the repetitive flute notes. He wanted to smoke out the

Japanese music and listen to Counting Crows. Instead, he just puffed deeper on his cigarette.

Marley loved to smoke. It was something he wasn't able to do around Jinn because of his insistent objections. In fact, his name really wasn't Marley at all. Friends had nicknamed him that back in the sixth grade because he was the only kid who could get through a pack of Marlboros in a day without coughing to death.

Marley could see from his vantage point that Jinn was getting restless. Jinn had stepped onto the stone path that skirted through the stone garden and was engaged in some of his obtuse Tai Chi positions.

"It looks like he's slicing through the wind," Marley remarked out loud to himself. "Like he's about to karate-chop a dragonfly."

Even though he was slightly older than Marley, Jinn reminded him of a stately gazelle, his neatly compact muscles oiled with the scent of jasmine and verbena, his skin the muted copper of a ginger bulb, his eyes always peering into Marley's as though they could see behind them. He was lithe and elegant, positioned like the tigers and snow leopards they had seen on their first chance encounter at the Tennoji Park Zoo.

"I can't stand to see them in those cages," Jinn had intimated that unremarkable afternoon they had met in October.

It was the kinship between Jinn and the animals that had first aroused Marley. It seemed as though they shared some sort of unspoken bond, the way the creatures eyed him carefully as they paced in their cells, rubbing their shiny black coats against the iron bars. It was as though Jinn held the leopards in a trance, much the same way he often paralyzed Marley with the penetrating gaze of his dark Italian eyes during sex.

"I wouldn't want to be them," Marley replied, a slight quiver in his throat.

"I wonder if they'd want to be us." Jinn smiled, staring through the cage bars.

Marley inhaled down to the filter tip. He broke from his memory and watched Jinn return to the terrace of the botanical gardens and move back onto a cushion. Jinn's limber legs crouched back into perfect form and his spine realigned, impossibly erect. Through the last tendrils of smoke Marley could almost envision Jinn floating over the raked Zen pond and into a cluster of clouds; he was that inscrutable sometimes.

Marley and Jinn rode the bus back to Marley's studio in downtown Osaka. Marley still couldn't get over how the two of them were still together after almost two months. Jinn worked most nights on his graduate degree in Malaysian philosophy and taught literature classes part-time during the day. Marley admired his discipline, how Jinn poured over his lesson plans and practiced his orations for hours. But there was something discouraging about his meticulous attention to his studies, as though Jinn couldn't find a way to crack the code and master the soul of it.

Even when he tried to show Jinn how to cut a tomato once, how to hold it in his fingers and roll the blade of the knife a certain way over the ripe skin, Jinn became exasperated: "Isn't there a book that gives better instructions on how to do this?"

There was something brooding underneath Jinn's exactness. Marley thought of the night when he was stirring together a cheddar polenta in his studio and noticed Jinn struggling with a passage in one of his textbooks. Jinn abruptly tore out a page in the opened tome and began pleating it with his shaking hands. He set the creased object on the counter for Marley. "A little gift for you." Jinn pursed his lips and with a gust of breath, he softly pushed the paper figure toward Marley.

Jinn had created an origami swan to float in Marley's kitchenette. The matchless bird had the words "Austronesian" and "doctrinal" printed on its feathered wings and seemed desolate, as though another swan needed to be formed out of paper to partner it. Marley studied the intricate folds that made the bird's beak and curved neck, but it seemed there would be no way of ever folding together another one quite like it.

On the surface, one could easily dismiss Jinn for being a pompous bookworm. He always carried around an electronic dictionary to look up any unfamiliar words he would happen upon. He practiced his Japanese language lessons faithfully and was quick to point out the history of the noble samurai. He understood what distinguished the

Edo period from the Heian, could detail the history of the renovation work that went on in the Osaka Palace after World War II, and could chat up people on the street well enough to get to where he needed to go.

But Jinn was sensual too at times and would sneak wet kisses in the back of the art house movie theater, place oily kernels of popcorn into Marley's mouth during some subtitled film, and rub his hand over Marley's thigh during certain on-screen moments of romantic tension.

Marley's favorite dining spot was an anomaly in the city of Osaka— an Italian restaurant with Japanese cooks and waiters. Jinn fed Marley soft quail eggs and anchovy salad, twirled langoustine ravioli with blood oranges onto a fork, blew on the sauced crust to cool it, then lightly placed the square on Marley's tongue.

"I love to watch your mouth when you chew," Jinn would remark, reaching for a napkin. "Here, let me wipe your chin."

"But when can I feed you?" Marley eyed the green beans and leeks.

"When we get home, of course," Jinn flirted recklessly. "You know the routine."

Jinn had no problem with displaying affection in public and had a way of getting to Marley with a well-timed embrace behind a park statue or a tongue kiss inside of a museum sarcophagus. The Japanese would often giggle or look away quickly; Jinn imagined the people of Osaka were simply shrugging off the behavior as something half-drunk American tourists do.

Once, Jinn let Marley go down on him in an open boiler room of an underground parking lot. Jinn's moans braided together with the hiss of steam pipes and just before he was about to explode in Marley's mouth, he pulled out. "Jesus, be careful." Marley gasped to see the panic that had suddenly creased Jinn's face.

Still, Jinn's way of lavishing Marley with affectionate glances and tugs endeared him to his companion. "My father never liked to hug anyone," he confided one night to Marley. "He was a simple man, pushed a fruit and vegetable cart over on the old Maxwell Street on the south side of Chicago."

"But you must have eaten well."

"I despised his profession. I had to stock that wagon every morning before going to school and I could never line up those freaking pomegranates the right way." Jinn began to recoil from Marley's embrace. "Sometimes kids would knock over the cart or throw spit wads at us. I could never act like it mattered because we had to show them how proud we were. The staunch Sicilians!"

"But that cart put you through Northwestern, didn't it?" Marley expected to hear Jinn talk about his illustrious academic life again.

"I was the monkey from Sicily because of my wide nose and frizzy hair. See this?" Jinn pointed to a nearly faded scar under his thick lower lip. "Someone threw a giant peach pit at me one morning. Called us ignorant dagos. I had to prove I was better than that, more than just an apple peddler."

"But you defended your dad's profession."

"My dad never defended mine."

"Yours?"

"My faghood." Jinn seemed to rub goosebumps off his arms. "I came out early in my teens and he said I was going to catch the virus if I continued my debauchery, as he put it. I remember being seventeen and working for my dad. I cut myself once on an artichoke and all the produce had to be tossed out, the cart hosed down. I could never reconcile any of that."

"Do you think your meditation practice can keep you safe?"

As Jinn drifted off, unable to respond, his eyes caught a moth fluttering over an orange neon tube outside. "It's late in the season to see any lepidoptera insects. It must be freezing."

"Maybe it would be better off in Malaysia?"

"I suppose all of us might be better off watching palm leaves blow in the wind and sipping cooled cups of Formosa tea." Jinn mustered up a tiny grin. "But there is no idée fixe, no perfect retreat. Did you know that HIV is spreading more rapidly in parts of Asia now than back in the States?"

Marley placed his hand on Jinn's belly and let it rest there, watching it rise subtly with each breath. He wondered what talisman could possibly protect the world from rampant diseases or natural disasters like the tsunami. Marley liked to compare sex to matzo ball soup, like a powerful cure or remedy. He used a condom but he resisted the notion that the drool in an amorous kiss might weaken him.

One night, Jinn paced around Marley's studio looking for a sweatshirt to throw on. It was interesting to note how much Marley resisted embracing Japanese culture. "For gosh sakes, we're in Osaka," Jinn looked exasperated. "Why do you have these posters of California surfers up?"

"I like to be reminded of my childhood spent in front of Frankie Avalon and Annette Funicello movies," Marley would grin. "Besides, I'm getting enough Japanese culture when I'm making my yakitori chicken at school."

Jinn was astonished to find tall stacks of American cookbooks in the closet that had been shipped to Marley from home. "You have an original copy of the first printing of Fannie Farmer's recipes?" Jinn gave an incredulous stare.

"Breathe on them and they all fall down," Marley cautioned.

Jinn took extra care in stepping backward to count the volumes, some of which seemed to be quite ancient. There were old issues of *Gourmet* magazine that Marley subscribed to, mixed in with recipes cut from the backs of tuna cans and pasta boxes, along with guides ranging from *Australian Cuisine* to *Tex-Mex in a Jiffy*.

"This is my favorite one," Marley said as he handed Jinn a handwritten copy of a nineteenth-century French cooking manual translated roughly into English.

"It's actually called a *grimoire*," Jinn noted as he read the calligraphy on the title page carefully.

Marley cleared his throat. "It tells the story of a magician's apprentice who learns how to cast spells through his recipes."

Jinn seemed genuinely curious as he held the fraying book binding in his hands.

"Through combinations of spices and pagan rituals, the apprentice could cause his acquaintances to give over their money, even fall in love with him."

"Have you ever tried making any of these dishes?" Jinn's brow arched.

Marley's eyes rolled back. "Why, have you fallen that deeply in love with me?"

Jinn's shoulders straightened rigidly as he took a deep breath. "I wouldn't want to leap into that chasm."

Marley took the weathered book back into his hands and lightly touched the frail cover. "I just like to read the ingredient lists and pretend that I'm the magician inhaling the steam, saying the occult words over the vapors." Marley's palm rotated in widening circles over the cover of the cookbook. "I like to think I'm the alchemist putting my sweat into the stew and ladling my magical soup from an enchanted tureen."

"Hey, be careful about which body secretions you're leaking into my bouillabaisse, okay?" Jinn drew back, covering his mouth with a dish towel.

"If you're suggesting I might stir in a deadly virus, relax." Marley gently shook his head. "Besides, authentic compassion would be the best anecdote to any such malady."

"Just a knee-jerk reaction. I know we're both tested and safe."

Marley pretended to hold a serving spoon to Jinn's lips. "Sip this, my dear." Jinn took Marley's extended finger into his mouth and gently sucked down to the knuckle, then pulled Marley onto the open futon and began caressing his back.

"In Borneo they eat something like Hawaiian poi." Jinn spoke through slow kisses. "You want some sweet poi, little boy?" Jinn always found a way of relating everything back to Malaysia or Kuala Lumpur or the length of the Malay Archipelago. In a few deep lip-locks, the cluttered apartment seemed to vanish and fade in a sitar-like symphony of long moans and sighs.

There was a comfort in the heft of each other's body and a familiarity that allowed Marley to act out his food fetish on Jinn. Sometimes he'd masturbate his partner with the slippery skin of a banana peel, or tie licorice whips around Jinn's scrotum. Jinn would giggle at Marley's attempt to make a butterscotch sundae out of his crotch, using puffs of marshmallow crème and chocolate mints. But when their elaborate devices for prolonging lust had run their course and the latex had been used up, a dour hush would descend upon them, Marley would peel at the grime wedged in between his cuticles and listen to Jinn's quiet breathing for hours.

When Jinn did speak it was usually about Asian philosophy or about a life he wasn't living in Malaysia. When he described the shrines of Penang Island, Marley would see himself there among the sightseers, pushing a cart laden with exotic dishes like murtabak, dumplings with shark's fin, steamed noodles with salted eggs, and crab sticks stuffed with fish paste. In one particular scenario, Marley would imagine himself led to a hidden cove nearby. Jinn would cover him with lychee fruit then gently eat the translucent wet globes off his warm skin, or drench him in coconut milk and a peppery curry then lick each crevice of his body.

But even in his dreams, Marley felt these novelties becoming tame. He imagined Jinn retreating inside himself after the disapproving gape of voyeuristic tourists. Then in his mind, he saw himself showering off the sticky residue of honey and salt after a fantasy bareback session with Jinn and left with a sense of dislocation, an overwhelming ennui with being his partner.

Still, it wasn't his naked cock that he wanted inside of Jinn after all, but his own voracious heart plugged into his companion's chest cavity, stripped to its core, unsheathed and vulnerable, beating in unison with Jinn's.

After making love, Jinn always fell into a kind of insular chill. To break the monotony of silence, he would sometimes improvise a tune that the Malaysian rice gatherers would sing in their native language. It had a melancholy tone to it and when Jinn sang the long dark chords the first time, Marley almost cried.

"Your voice makes me think of those characters on the Honda Heihachiro folding screens." Marley swallowed the cool air. "The way their heads are tilted as they listen to the lutes playing, as though they're levitating into the gold background."

Jinn had a way of leaving pauses in place of sentiment and allowing emptiness to enter between the two of them. A hundred thousand lifetimes seemed to pass in those quiet spaces and Marley sometimes felt burdened to fill it up with something, a perfect language that would leave him scrubbed and sagelike in Jinn's eyes. But Marley was a tourist. Not only here in Osaka, but with Jinn. He had no language skills to conquer the terrain.

Jinn had his perfectly memorized recitations of Robert Pirsig, his slow breathing meditations, and his three-day fasting and charcoal-filtered colonics. But there were other habits that kept Marley stuck on Jinn. Like the way Jinn gently sucked on Marley's lower lip while kissing. Or how Jinn would read from *The Tao of Pooh* and Marley would fall asleep on his chest. Or how during Sunday excursions to the Kuromon food market, Marley would gape at the assortment of preparations for Japanese duck, the soft-shelled crabs, the simmering curries, the hanging soba noodles, the metal vats of tripe soup and boiled gizzards, and the gelatinous balls of dough filled with squid and ground pork.

The foodstuffs were nothing compared to what Marley worked with; still he loved cooking at the American diner downtown and the challenge of turning something fairly simple like chicken-fried steak into a culinary masterpiece.

He remembered the time when Jinn had come into the diner for a surprise visit. Jinn had just finished lecturing at his college on Canton-ese logic. When he stepped through the door, Marley's face nearly burned to match the ketchup dispenser on the counter.

"I don't see anything for vegetarians on the carte du jour." Jinn looked almost stupefied at the plastic-coated menu with pictures of submarines and french fry-laden grill steaks.

"I can make you a salad if you don't mind shredded cabbage and iceberg." Marley kept wiping his hands on his soiled apron, hoping Jinn wouldn't be too critical.

"No, thanks. I prefer the crowded noodle shop down the street."

"Oh, but check this out." Slowly Marley unwrapped a tuna steak one of the cooks had just purchased. "If you can wait a few minutes." Marley noticed how rigid Jinn's shoulders had become, almost as if he were going into one of his warrior positions he was so fond of in yoga.

"I'll pass on it." Jinn moved to the corner of the diner and began to sip on some verbena-infused iced tea.

Marley didn't understand how to break the shell that sometimes held in his lover. He knew how to peel an onion without crying and debone an entire chicken in less than three minutes. He knew the right amount of cumin to sprinkle into chili and the temperature an oiled pan must reach in order to sear meat. And now that he knew Jinn, he understood something about desire and instinct, where kisses could take him if he would just let himself follow. But it was like a treasure box being opened for only as long as their lovemaking lasted. Once the careful kisses stopped, the jewels were hidden away, and only another erotic encounter could undo the latch again.

"Are you happy?" Marley innocently asked once after a prolonged sex session.

"Well, happier than you are when you're flipping those 'chik-a-patties,' right?" Jinn's remark sounded like the definitive whack of a blade going swiftly through to a butcher block.

He wondered if Jinn would have said that if he were supervising a staff of sous chefs at Le Bouchon, or hawking his own culinary books on *The Oprah Winfrey Show* like Charlie Trotter or Wolfgang Puck? For someone so elevated in their thinking, someone so seemingly devoted to Eastern thought, Marley thought it seemed out of character to challenge someone's status in life or identify their whole destiny with their work. But Marley just shrugged and quietly declared he was happy with his current livelihood.

He loved to work with collard greens and crayfish tamales and he was teaching himself how to make an amazing balsamic reduction and, for now, that was enough. Marley found transcendence in the pouring and stirring, with his moist brow hovering over each new food creation. When he made his cornflake-crusted tripe he knew just what Siddhartha must have felt like when he woke up from under the bo tree and saw the world dancing in shimmers of light. And he would trade those fat textbooks on Islamic customs and Malayo-Poly-nesian languages that fell out of Jinn's backpack for recipes on Viet-namese spring rolls and satay anytime.

Marley didn't say a word. He moved across the room and into the bathroom, then lit a cigarette. Next to the shower stall, Marley had made a shrine to his smoking addiction with Marlboro cigarette para-phernalia that had been loaded onto him by friends in high school. A Marlboro mirror sat over the sink in the bathroom with sink knobs in the shape of Stetson cowboy hats. Marley was hardly kindred to the smoking cowboy, but his association with the brand stuck to him as much as the smell of stale tobacco permeated the cloth shower curtain and towels. At times it seemed that the whole room could start clouding up with nicotine fog.

"You mentioned Nietzsche this afternoon." Jinn's voice broke the quiet as he called from the living room. "You've read his book, *The Birth of Tragedy?*"

"No, I was just thinking that Japanese stone garden was kind of useless. I mean, unless you were to set up a little hibachi or something in the middle."

Jinn smiled. "It's a place to breathe and contemplate. You know Nietzsche said that falling into silence can cause humans to perceive their own life as meaningless and absurd."

Marley crushed out the half-smoked cigarette in the bathroom sink. For a moment, he felt sorry for his sophisticated companion. He thought of Jinn hunched over a toppled fruit cart in the Chicago marketplace, wiping spit off his brown cheek and not being able to fall into his father's arms. He tried to imagine Jinn as a little boy, a kid who pinched his nose at night with a clothing pin, who rejected the earth-sodden smell of rotten pomegranates and avocados; someone who took refuge in a book, someone shy with risks.

"I do have a real job." Marley called out from the bathroom. He looked at his face in the Marlboro mirror and stared at the way it seemed chopped up, discombobulated and partitioned into irretrievable sections.

Jinn walked into the room waving his hand in front of his face trying to fan away the smoke. "What are you going to do? Spend the rest of your life as a grill chef at the American diner in Japan? How very quaint!"

"I like making Americans feel like they're at home." Marley was resolute as he exhaled over the sink. "So what if someone in Osaka feels more comfortable because they can order a hamburger the way they'd get it in Chicago? What's wrong with that?"

"And that's it? The ugly American with your loud Hawaii shirts and Bermuda shorts and your Green Day?" Jinn bolted from the doorway.

Marley turned the ceiling fan on to clear away the smoke and washed out the ashes in the basin. He walked from the bathroom to find Jinn had lit a candle and retreated into his insular lotus position. He bent over to kiss Jinn on the cheek, but it was as though his friend had already risen into the bodhisattva's fifth heaven, impenetrable and safe. For a moment, he wished he could chant a magical rhyme over Jinn's head, or sing a song to get inside of him, but instead he just stood there, silently watching the ascending yogi.

Marley found himself calling Sol the next day to meet up at the American Beauty. Even though Jinn had two tickets to see the Kurosawa film fest at the National Museum of Art, fresh-brewed beer sounded much more satisfying.

"I'd rather walk around Universal Studios Japan," Marley snorted. Besides, he didn't want to risk having to walk through the displays of painted scrolls and ancient deity sculptures at the museum. "Who needed another history lesson from Jinn on the Japanese woodblock prints of Hiroshige? So what if this artist inspired Whistler? So what if he perfected color-etching in the eighteenth century?"

None of Jinn's shared insight into meditation or artistic discipline or Asian art seemed to matter at the moment. All that mattered was the foggy din in Marley's favorite barroom and the sweaty grip of husky wrestlers on a giant television screen.

"Order two pitchers." Marley's instructions to Sol were definitive as he exhaled smoke through his nostrils.

"What's that edge in your voice?" Sol motioned to get the attention of the bartender.

"I just want to shut off."

"Have a sip and take your mind off Jinn." Sol's solace seemed to hang in the air like a far-off bleating foghorn.

Marley gulped down the contents of his cold mug and stared at the sumo wrestlers on the big screen. As he watched, there was an uneasy tremble in the pitch of the arena crowd. It appeared that one of the wrestlers was really bleeding and it seemed as though someone would hurl grenades into the ring. One of the men was taunting some reveler in the audience in Japanese. Marley tried to focus but some kind of static was dancing over the wrestlers, like sudden snow flurries on the lakefront or the haze from an exhaust pipe.

"I can barely make out what they're doing." Marley sounded more annoyed and with each complaint, Sol poured another glassful. *"Evening Rain at the Ethai Bridge."*

Sol looked perplexed. "What did you say, Marls?"

"That's the name of that goddamn painting by Hiroshige."

"You're thinking of a painting right now?"

The hazy reception on the widescreen had somehow made Marley think of one of the color woodblocks Jinn had shown him at the museum. It was a scene of incandescent moonlight and rain, faerie mist, and three oblong boats steered by dark figures with long paddles. Marley remembered wanting to be a figure on the edge of one of those narrow canoes that afternoon Jinn pointed it out to him. There were the arches of a bridge and wisps of rain and the sky in the painting was charcoal gray hues streaked at the horizon.

"Don't you see the other boat?" Jinn raised his finger to trace the outline of another sidelong watercraft. "He's trying to catch up with the other one."

"No." There was an absolute assuredness about Marley's response. "They're just passing each other by. There are dangerous eddies and the edges of the shoreline are black and the boatmen are barely noticing one another. They're not even waving."

Jinn squinted and leaned forward a bit to scrutinize the scene. "As I recall, the artist's philosophy was to see life as a stream. A man floats, and his way is smooth. The same man turned upstream exhausts himself. To be one with the universe, each must find his true path and follow it."

Marley seemed unmoved by Jinn's anecdote. "But look at the way they hold their bodies after passing so close. They're still so stiff, so formal, unmoved by the whole encounter. I wonder if their oars even brushed against each other or if the uneven current even made them waver a bit. If one toppled over, would the other come to his rescue?"

Marley seemed to recall every detail of the painting, every word of his conversation that afternoon in the Asian art gallery with Jinn. It all seemed fresh in his mind, even while the wrestlers on the screen were being buried by gray snow and static, vanishing.

"I'm done with this for now." Marley cleared a path for himself through the bleary haze of the bar, leaving Sol bewildered. He stopped for a moment to look at some half-drunk patron fumbling at the karaoke microphone in a pink Hello Kitty sweatshirt, trying to follow the words flashing across a video screen in order to correctly pronounce the lyrics to "Hotel California." In that flash second, Marley felt despondent. He had kept himself insular from the world and, despite being in Osaka and meshing with Japanese culture, he was still cocooned in his little hometown in America.

He went to catch a bus back up to his studio apartment. He looked at his legs in the cold air and wondered why he didn't own one pair of jeans that didn't have a mustard splotch or grease stain on them from working at the restaurant. He thought of watching the Food Network on cable television back in the States and Emeril Lagasse's starched white chef's smock. How sometimes by the end of the show, after making love to a pork loin or rows of garlic cloves, he would be mottled in extra virgin olive oil and New Orleans hot sauce. How the audience would shout "Bam!" when the plates were finessed with ground red pepper and oven-smoked garlic.

Marley wanted to feel that sense of connection with food, with life. He wanted his naked hands to be kneading and toiling. He wanted them buttery and submerged into bowls of peeled artichokes and grated potatoes. It might be risky, too much salt, a casserole over-cooked, but he wanted to feed people, to give them nourishment, to see those who ate his meals achieve a sense of being at home or, as Jinn would say, "centered."

The temperature had dropped and the cloudy vapor from his breath made it look as though he were exhaling from one of his cigarettes, but he had left almost a full pack on the counter of the bar and he wasn't going to go back for them. He kept imagining himself and Jinn as wrestlers trapped in a phony pin. Jinn would throw a judo kick at Marley and he would miss. The crowds would shout out, "Don't touch the blood! Stay away from the blood, you dumb queers!" Then Jinn would wrap Marley up in plastic cellophane, like leftover sushi, and walk out of the ring.

Before boarding the downtown bus that would take him to his studio, Marley walked through an underground arcade crowded with clusters of exuberant shoppers. He imagined himself, in a way, as someone entirely invisible, as if he were moving through the throngs of bargain hunters as some sort of living ghost.

He stopped to stare at the yellow tigers made from a traditional Japanese papier-mâché process known as *hariko*. He stared intently at the benign talismans, their jaws left open to reveal their tiny wooden fangs and the detail on their rose-painted tongues. For a moment, he caught his own reflection in the glass pane, his drawn face transposed over the paper figurines.

When Marley finally arrived home, he discovered that his studio was chilly. He thought that the hot-water pipes had probably frozen up again because the tenant downstairs was just now beginning to bang pans on the radiator. But Marley noticed that a bit of steam was wheezing through the painted radiators, and that tiny push of mist through the pipes almost sounded like the ache in Jinn's voice when he would sing that Malaysian song.

Marley took out a little cardboard box of leftover dim sum from the refrigerator. It was a fried ball of crusty coconut layered over a caramelized mixture of rice and pork. Marley took a bite thinking of the cook who had prepared the dough, who ground up the fish and seasoned it with cilantro, who spoke over it in a foreign tongue then rolled the orb in his warm hands. He thought of the fingers of the chef as he chopped the shallots. Of the exactitude and skill used to make this common ball of fish paste and sprouts. How this seafood had been transformed into this rolled-up world just for Marley.

Marley scrutinized the appetizer and passed his hands over it like a magician would before biting into its core. "Heart of simple fish, herb leaf of true desire, blend into me." Even chilled, it was like taking in a lover's long tongue kiss.

Marley was still shivery and went into the bathroom to feel some warmth from the rising steam emanating from his soaking tub. He kneeled down, rested his head on his arm. He smelled like his familiar stale cigarette smoke odor, like the prep kitchen at work, like garlicky shallots and Crisco and patties of pressed chicken and paprika.

He turned the spigot to let a trickle of lukewarm water run over his hand. It dripped over his palm like iridescent pearls, small clear gems that exploded over his fingers. He watched the water slowly begin to fill up over the rusted drain. He looked at the chipped porcelain white of the bathtub. He watched tiny ripples dance over cold, hard white and thought of small white stones and of the Zen garden he'd seen earlier that week.

He imagined himself as simply himself, wandering in that Japanese enclosure, without his Keds, without his flip-flops or fraying Birkenstock sandals, even without his cigarettes. He was there, tiptoeing over the edges of long white slate, dancing over granite islands and quietly leaning over the blanched, frozen waves of the Zen garden.

He thought of Malaysia and all the places he'd never been to. He didn't mind being alone; he didn't even mind feeling slightly out of place, a little bit like Nietzsche contemplating his shadow, perhaps.

Marley surrendered to the detached feeling and, if he looked closely in the corner of the remembered garden, he could almost see Jinn striding into a little replica of a Japanese hut, running into what seemed to be a birdhouse or a fabricated sparrow's nest.

In Marley's mind, Jinn had now become someone just that tiny, who could step through that little door frame and never walk back out again.

Holding Pattern

Flipping through the complementary in-flight magazine on board my flight to Casablanca, I read about all of the places I have never been to. I'm convinced after skimming the feature story on Jakarta that I should be booking a flight there this season since, according to the author, airfares and hotel rates are plummeting due to widespread fears of another possible tsunami disaster. I note that it's a virtual bargain basement for those seeking Shangri-la.

No mention of the choking air pollution, heroin addiction in the overcrowded slums, rampant prostitution rings, and desperate poverty that exists on the island of Java, only that luxury hotels are offering enticing discounts and that I can pepper my stay with a five-star property's exclusive in-room massage service, visits to an on-site health club, three oversized plunge pools, high-speed Internet access in every suite, and business-courier amenities offered at no extra charge.

The photographs anchoring the travel article reveal fertile palm trees flourishing in the middle of the high traffic boulevards with blurred images of glammed-out tourists under ghost trails of neon, euphoric in the midst of a decadent nightlife that reportedly rivals even Singapore and New York.

I slip the magazine back into the seat pocket in front of me and for a moment I am in that glossy image on the cover, sun-tanned and giddy, with my handsomely fabricated companion holding gold-tipped chopsticks up to my mouth as I sample the fresh Japanese sushi under a hanging paper lantern. I close my eyes as the jet moves into Greenwich mean time and continue to airbrush that image in my mind until I am nearly indistinguishable from the soft-focused haze around me.

Postcards from Heartthrob Town: A Gay Man's Travel Tales
Published by The Haworth Press, Inc., 2006. All rights reserved.
doi:10.1300/5732_07

*   *   *

I am plugged into my portable compact disc player listening to the Bryan Ferry CD I purchased before boarding this delayed flight to Morocco. The music stall at the JFK airport terminal offered discounts on old titles and I couldn't resist picking up a vintage Everything but the Girl album, before the duo went techno, along with *The Best of Basia* and Ferry's classic *Bête Noire*.

Listening to Ferry sing "Limbo" again, I am transported back to that half-naked luau party on Kehena Beach nearly ten years ago. I had thrown up in a patch of purple bougainvillea from the seaweed and coconut-shredded poi, but still my relentless companion kept on trying to get me to bury him in the black sand.

"I came here for the live volcanoes," I kept repeating to my soon to be ex-lover.

"Screw the damn volcanoes. I'd rather see your own hot lava flow."

I came to Hawaii to see the ancient petroglyphs, to take pictures of the pit craters and rock moulds made from burnt-out tree trunks. To gape at the late-night torch twirlers on the beach and learn how to fold together a perfect origami crane.

My partner at the time wanted to sip the sweet liquor squeezed from island-grown cacao pods and sneak kisses with me from inside of a cinder cone. He wanted to dance around a roasting pig on a spit sporting his white jasmine lei and the torn edges of a grass hula skirt. He wanted to match the red eyes of the carved tiki masks in the lobby of our hotel by lounging all afternoon near a pool, wearing a straw hat and guzzling down a series of rum-infused cocktails.

I was in my late thirties back then, touring the Big Island with my partner and mindlessly nodding my head to Ferry's cloying drumbeats and his lyrics about voodoo love, the lion-headed Egyptian goddess Sekhmet, and a suffocating obsession for delusional romance.

I believed back then that I could prance through some hashish-infused discothèque until closing time and subsist on a series of sugared lattes for the rest of the day. I believed I could enter and reenter a progression of so-called serious relationships, undressing in front of a string of ill-matched suitors, and go through my temporary lives with them, one life supplanting the next, without much visible consequence.

Four songs into the CD now and I realize that I didn't purchase this lounge-life opus because I was nostalgic for the songs themselves. I bought the album because I want to remember that person I once was.

The shirtless rhythm bunny on a strobe-lit dance floor, jutting out his torso to a Jimmy Somerville remix, still toned enough to be mistaken for a reckless twink. The flushed novice in the backseat of the blue-black convertible, arms and fingers and sockless toes raised into the starless swatch of sky. The interminably fresh-faced kid who always shrugged his shoulders at the notion of boundaries and of getting older and of ever being anything less than handsomely draped in to-the-minute Armani couture.

I remove my headphones and the music continues to play with Ferry's rhythms becoming tinny and vacant as they mesh into the droning hum of the jet. My head falls back on the spongy travel pillow and I begin to move through the disequilibrium, the music now completely muffled by the subsequent popping of my inner ear canals as the plane moves from one altitude to the next.

* * *

I order an iced ginger ale because Royal Air Maroc doesn't stock 7 Up. I'm thinking the limey carbonation will settle my stomach and somehow reinforce the effect of the Dramamine tablets that I took hours ago back at the New York terminal.

I fold down my tray table and the flight attendant places a clear plastic cup on a red and gold cocktail napkin and sets down a covered oval plate with tonight's menu: foie gras, smoked salmon, a wrapped container of spreadable imitation cheese, and a wedge of melon on the side as a garnish. I unwrap my napkin and silverware and begin to cut the unripe cantaloupe into small pieces.

The seat beside me is empty so I am relieved of the irksome necessity of having to drudge up a few well-chosen remarks between bites of my meal. For a moment, however, as I spear the fruit wedges onto my fork, I think to myself that I am starkly lonely. I wonder if perhaps having to force myself into a conversation with a stranger right now might alleviate some of my feelings of isolation.

Surrounded by other passengers busily engaged in chewing their bits of pink fish flesh, listening on their earphones to the airline's programmed music, or scanning their folded-over newspapers, I'm struck at how I feel no camaraderie or fellowship whatsoever with anyone on board. I am relegated to the status of tourist, a virtual outsider with a boarding pass receipt on an airplane moving through clouds and sudden bumps of air gusts, flickering lights, and vague currents of storm electricity.

A female voice announces over the intercom in a heavy foreign accent that all passengers need to buckle up and remain seated, as "we will be experiencing some potentially bumpy and static conditions."

Outside the window is the bluster of wind and gaseous air dust passing by the blinking red lights of the extended plane wing. I can only make out the transparent image of my blank face, looking back at me in the rain-spattered window glass. I look like a bewildered excursionist, a disheveled exile wiping the dribble of melon juice off of my chin, as I attempt to imagine what this waylaid jet might be flying over at this disquieting moment.

Are we suspended over the vastness of the Atlantic Ocean or the Moroccan desert beloved by American expatriate writer Paul Bowels? The Islamic rooftops of Tangier or the sprawling marketplace stalls of some open trading post? A trail of camels and robed Bedouin tribesmen or the tennis courts and swimming pool of the Hilton Rabat? The ancient walled fortress of the casbah or a concrete-paved landing strip?

As I try to pull apart the sinewy salmon, I realize that, aside from a brief stay once in Tangier, Morocco has really only existed for me in books, geography lessons, and black-and-white movies. That in this moment as I try to fathom the actual solidity of the adobe forts below me, with their candlelit slit windows or the smell of pistachio-infused couscous simmering in an open kitchen, all that really matters is this part of the journey I'm on right now.

In my mind I continue to build on half-truths, myths forwarded by the bohemian stories of sex-crazed artists like William Burroughs and Jean Genet, and the symbolic, if not dated, abstractions floating in my imagination. A red fez cap filled with cocaine. The entrance to a mosque painted in shades of canary yellow. A dark tunnel running under ancient ruins. A series of seaside hills with no drawn maps available for tourists who wish to traverse their roads.

I habitually invent a succession of dreamy escapades in these far-off cities. In one fantasy I'm the irresistible bon vivant, welcomed into a colony of gay artists, perhaps. In another, I'm a charming poet who is quickly ushered into a Moroccan prince's all male harem and handed the long hose of a lit hookah.

Before the arrival is always the motive for getting there. I recognize now in my solitude that I can't neglect that part of me that simply longs to drift in my lopsided fabrications. That cross-eyed inner child who wants to inhabit the movie-set charm of Bogart's archetypal Rick's Café, wander the crooked streets and alleys of the medina, or be taken over by the lure of some handsome carpet vendor's seduction in a sequestered back room.

Somehow the worn, outdated fabric of the airplane seat around me and the cramped, confined space I am traveling in is providing an opportunity for this long-winded interior monologue, allowing me to dissect in piecemeal what it is exactly I am hoping to discover once the jet makes contact with the continent of Africa.

I consider that perhaps it is enough to simply be moving. To be caught up in the arc of crossing a dog-eared atlas, slinging my luggage from over my shoulder to an overhead storage bin. Checking the arrival and departure schedules at airport and train terminals. Following the suggested trek of trustworthy tour guides or breaking completely with their recommendations. It is enough, I tell myself, to simply be en route to elsewhere, in a perpetual state of flux, with the potential of acquainting myself with someone—anyone—I've never met before.

The plane lunges for a moment and my ginger ale topples off of my extended tray table and onto the empty seat beside me. As I wipe up the spilled soda with my lap napkin, a hand from the seat behind me reaches over the headrest.

"Did you lose your cup?" The male voice is somewhat formal but nearly arches over into a sense of friendliness. As I turn around I can only see the gentleman's extended shirtsleeve and the top of his well-groomed head of hair.

I retrieve the glass and offer my thanks to the passenger seated behind me. I'm somehow grateful for this momentary encounter with another traveler, a camerado. I'm contented by the contact I just made with another person on board, even as negligible as this one was, as I note the sudden white flashes of lightning outside the window and the increasing frequency of dips and lurches within the cabin.

If the pilot should lose control of the plane, if we should suddenly plummet to earth, if I should never reach the Casablanca of my dreams, at least I will have this small, final affirmation that I wasn't completely alone.

*   *   *

I'm on assignment in Morocco to write a story about exotic sojourns. I will probably write about my first brief encounter with the city of Tangier several years ago, when I traveled by train from Spain to the breezy northwest coast of Africa.

My traveling companion at the time was my lover of one year, although it was still during that time I used the abstract word *lover* to encompass anyone who I discovered a rapid affinity for and who could share the rent on a tiny loft in downtown Chicago. We had been living together for just six months and he insisted that we bring back a handmade rug for our front entranceway.

"Every time we walk into the apartment we'll remember our trip," he said.

"We can purchase one but, just remember, you're strapping it to your back and carrying it home."

Tangier is the closest African city to Europe with a growing population that reaches well over half a million. Notable for its Islamic architecture and breathtaking vistas, the city became beloved by American and European artists who came seeking inspiration and license to express the bohemian attitude. While luxury hotels and five-star restaurants are well entrenched in the cosmopolitan city today, many of the inhabitants, most of whom are Muslim, struggle to make ends meet.

Stepping off the train we were initially accosted by a throng of young children shouting for us to give up our spare coins, holding up metal bracelets and waving colorful djellabas at us. The air was infused with the vague scent of coriander and diesel fuel as we tried to orient ourselves to the twisting web of streets.

As we walked from the platform to the busy sidewalk, we encountered a chain of Morocco's disenfranchised and destitute: a teenage amputee leaning on his crutch with a begging cup, a half-veiled elderly woman seated at the curb with a sign written in French and English requesting to PLEASE HELP, and a group of seemingly stoned-out scruffy hippies who held up their empty woven baskets to a mostly indifferent stream of new arrivals.

We stayed in a dank-smelling guesthouse in the mud-walled Casbah, the old fortress overlooking the crowded metropolitan area. The landlord was an amiable ex-pat who had sought refuge from the Vietnam War back in the seventies. Our lodgings were decorated with tiny painted canvasses that reflected his love of the beach and the shell-pink sunsets over the Mediterranean.

We unpacked, changed, and crossed over to the medina, where we took photographs of vendor tables filled with ripe green olives, caged live chickens, almonds and wrapped confections, mosaic tabletops, and exquisitely shaped caramel-glazed pottery.

As we sought out the source of Tangier's allurement, we made note of the emerald-painted doorways, the blue-tinted shutters, and the scarred walls occasionally splashed with hues of turquoise and rose burning to lavender. The influence of modern culture was not lost on the old town either, with signs in English screaming FAX and silver satellite dishes poking out from the pink stucco rooftops.

In the center of the old town is the Petit Socco, a wide-open square where we purchased a cup of steaming mint tea at a terrace café and chased the ghosts of gay literati William Burroughs, Tennessee Williams, Truman Capote, and Jack Kerouac.

"Can you sense the sleazy homo vibe pulsing in this square?" I ask my distracted partner who was fanning himself with the menu. "According to the guidebook, we may be seated exactly where Jean Genet once took his coffee."

"Yeah. I can't tell if I'm being cruised right now or that row of guys over there are simply curious."

"Or better yet, if they want to drop your pants so they can nab your money belt," I cautioned.

"I think that's a risk I'd be willing to take with the stud on the right."

While my partner and I had seldom discussed the notion of monogamy between us, it was something that I assumed at this early stage of our alliance would either galvanize the relationship or become a point of bitter contention.

We finished our brew, resolving to ignore the persistent stares of the precarious olive-skinned men, the sensual furtive beckoning from their dark eyes that seemed to promise anything in their overt seduction.

I paid our bill and we proceeded to meander up the Rue de la Marine past wooden peddler stalls, tailors and carpenter shops, and huddled groups of robed Berber men. According to the guidebook, the crooked, tunneled path eventually led toward the grand mosque, so we slowly snaked our way toward the noted tourist site.

"Hang on; I want to take a look at these rugs over here," my companion called back at me from a well-stocked carpet stall. "I'll catch up with you later."

"Don't forget to barter firmly!" I shouted back as my eye caught the muscled arm of the handsome cruiser from earlier in the square.

I watched as the two of them drew closer together, my companion utterly spellbound by the magnetism of the sculpted bronzed man in his tight green T-shirt.

While Morocco has no established network such as bars or bathhouses to service openly gay clientele, there seems to be the quiet acknowledgment that what goes on behind closed doors will remain covert. I felt a sense that there are few sexual lines drawn in this country and, while bisexual activity may not be supported openly, it comes as no shock to the indigenous population.

As the spurious allies turned down a shadowed side alley, I drew a blank. I stuttered, nearly gasping as I attempted to recall my companion's first name. Who was it that I had boarded a plane with just two weeks earlier, danced with until the morning hours on the beaches of Ibiza, and traveled by train down to this legendary port to be with? I was struck with a sudden paralyzing amnesia.

A robed man approached me with a fez-capped monkey on his shoulder and in a mix of Spanish and broken English asked me if he could tell my fortune.

"*Fortuna,* fortune?" His tattooed hand kept pointing to the tiny monkey climbing up his neck.

"It's not necessary," I shook my head as the monkey reached out to touch my ear. "I think I get it now."

I watched then as the street became a kind of hazy whirlpool, with television antennae falling into the crooked flat-topped roofs, pestering touts dashing in and out of the labyrinthine side streets, and the clacking tongues of wildly gesturing vendors all blending into one single scream.

I left the collapsing blur and walked aimlessly through crowds and various quarters, past unreadable signs posted in Arabic, through alleys and tunnels that seemed to lead in one direction, but ultimately ended up turning me around to where I had just started. Nothing in Tangier was what it appeared to be.

I finally reached the ramparts of the old city and rested for a moment. I stood near a small plot of garden and examined the tiny buds of desert flowers on some low-growing plant, the edges of its petals and leaves singed by the relentless sun. I looked up at the gray stone alls set before me that were built in the fifteenth century, the crumbling turrets outlined in the vanishing light.

For a moment, Tangier felt like an oppressive weight upon me, but I was somehow challenged by the opportunity to finish my stay here alone. I reached into my backpack and pulled out my guidebook, trying to find the name of the hotel where Matisse always stayed.

I had this notion that if I could take in the view from the window of the guest room where he painted, I would feel like someone more myself. I was determined to see the vista from the Hotel Villa de France, the streets that curved around salt-white houses and the expanse of blue waters that crept up onto the bay's shore. I wanted to see for myself the iridescent light that Matisse tried to capture in his drawings and perhaps, for a moment, understand how I came to arrive at what I felt to be a kind of crossroads.

When I arrived at the Rue de Belgique, the sun had completely set and no tours were being allowed into the room where the famous artist had once painted. I proceeded to the lobby and requested single accommodations for myself at the famous hotel.

I had no desire to return to my shared room in the Casbah or to even converse with my now former traveling companion. In my mind I had him wrapped up in his sought-after, rolled-up, thick wool carpet, securely attached to the young man who approached him in the Petit Socco earlier in the day.

When the sun rose in the morning I could see exactly what it was that led Matisse to this dreamscape city. I wrote in my journal about the changing hues of the sky and the way the light tiptoed off the turquoise waters and onto the stone walls of the city. It was as if the light in Tangier had the power to somehow cleanse everything that it touched.

I stood for a long time looking up at the sun on my hotel terrace, taking in glimpses of where the Atlantic mixes with the Mediterranean, allowing the penetrating rays of light to wash over my face, hoping that by late afternoon, any trace of my former life would somehow be burned away.

*   *   *

"Maybe there's an Algerian dust storm in the Sahara," I hear a passenger remark in a somewhat alarming tone. "Perhaps there are high winds blowing through Marrakech, blowing us way off course."

For nearly an hour the plane has been rattling through disabling air currents and rain clouds provoking the air stewards to prematurely gather up the plastic dinner dishes and cups and insist that passengers tighten their seat belts.

"We're in a holding pattern," one of the flight attendants says as she hands an elderly woman a patterned blanket. "The captain is doing everything he can to safely land the aircraft, but for now we need to be patient."

I stow my compact disc player away and stare straight into the high back of the seat in front of me. The cabin seems to wheeze a little bit every time the jet navigates through another pocket of wind and I find that there is little to console myself with.

I pull the white panel shade of my window down and think of a painting I once saw at the Art Institute of Chicago, a representation of a man riding on the back of a horse that is wildly bucking a lion's attack.

Eugène Delacroix rendered the famous oil titled *Arab Horseman Attacked by a Lion* in the mid-1800's. It depicts a gilded white stallion with its strong head askew and its upper body cocked back in an exaggerated manner. Its front legs are raised against the penetrating open jaws of a lion, while the red-caped rider wields a long blade against the aggressor's ratted mane.

Delacroix, the leader of the Romantic movement in French painting, visited Africa, including Tangier, and found inspiration for many of his works there. He tried to infuse his paintings with a kind of visceral passion. He attempted in his artwork to locate the furious pulse of his chosen subjects through charged colors and movement.

I don't know why I am drawn to that image floating through my mind at this particular moment. Only that I have always wondered about the outcome of that frozen bloody encounter.

Will the startled horse run off leaving the man to fend off the lion on his own? Will the lion overtake both the rider and the horse, leaving their entrails as carrion for the morning? Or can the stomping horse distract the lion long enough for the turbaned fellow to fatally skewer the beast?

The jet seems to be curving downward at the moment, slowly turning around in the gray-black rain. I imagine that the plane is suspended over a vast expanse of desert. At the moment, it seems impossible to create in my mind the boulevards, infrastructure, and architecture of a city like Casablanca.

Have the art deco buildings and colonial influences of the old city been covered over by sand? Where are the modern skyscrapers and the ancient mosques? Why does my mind resist its typical inclination to conjure an image of this famous locale?

I'm in a holding pattern. Circling and floating and jostling through time and space, over a dusty atlas with no recognizable time zones or tundras, oceans or cities. No shaped continent on a map that would seem even remotely familiar to me.

The hum of the plane's engine seems to drive out any recollection of past lovers, cherished visits to foreign places, or moments of pure transcendence when I might have once completely understood what it is that provokes me to travel in the first, what moves me from one city, one set of arms, to another.

I remember from an art history course in college that in the early part of Delacroix's life, he believed things happened randomly and considered himself to be an agnostic. As his career progressed, he began to believe in the notion of a divine being and wrote in his journal that "God was within" each and every individual. Even his later work reflected that there was an inner force that guided every soul toward what was good and righteous.

I am floating in an imprecise and starless sky tonight, waiting to hear that same celestial voice that spoke to Delacroix. That same holy force that moved the artist's hand across the canvas.

I am waiting to locate a transcendent presence that would suggest I have a purpose on this journey. I am searching for the conviction and recognition that I am a pilgrim with a resolution and that I know exactly where I'm going.

Smoke Follows Beauty

Berlin Brandenburg International Airport

I don't care that I'm half-German. I don't care that my mother named me Gerhard after the German painter Gerhard Richter. I don't care that I was raised on a steady diet of Wiener schnitzel and sauerkraut while listening to Wagner's interminable *Ring Cycle* playing in the background. I won't even attempt to speak a word of this incomprehensible language while staying in Germany.

"Don't think I'm going to be your patsy and translate everything here in Berlin for you," Franz insists while flashing his inscrutable grin.

"I'm not asking you to, my sweetmeat. Just teach me the proper German words for *condom* and *suck* and I'll get by just fine."

"You hardly need words for those simple universals," Franz offers me a wry side-glance as his roll-away luggage tips over while coming off the moving sidewalk. Rolled-up socks and boxer shorts and a shaving kit filled with miniature shampoo bottles stolen from our Amsterdam pension spill out onto the floor and scatter in every direction.

"You should have zipped up better, baby." I'm laughing as I pull my own wheel-away off the conveyer belt.

"That's what my mother told me, but did I listen?" Franz heads toward a newspaper kiosk to retrieve his spilled stash, while I head for the restroom. I pull my carry-on next to the urinal and quickly realize there is more than just peeing going on in this public restroom. There is an engorged uncut pecker to the left of me and on my right, a burning stare grazing my own stiffening cock.

I live for these moments of spontaneous combustion, as my two unnamed partners and I reach out for a friendly but discreet whack.

Postcards from Heartthrob Town: A Gay Man's Travel Tales
Published by The Haworth Press, Inc., 2006. All rights reserved.
doi:10.1300/5732_08

What astonishes me most of all is that men come in and out of the latrine and go on whizzing right next to us, oblivious to the frenetic gesturing that's going on just a few steps away from them.

The rhythmic motion of our open masturbating reminds me of Franz' violin bow. Back and forth, the wand divines the secret code written into his quirky compositions. The to-and-fro of Franz's arm reaches a frenzied pitch, particularly when he is playing in concert, and all at once the musician has alchemized into the music itself. I love to watch him close his eyes and get lost in the drone of those taut strings. I live to watch those tiny beads of perspiration that form on my friend's forehead, the way his head falls back and his body trembles with the rising chords of the composition. I think of his passionate playing as I spew into the drain and watch as my jizm is gently sprayed away with the whoosh of the urinal water.

I make my way back to my companion, who has gathered up the contents of his boarding tote. His Stradivarius case is strapped tightly around his shoulder and he's looking hungrily at some svelte blond crew cut.

"You're insatiable," I laugh, as I put my hand on his shoulder. Franz gestures at the masculine Aryan vision: the broad shoulders, the stealthy frame, and the eyes that suggest a complete detachment from the moment.

"Put him in a uniform and we could play all night," Franz whispers to me.

The voice on the intercom is announcing flights to New York. For a moment I think of our apartment on the Lower East Side and why we came here in the first place. I think of our dream to compose songs together, Franz writing the music and me scribbling at the lyrics.

"Rodgers and Hammerstein," I always say to him.

"No way," he corrects. "Gilbert and Sullivan."

I think of how we decided to wander through Europe to simply absorb the tumult of it all. To soak up inspiration wherever we might find it, be it in an opera house or a bathhouse. I think of the warmth we find in each other's company. To simply snooze in each other's arms, while sharing a bed together in some foreign locale with no formal attachments to each other, no false dependencies. Or so I tell myself.

I'm wiping the dried residue of my restroom encounter off the crease in my khakis while Franz seems lost in his cruise.

"Franz, how do you say the word *wantonly* in German?"

"My darling, why say it, when you can make your whole life into that fatal gesture?"

Volkspark Friedrichshain

I don't know why all the beautiful men in Berlin seem to linger near the Fairy Tale Fountain at the entrance to Friedrichshain Park, but this neo-Baroque structure made up of characters from Grimm's stories seems to be whispering to amorous strangers from everywhere in Europe to connect. Franz and I are seated near a water-spraying limestone frog. I'm eyeing the cruisy promenade of hunky potentials, who make their connections then disappear down a crooked hedge path. Franz seems more annoyed than anything since his pen won't write.

"Why is it when I'm completely inspired to create music, I can't seem to locate any free-flowing ink?" Franz dabs the tip of his leaky ballpoint to his tongue.

"Check out the melody that's passing by us right now."

All eyes are on the striking man in tight tan jeans and tank top. Like a caricature from one of Tom of Finland's drawing boards, the brown-haired stranger with the exaggerated bulges seems to be magnetized by Franz' subtly erotic movements. Maybe because my companion is entirely absorbed in finding a pen that will create a correction mark rather than drooling over this sexy man's visage, the swarthy presence leans on a railing that places him directly in Franz' sight lines.

"I think you've got a potential new boyfriend, darling."

Franz glances up rather abruptly, then turns around to shade his notebook and hunches over to scribble notes onto his lined paper. "Amuse yourself, Gerhard. My musical muse is calling."

"I don't think you understand," I caution. "Your muse is pointing straight out at you and, I'm telling you, it's not his finger."

The well-endowed cruiser adjusts his shorts several times, pulling at the ever-growing outline in his shrinking pants, before finally heading over to the other end of the water mélange. I toss a schilling into the central fountain where Hansel and Gretel seem content to float separately on the backs of two ducks and Puss in Boots seems ready to lick his whiskers, before I decide to wander down one of the narrow hedge lanes.

It's easy to see the small breaks in the tall bushes where covert strangers can slip away. By following a small foot trail laced with condom wrappers and cigarette butts, hardly the bread crumbs left by Hansel and his sister, I reach a small opening where Franz' hopeful suitor is holding court. Leaning back onto the trunk of tree, the beautiful man's shorts are now stretched around his ankles and his perspiration-soaked T-shirt is hoisted above his thick nipples. A devotee kneels before the bejeweled royal scepter and takes slow, careful tastes of the rock-hard phallus.

In the distance I can hear the trickle of water spewing from the mouths of lions and green, weathered vases. I think of Franz and his hand drawing the silent notes onto a page. And in the shadow of Sleeping Beauty's statue, I imagine that the notes are coming off the paper and taking flight over the captured storybook creatures.

Another hungry minion takes the captive stud from behind and I draw closer to touch one of his large, amber nipples. The licking and sucking braids into the gentle gurgle from the fountain, and I imagine again Franz' symphonic score coming into being. Bluebeard and Little Red Riding Hood are beginning to awaken and suddenly the spring is alight with mythical heroes. The ancient spell that has kept them imprisoned in stone has been broken. Alive and supple and hungry for touch, the faerie world summons its inhabitants to join in a sensual dance.

"You like mouth to mouth?" the aggressor posits in broken English.

With that I begin kissing the handsome prince full on. He is probing the sweaty crevice of my ass with his fingers and moaning something that vaguely sounds like the word "baby." I can sense the restless music in the trees enveloping us as he quickly gushes into the mouth of his kneeling servant. I leave his wet saliva on my lips and cheek as I make my way back toward Franz.

"Back so soon?" Franz hardly looks up from his writing.

I know something now about the enchantment that breathes in the arteries of a forest and about the winged creatures who watch from the balustrade of a fountain, spinning magical rings that allow men to be invisible to the patrolling security guards who walk amid the clandestine leafy paths.

Franz is still hovering over his work as I gently lean into his shoulder.

"Still with your other muse?" My voice is deliberately soft and far away.

For a moment he rests his pen and sighs, letting his head sink gently onto my cheek. Then he resumes his careful notations, as though the whole world has simply vanished.

Charlottenburg Municipal Baths

Franz wants to linger all day in the medieval core of the city. He seems enamored with the western bank of the Spree River. He's not interested in seeing the remnants of the Berlin Wall or in hanging out in the raucous taverns or taking a bus tour past the financial districts and monuments.

"I want to feel the old Germantown," Franz remarks emphatically while eyeing a tourist map of gay Berlin. "I'm not interested in the digital masturbation diary exhibit at the Underground Phallic Film Festival or watching simulation intercourse backed by a morosely dark ambient soundtrack."

"So after our bratwursts and cherry beers, can we get the cheap seats at the opera?"

Franz closes his eyes tightly, which means he is peeved. "And I could care less about hearing Lucia di Lammermoor at the State Opera House tonight."

"But the notes at the end are so amazing," I begin a plea that sounds like an off-kilter whine from his fiddle. "I love it when she's dying."

"Gerhard, you hate opera."

I can't argue with Franz. I'm not an opera buff. But I remember my parents taking me to Donizetti's *Lucia* when I was just nine. I was struck by those subhuman sounds, often resembling something like a wounded bird, somehow emanating from the diva's throat. How her suitor Edgardo could be so easily tricked into thinking Lucia was actually unfaithful, I always wondered. How could he not hold onto their pledge of undying adoration?

"Just this one time." I tug on his violin case.

"We'll check at the concierge desk if there are inexpensive spaces when we get back. But first, I'm in desperate need of a steam."

When Franz goes to the baths he makes an event out of it. He walks in with his own monogrammed posing towel, baby powder-scented soap, and a tall spray bottle of expensive toilet water. He takes his time, sauntering from the oversized hot tub to the steam room to the cooling pools, then, finally, to a reclining chaise. It's something of a savored ritual.

After getting briefly lost on the U-Bahn, we finally make our way into the cruisy shower room where Franz announces happily, "It's nude swim night; forget the bathing trunks."

Sculpted men and not-so-toned daddies splash and frolic in the facility's large swimming area. Franz and I watch from a lounge chair and try to conceal our hard-ons with towels.

"I need to make like a shark," Franz leaps into the tepid water and begins to coyly float next to the broad-shouldered hunk who is leaning against one side of the pool, pushing slightly on the palms of his hands to reveal the most perfectly rounded white buttocks I've ever seen.

I watch Franz back-floating on the surface of the water. I think of high school and the first time I saw him in the locker room. I was fifteen and had barely sprouted pubic hair. Franz seemed to take tremendous pride in shamelessly peeling off his jockstrap and revealing his bushy, half-erect penis. He was matter-of-fact when he pranced around the dressing area, his proud manhood dangling from under his long, slender torso. No one would have spotted Franz for being queer, even though most of his classmates thought of him as a nerdy introvert because he was always more interested in composing music rather than being social.

I loved the way his eyes flashed when he talked to me about Paganini. How we stood together in the shower room, the water spraying over our backs, as he smiled curiously at me, not uttering a word.

From sophomore year on, I could only think of Franz. I waited until his class got out and we rode the bus home together. He was always showing me what different chords stood for, which never made sense to me. But I listened intently, waiting for our legs to touch under the spread-open notebook resting over our kneecaps, ready to feel the rush of blood to my chest and the tingle on my skin from his heat.

"What do you like in a guy?" I remember bravely asking one afternoon.

"It's hard to say what I'm drawn to," he'd tell me reassuringly. "But don't be frustrated that I can't seem to help that it's not you. You're like my brother. And that's pretty special, isn't it?"

It was enough to linger in the scent of him, the whirl of his brilliance, to orbit around his innate magnetism. Something about the way he wanted to translate the world into music made me want to be a better poet. Live up to my own craft, and have that music he felt inside of him be paired with my carefully chosen words. I didn't have to kiss Franz, or taste his warm cock inside my mouth, or come with him thrusting inside of me, to know the essence of his beauty.

Franz has connected with the man with the firm rump and they head off to one of the changing rooms to cavort. I tiptoe to the far end of the room where I conceal myself behind a half-open locker door. I can see they are gently touching each other's chests. I watch my companion's eyes roll back in his head and I begin to grab my own sex.

It's not the first time I've been a voyeur to his exploits. After graduating high school, we became jerk-off buddies down at the Manhattan "Y," with me keeping careful guard duty in the shower room.

Watching Franz tonight, engaged in spurious sex with his desired target, is enough for me, I tell myself. Seeing him aroused provokes a kind of fire in my belly. Sort of like the first time he slipped his tongue into my mouth in the back of the school bus when no one was looking.

"I was only joking with you," he later admonished after I wrote him a sappy love poem on the back of a chamber music program to a concert we had attended together. "You weren't supposed to take me that seriously."

So I watch him from a distance tonight, as always, very seriously. With my eyes intent on the movement of Eros though his veins. Watching for any sign of his infidelity. I don't care if some stranger with a gorgeous butt has him pinned against a grimy wall, captivating him in the moment. At the end of the night, we'll go back to our private hotel room and sleep together, body heat melding, in each other's watchful keep.

When I come, I come watching Franz. At the moment I ejaculate, I gasp and moan, almost imperceptibly, making little bird noises, the way Lucia might. A little wounded, a little crazy, and maybe even a little hopeful that things might still work out.

Bahnhof Zoo

"Tiger, tiger, burning brightly." I'm waving at the captured animal behind the bars.

"Do you think he understands William Blake?" Franz is reading the back of the box of German chocolates.

"I'd like to think everyone does," I proffer. "After all, he wrote a lot of poems for even children to understand."

"Write me something I'll understand then."

I pluck a pen out of Franz' day satchel and begin to write on the back of the magazine guide I've been carrying around with me all afternoon. Franz smiles and moves toward the pacing snow leopard in the cage at the other end of the lion house.

"And none of that love poetry you and Anne Sexton are so famous for."

"Sexton died for love!" I shout back. "And I can think of nothing more tragically noble."

The tiger is trying to push his mouth through the space in the bars. He rubs his forehead against the front of the cage and it seems he is trying to escape into freedom. A rowdy group of teenagers keeps taking swigs from an open can and spitting the saliva and beer toward the front of the cage. The tiger moves back for a moment, only to rejoin his attempts to push through.

One of the roughnecks gives the finger to the animal and shouts *"der Kacker,"* at which the entire group breaks into thunderous laughter. I know enough German slang to know they've called the imprisoned animal a vulgar term referring to feces. I shake my head and continue to compose something, trying to imagine what the caged tigers might sometimes dream of.

After a few more jeers from the strident group, I walk toward the end of the cages, but Franz is nowhere to be found. I walk slowly toward the outside and spy him chatting up what appears to be a young rent boy. As I approach, I can hear them speaking in German, but the language is impossible to my ears.

"This is Ziggy," Franz announces as I step into their presence. "He'll do both of us for cheap."

"You and me?" I pause with a look of bewilderment. "Right here?"

"Or at the hotel if you prefer," Franz looks completely enamored with the soft blond hair on the young chap's head.

Men are cruising one another in front of the reptile house. I watch them go into the entrance of a hollowed-out structure built to resemble a rocky cave and linger there. I point toward the notorious spot and the three of us enter the faux stone mountain. Franz hands Ziggy some paper money before the light at the mouth of the cave dims and we sequester ourselves in a carved-out husk. Franz whispers in German to the boy and on the words *"der Zugenkuss,"* Ziggy bends down to embrace my friend's torso.

It's difficult to make out what's happening in the musky dark, but the sparse shards of light that remain in the cave seem to fleck off Ziggy's blond halo. His frothy suction seems to fill up the cavern as he moves rapidly next to the snatch of hair shooting up toward Franz' belly button. Ziggy abruptly stops, then begins to finger the zipper on my jeans.

"I want to watch," I say emphatically. I reach for Franz' violin case and hold it like a fragile infant in my arms.

"*Nein!*" Franz guides Ziggy's mouth back onto his wet shaft, and the paid cherub continues.

Franz begins to breathe rapidly, and with one deep exhalation, he is relieved of all of his tension. It's enough that I can be next to him; his sighing "*Gottverdammt*" resounds like an otherworldly melodic key that echoes off the walls.

Before Franz has a chance to compose himself, Ziggy has made his way out of the cave and melded back into the oblivious crowds. I put my arm around Franz' waist and escort him back toward the stifling October light.

"Your money belt." I halt at the point where the sunlight crests in. "You just had it with you didn't you?"

"I had it when I paid him," Franz begins to paw himself frantically, checking his day satchel and pockets. "Oh, God!"

When I was sixteen, I was always getting teased in high school for not being boy enough. For wanting to read poetry and hang out with the girls. During my senior year someone broke into my locker and spray-painted FAG over the door. They stole all of my books and papers, and even smashed a final project I had been working on for a science class. Franz had been there to lend me his books and make Xerox copies of lost assignments, and he helped to rebuild my miniature volcano. Now, it is my turn.

Later that night in our Berlin hotel, after police reports have been filled out and careful descriptions of the thief have been taken down, I touch the loose brown curls on Franz' head as he sinks into the pillow.

"What are you thinking about?" I keep my voice as unobtrusive as possible.

"I'm thinking you never shared that rhapsody you wrote for me today."

I pause to let silence float through the room. After a few minutes I move quietly to retrieve the folded lyrics from the pocket of my trousers, which I had thrown on the floor. By the time I reach the bed, Franz is breathing heavily, drifting into a heady slumber. I read the poem silently to myself, then fell asleep too, dreaming of my cohort and me riding the back of a flaming tiger.

Franz is playing his violin like Izthak Pearlman and both of us are straddled around the concrete ribs of the beast, leaping over everyone's astonished heads, and bounding into the distance, into the shining universe that is just beginning to come alive.

Siegessäule

"I'm so over my fantasy about SS officers," Franz remarks while buying a ticket and walking into the Deutsche Guggenheim.

"There comes a time when you have to surrender your fantasy, my dear sweetmeat."

"Not every fantasy," Franz licks his lips at a youthful specimen eyeing him from the entrance to the gift shop.

"Why don't I meet you back at the front desk in, say—oh, an hour?"

"When his big hand is on my cock." Franz winks and makes his way toward his new conquest.

I move into the upper gallery and locate a series of Gerhard Richter's abstract paintings titled *Acht Grau*. I've made this pilgrimage to see what my namesake has left to the world. Richter's attempts at painting the philosophical concept of nothingness are striking, even the neutral, almost slate, palette makes everything in his world a moving blur. Something like smoke devouring everything in sight, or what it looks like while taking pictures from the window of a fast-moving car. Richter's fluid brushwork seems to be spontaneous, but it's actually very strictly calculated to achieve those wide spatial effects he's become so famous for.

I stare into one of the large enameled monochromes and lose myself. I'm floating into Franz' head. I'm the thought that runs through his synapses. The charge that fires and animates his urgent hand over the violin. I am the beads of sweat on his neck at the end of an exhaustive concert. I am the tremor in his throat as his bow reaches up into the air, again and again, as if trying to puncture through to another side of reality.

Franz always says "Smoke follows beauty." I am that gray tendril that wraps around my hidden thoughts that invent this fantasy with my beloved, the nearly transparent line of smoke you can barely trace in the air that becomes an umbilical cord between my heart and my inescapable fate.

When I return to the front desk, Franz is waiting like a clump of withered violets. It seems everything has been drawn out of him. I want to translate what I'm feeling for him, speak the secret language of desire that has lingered inside me for almost a decade.

"Did time stand still for you, my friend?" I smile knowingly.

"I think I'm overwound a bit."

"Let's take a taxi to the Victory Column," I say with a forced cheerfulness. "My treat."

A dank chill has set in as we walk through Berlin's "Central Park" known as Tiergarten and we arrive at the entrance to the city's most famously phallic pillar, the Siegessäule. I almost blink twice, thinking I see one of Wim Wenders' trench-coat angels standing on the rim of the structure's perilous lookout point.

We ride to the top of the tower to see that twilight has brought with it a blanket of cushioning fog. There are just a few peevish tourists peering through the tall fence of the observation deck as the tiny lights go on throughout the city.

"If only we had wings to fly across that skyline," I half-sing.

"Is that the best poetry I'm going to get from you this whole trip?"

Franz takes out his oiled violin and begins to play something slow and melancholy. As if the whole heart of Berlin were about to break listening to the buttery notes that pour out of his instrument, I stand back, still amazed. A few tourists nod and one even drops a handful of coins at his boot. Franz is in rapture; his notes are laced upon the thickening champagne air. I look at him and realize that he is officially lost on whatever planet he seems to be wandering through at this moment.

For a half-breath, in the thickening fog moving over us like a blanket of clouds, I think of Richter's suspicion with reality. How he painted to create a doorway into possibility, a path away from artifice. My current frame of reality shape-shifts before my eyes. I'm looking and not seeing. Everything seems to tilt and disassociate, meld into the abstract. I feel I am in my body, but I am also in my companion's, and we are bound to move to the same music, to the same clandestine notes.

This is the landscape Richter tried to show me. And it is the same world I stepped into the day I met Franz.

After a while, the tourists who have paused to listen turn away, and Franz moves to the absolute edge of the lookout. I follow him without thinking.

"Is that tune you're playing Gilbert and Sullivan?" I murmur softly.

"Don't you recognize the song 'Edelweiss'?" he half-sings. "It's Rodgers and Hammerstein of course."

"Of course." I'm suddenly hotly blushing.

He continues to play, his bow moving gently over the strings, his gaze somewhere far off in the distance. As the music changes to one of Franz' original compositions, I gingerly approach my muse, my still-elusive triumph, from behind.

"Can I share with you my poem now?" I whisper into the back of his head, my lips brushing against the edges of his flowering curls. "I think it's just about finished."

The musical notes from his violin keep rising and get lost in the soupy fog. I tell myself that no one can see us, two foreigners stumbling into each other at the top of the indifferent city.

I fold my arms around his narrow waist, so that he can barely feel the yank of my gravity. I tell myself I have turned into something vaguely resembling a pink cumulus cloud or a delicate pair of fluttering, feathered wings. Though I have begun to vaporize, I can sense the rising heat between where my arms are resting and his narrow hips.

"Can you imagine the lyrics I've created to compliment your music?"

Franz keeps playing his violin, not moving, not altering his devotion to the tune. I wonder if he can recognize that I am still here with him, though I have begun to disappear from off his map.

In this moment, it feels as though I am barely present, a nearly weightless creature, negligible in worth even, an outline of something almost angelic, nearly human, hovering imperceptibly, barely noticed, and hardly ever touching the surface of things.

This Man Is an Island

It was clear that Olin had become the enormous boulder he was resting upon. Somehow he was able to seamlessly metamorphose into that craggy stone overlooking the turgid roil of the ocean and vanish into the jagged topography of the mountain overlook. There was a part of me that wanted to walk away from him then. To leave him there, a porous stone formed from the ash of volcanic fire, hanging over this wild stretch of Italy's Ligurian coast. But I didn't walk away. I lingered at the weedy trailhead, trying to remember the words that might call him back from his frozen state. What intimate name might break the hard igneous shell encased around him? "My sweet Ollie. My poison apple. My heart's compass." What soft intonation, what secret code might crack the cold phosphorous that had encapsulated the man I once recognized as my lover of four years?

"I found all these dead ladybugs here!" I shouted from the overgrown path where a heap of dead beetle carcasses lay on the pebbly dirt. "You've simply got to come here and see this."

Olin emerged from the precipice with a disgruntled look after several long moments and seemed only half-present, if not utterly distracted, by my request. He cast his eyes down at the layered mound of black-dotted orange spheres.

"Isn't it the strangest thing?" I peered up at Olin who merely shrugged and rolled his eyes. "What do you think happened to them?"

"They didn't fly away home like they were supposed to." Olin muttered to the line of gray-green olive trees in the distance. "How the hell should I know? Let's go have lunch."

It was Olin who insisted on coming to the Italian region known famously as the Cinqueterre, an isolated string of five islands located just southeast of Genoa. Referred to by travel brochures as the "real Italian Riviera," Olin was convinced that coming here would offer us

Postcards from Heartthrob Town: A Gay Man's Travel Tales
Published by The Haworth Press, Inc., 2006. All rights reserved.
doi:10.1300/5732_09

the best of all worlds. "We can rub up against real authentic Italian tourists and not just other American tourists," he enthused before convincing me we had to spend our so-named second honeymoon somewhere that was a bit off the beaten path.

But the path that led us to this Italian paradise was the only thing that seemed to be beating us down. A damp chill had somehow lodged itself into Olin's persona. For months leading up to our trip here, he would become easily distracted or moody, spend hours before coming to bed roaming the Internet. Often he would collapse into a kind of languid numbness as we'd attempt to make love at night, then he'd turn over and fall asleep with his iPod earphones plugged into the *Phantom of the Opera* soundtrack or a dolorous Mahler symphony.

Admittedly, it had become more and more difficult for me to retrieve what had brought our skins to fire in the first place. For the first few years we spent together, our bodies provided the only proof of love we truly needed. Our blood aptly registered the currents of electric attraction we felt toward each other and our trustworthy limbic systems repeatedly sent signals that would send our adrenaline pumping, our glands pulsing. But after so much time together, a shared apartment, two needy cats, the routine of work schedules that seemed to sometimes oppose each other, it seemed the erotic throb had waned, and secretly I carried hopes that the mythological blue of the Italian sea and the bend of the footpaths through the cypress groves that cradled the town of Corniglia might revive what had seemingly become irretrievably lost.

"I'd like the risotto a mariana, please," Olin politely handed the midday menu to the waiter as I helped myself to the breadbasket. "Don't stuff your face with empty carbs, Lowell. You'll be too bloated for the specialty tiramisu."

I ripped the tiny loaf rather dramatically with a toothy, somewhat savage grin. "As if the carbs in your cream-covered rice dish are going to be so much fuller for you," I snapped back, as the hard crust of bread fell onto the yellow flowered tablecloth.

I was convinced that our constant bickering had come to annoy Olin just as much as it irritated me. Our incessant quarreling was even more pronounced since we were planted in such an idyllic setting. Our outdoor restaurant was situated in the center of a lovely piazza next to the nearly imperceptible trickle of an ancient fountain that had been cast in the late eighteenth century. We sat under a perfect azure sky, the kind that only Condé Naste can airbrush, with the creak of fishing boats moored at a pier just a few steps down. Our red and gold café umbrella twirled lavishly in a sun-splayed breeze as I watched my companion stare at some horizon point beyond the pier.

"Why don't we go for a longer hike later?" I suggested, taking a slow sip of my grappa. "There is a footpath that runs through part of a vineyard running between Riomaggiore and the town of Manarola."

"Lowell, I'm sorry, but that's just a bit too daunting for me today," Olin had placed his sunglasses on as he fanned himself with a folded map. "I thought we could just kick around the beach today, unless you would rather go off on your own."

We'd spent only five days of our planned two-week holiday on the Cinqueterre and for much of the time I had found myself wandering the breezy villages alone. Granted, I enjoyed meandering around the twisting alleys and belvederes and taking Polaroid snapshots of the four-story houses painted in shades of burnt caramel and canary yellow. But it seemed rather odd that Olin could not shake himself from what he described as the repeated onset of a migraine induced by jet lag.

I stared icily at my partner. "The question is, would you rather I go off on my own?"

Olin drew in a deep breath as the waiter set down a warm bowl of Parmesan-crusted risotto. "You know, Lowell, I wouldn't mind it if you did take off this afternoon," he spoke softly as he blew onto the wet rice kernels clinging to his steaming fork. "I think we could catch up this evening, maybe visit that wine tasting you mentioned earlier? I really could use a long nap."

"So the balmy breezes of the Italian coast are inducing sleep in you, are they?" I stared into my cooled bowl of seafood bisque. "I had no idea our second honeymoon would be hallmarked by your acute somnambulism."

The rest of lunch consisted of me folding and unfolding a map of hiking trails that string together the five connected islands, while Olin adjusted himself uncomfortably in his slatted chair, staring at the lion-headed fountain spigot and pushing away most of his lunch. We walked back to our rented apartment without a word to each other. Once inside, Olin closed the metal shutters on a perfectly framed view of the sea and collapsed onto the bed.

"See you in a few hours," he moaned listlessly as I proceeded to fill a small pack with bottled water, some sunscreen, and my camera. "Go and enjoy yourself. This is Italy in August, after all."

I tossed the travel backpack over my shoulder and headed out the door swallowing every sarcastic remark inside of me that was looking for an outlet. I walked rapidly without even an *arrivederci,* trying to see if I could manage a swift pace and break a small sweat in order to dissipate some of the tension I was feeling. I moved quickly past the small trattorias and vegetable and fruit stalls. Two men pulled a wooden cart with an oil tarp covering what appeared to be the day's ocean catch. A women's choir practiced in low tones as I walked past the Church of San Pietro, a fourteenth-century landmark with prayer-book peddlers standing beneath its salmon-colored stained-glass windows.

But I didn't linger. I moved rapidly up the switchback stone steps in order to get back to the hiking trail. Back to the olive groves and fragrant lemon orchards. Back to the little hens wandering about the pomegranate trees covered with red fruits. Back to my own rhythm where I might be able to make sense of Olin's detachment. I wanted to merge with the snaky foot trail, to lose myself in the stark views of the terraced hillsides that plummeted into the sea. I wanted to take back a souvenir of this trip that didn't consist of me watching Olin slip into a distracted state of mind.

I paused at a rocky promontory overlooking the tiny harbors, the wooden boats chafing one another, the sheer cliffs that seemed oblivious to everything beyond them. Everything here seemed fragile. The little ferry carrying tourists back and forth between the mainland and the island shore looked precarious, as if a strong wind might easily topple it over. The few brave tourists sunning themselves on the rocks of the gray pebble beach seemed as if they could cave in and be swallowed up by the incoming waves.

Though it was everything Olin had promised, a pervasive gloom seemed to tint the stagy views around me. Cars had to be parked on the outskirts of the villages and no tour buses were allowed in. It was easy enough to become enamored with the pre-Roman rustic charm of this place with it's unadorned simplicity: the laundry flapping in the wind, the capped fishermen lingering at the quay, the terraced vineyards, the constant scent of lavender and lemon leaves, the farmers picking green grapes from ladders propped against flaking retaining walls. It all had a certain bucolic appeal. Granted, the region had been placed on UNESCO's world heritage list as well, but that didn't stop me from sinking into a state of disenchantment.

"We'll make love off one of the footpaths," Olin had promised me, months before we even made our plane reservations. "I'll feed you a picnic of basil pesto pasta and antipasti al mare with squid and anchovies. We'll get drunk on the local white wine and sunbathe naked on some remote rock shelf. You'll see, Lowell; just wait."

I had imagined that the roll of the Ligurian Sea would bring our fine hairs to fire again. That we'd somehow feel the way we did on our first honeymoon, the one in Venice when we stayed at a small hotel and didn't come out for the first two days because we were so enamored with each other's young faces. Olin was Sicilian and his soft olive skin, dark flashing eyes, and thick lips were in stark contrast to my own fair Nordic features. Olin had arranged for a Venetian gondola ride the last night we were there, and it was only then that I began to see the city emerge around us, only then that the stone bridges and looming towers began to register as a backdrop to our languorous romance. I remember thinking that that was how any first-time tourist should inhabit a new place, through the bond that is shared with his partner, through the alliance that is knit through the connection with his beloved.

I noticed as the afternoon went on that hikers were becoming more and more prevalent on the trail. I made note of how many pairs there were, leaning into their dog-eared travel guides, pointing beyond a distant bluff or toward a stucco hillside chapel. What did it feel like, I wondered, to be that joined to another as you moved through foreign terrain? What must it be like to encounter each new vista through the eyes of someone you adore? I tried to recall my former trip to Venice with Olin, but that memory path seemed inaccessible to me at the moment.

"What is Olin dreaming of right now?" I whispered under my breath as the sun loomed large in the late-afternoon sky. I pictured him slack on the bedspread, his ears cushioned between his mini head-phones, lost in the Italian songs of Amedeo Minghi or Andrea Bocelli. Was he waiting for me to return? To feed him handpicked olives or sun-warmed plum tomatoes? To tell him of the donkey paths and the overhead views of slate-roofed, pastel-colored stone structures? Was he wondering what I was seeing? If I had taken a wrong turn? Slipped off the side of one of the stony inclines?

"Do you speak English?" A young woman in her twenties approached me, her male companion wrapped tightly around her slender shoulders. "We need some directions."

"I'm a stumbling sightseer here myself," I stuttered a bit shyly.

"We're looking for the Via dell'Amore," the sprightly traveler grinned. "You know, the part of the hike that they call 'the kissing path.'"

I had read that the southern end of the trail, the one leading around the town of Manarola, was also known as "the lover's walk." I had pointed it out to Olin on the plane ride over and he simply nodded and told me to underline it.

I showed the bubbly couple the notation in my guidebook and they thanked me for my help. I watched them skip lightly up the brick steps and vanish behind a cluster of trees. I felt better knowing that even though I myself would never seek out the Via dell'Amore with my close companion, I had assisted someone else in locating that landmark of Eros.

Turning back around, I stumbled off the marked foot trail. I moved through an opening in the dark olive woods, toward the edge of the sloping landscape. Wild cactus, aloe, and belladonna brushed my trousers. I moved toward a clearing where I stood toe-to-toe with the blue open sea and sky. Below I saw the great rusty iron rings and mooring chains, capstans, and fragments of old masts and spars from an ancient shipwreck. I knelt down on the stony earth and took in a deep breath. The salt air mixed with basil and orange made me feel a bit inebriated. I fumbled through my backpack for my bottled water. "Was this the place Olin had imagined we'd make love?" I wondered.

Rustling through the sack, I realized my San Pellegrino had leaked onto the contents of the carryall. I dumped out the books and papers, realizing as I did that I had been carrying Olin's knapsack all along. As I carefully unfolded the damp sheets of paper, I realized that they were e-mail letters addressed to my partner, correspondence from someone named Roberto, a university student, I read, who was studying art and graphic design in Florence, and ironically, vacationing in the village of Corniglia at the same time we were.

The afternoon ocean breeze quickly dried the clutch of e-mails revealing photos of a good-looking, curly-haired Italian man with a strong physique, notes on several rendezvous points along the string of the islands, cell phone numbers and local addresses, and details of various remote locales throughout the Cinqueterre where "no one will be able to interrupt our time together."

I froze in the sun-warmed gales sweeping through the landscape. "We'll slip off and head toward the town of La Spezia," Roberto wrote in one of his furtive love letters, "and we'll wander the Golfo dei Poeti where Byron and George Sand were inspired to create their greatest love poems."

For a moment I imagined myself tumbling off the side of the steep hill. I imagined my bones becoming indistinguishable from the spiky weathered boards of the shipwreck below. I imagined taking my last breath, looking up at the gulls, my eyes fixed on some little fenced-in garden on the side of the coast, my broken body surrendering to the pull of the tide as workers went on picking grapes in the late summer sun, oblivious to my moans.

As I slowly gathered my senses, I picked up the spilled contents of the knapsack from the ground. A recent snapshot of Olin and me, our faces leaning into each other's, had slipped out of the guidebook.

"Would you take a picture of us?" I suddenly recalled Olin asking one of the airline attendants before we boarded the plane for Italy. "I want to frame this when we get back."

I studied our faces carefully for a moment, tried to glean some kind of sincerity in the manner that Olin had wrapped his arm around my shoulder, or the way his lips were pursed, as if ready to offer up a parting kiss. I wedged the snapshot into a v-shaped branch on a stunted lemon tree and turned to go.

It must have been a few hours before I finally went down the narrow steps to the village. Fireflies had begun to emerge from the dense thicket and the harbor cafés were brightly lit and beginning to serve up plates of cheese-filled focaccia and homemade spaghetti. I let myself inhale the air of the village. The damp ocean air seemed to pervade everything. For a moment, a familiar laugh broke through. I turned around, half-expecting Olin to be raising an aperitif glass of Sambucca in the air, balancing a coffee bean between his teeth, his dark hair mixing with the blackness of the encroaching night.

When I returned to the flat, it was deserted. The air was filled with the scent of Olin's cologne combined with the dank odor of mildew and sea brine. Next to the bed was a plate of peeled blood oranges and the bitten-through flesh of a ripe pear. On the bureau mirror, Olin had scrawled a note saying he went into town to "try and wake up" and would return later.

I quickly threw my belongings together, hoisted my satchel over my shoulder, and closed the door behind me. My stomach seemed to lurch a little as I took my first steps out into the evening air. Sparks from the fireflies haloed around me and seemed to somehow assure me; their alternating glow seemed to be sending me a code that it was all right to leave this way.

It wasn't until I reached the train station and purchased my ticket back to Genoa that I realized I had left all my guidebooks back in the apartment. It occurred to me that once I arrived in Genoa I would be without a compass. I would simply wander about, looking for a late-night pizza stand and a cheap room, and then, much later, decide where to go from there.

On the train, I imagined Olin and Roberto languishing on their island sanctuary. But in my mind, it was difficult to distinguish Olin from the actual landscape. Somehow in every imagined scenario, he would vanish into a line of olive trees. I imagined him rubbing oil on the back of his new lover Roberto, then he would pulverize into flecks of gray sand or merge with an olive tree or an overturned rowboat. I'd see the two of them sitting in the piazza, their legs just barely touching under the table, their gazes steady on each other, and then all at once, Olin would meld into the fountain. He would become so transparent, that Roberto would simply walk right through him.

The train reached its destination of Genoa and I set off to locate a tourist bureau to make some kind of reservations for a room. I stood behind a short line of other weary tourists, mostly couples traveling together, suntanned from long walks along the rugged coast, seemingly content and filled with amorous memories.

A woman called after her toddler in Italian. The child's name seemed indistinguishable from the rest of her clipped phrasing. It was in that moment I remembered my own name. "Lowell," I began to say under my breath.

I repeated it over and over. "My darling Lowell, my lost one, my little one," as if saying it over and over could somehow resurrect my spirit, or comfort me enough to continue going farther and farther away from the familiarity of my past life with Olin.

I looked up at the row of stark lightbulbs lining the concave roof of the train station. Clusters of little beetles crawled about the edges of the glass globes. "Are they my ladybugs, come back to life?" I spoke in the direction of the train station.

As a child, I solemnly understood that seeing a ladybug warranted respect. I knew that the gentle, winged creatures needed to return home, to their little houses that had been engulfed by boundless flames. They needed to rescue their offspring who had been neglected and thoughtlessly abandoned. They needed to go home.

"How long are you looking for a place to stay?" the woman behind the desk inquired without looking up.

For a moment, I thought of my return airplane ticket back to the States. I thought of the life I had built with Olin in a mortgaged house in the suburbs. I remembered the modern paintings we'd purchased together on our first trip. The rusted keychain, a stolen souvenir from our hotel in Venice, that would always open the front door of our townhouse. The burnt sienna color of our bedroom walls, chosen to duplicate a wine cellar we dined in over our honeymoon. The amber Venetian glass on the fireplace mantel that always seemed to be lit from within. The terrarium made from a pickle jar. All of that seemed to deteriorate suddenly, like Roberto's discovered e-mails to Olin, dampened and fragile, shredded in the swift Mediterranean breeze.

I thought for a moment that I had no place to belong to, that, like any exile, I belonged to the environs I found myself exploring, owned by whatever fragmentary moment I happened to be immersed in. But like the stray ladybugs, I had gone toward some strange light, some other luminous calling, and left everything behind me in flames.

I handed the woman at the desk my flash camera and asked her in polite English to take a photograph so that I might remember my brief stay in Italy. As she snapped the Polaroid, I looked up again at the row of bright lightbulbs around the train station, suddenly stark and bare and without any trace of the mysterious winged beetles.

Slowly, my own face began to emerge in the photograph. My own face, without Olin's, with a strange Italian city as a backdrop. All at once, the details of my eyes, the features of my lips and hair, all began to sharpen in this city filled with other tourists and strangers I could barely converse with. I knew that I could take another train leaving in four hours destined to arrive in Venice, and that from there, I could keep moving on, creating my own journey, managing my own self-driven travelogue.

I drew back from the reservations desk and blew slowly and steadily on the Polaroid snapshot, waving it gently back and forth in the night air, to see if the image captured there could come in any clearer.

Pagan Love Child

Lammas

He's shaking his head to Skankin' Pickle punk band and chewing
on half of a crumbling MoonPie as he draws my face up to his. I pick
up the scent of ambergris and dried sweat clinging to his ash-blond
dreads. His nipple ring is a cool twinge on my breastbone. I lick the
flakes of marshmallow and pie crust from his lips and trace the outline
of an Egyptian ankh that he has tattooed onto his right shoulder
blade. His palms are callused from operating a sheet metal punch
press all day. He covers my ears with both of his hands and whispers
to me, "Listen." For a moment, the muffled ska beat meshes with my
own heart rhythm. The world is morphing. His warm fingers cupped
around my head become conch shells where I can hear the sea breathe,
tumble into a wave, a "bliss wave" as Derek so often tells me just before he's about to cum. He rests his tongue tip on the dart of my nipple and the nerve endings just beneath my skin bleat an urgent primal
code: *man-to-man, man loving man.* He buries his scratchy braids into
my crotch and I am caught in the rabid undertow. He covers my
mouth with his wet mustache. And I drown.

Beltane

He's singing Zen koans to himself in a low, breathy moan. He
lights a marigold-scented incense wand and traces a pentagram in the
air with its soft trails of smoke. He's wearing a Pansy Division T-shirt

This chapter appeared originally under the same title in *Best Gay Erotica 1998* (San Francisco:
Cleis Press, 1999). Copyright 1999 Gerard Wozek. Reprinted with permission of the author.

and cutoff army fatigues beaded with turquoise buttons and faux emeralds. He fills a seashell with water from the bathroom faucet and places it in front of an effigy of Our Lady of Guadeloupe. He dusts the top bedsheet with rose petal talcum powder and lies down. I light a tall votive with a decal of Saint Lucia on it and curl beside him. Derek tells me to hold still. The thin hairs on my forearms conduct palpable electric currents as they brush against his skin. We lie on our backs and our slow breathing begins to rhyme. We don't touch each other, but I can sense Derek's cock getting hard and feel my own sap rising in synchronicity. I am caught somewhere between memory and anticipation. I am twelve years old and my brother and I are breaking ice puddles with our snow boots. I am fifteen and touching myself in the lilac bushes behind my mother's garden shed. I am twenty and traveling alone in Europe for the first time and my leg is resting on another man's knee on the Paris metro. I am twenty-seven and I am lying next to Derek's naked body in an apartment in Seattle.

He takes his index finger and runs it along the line of hair below my belly button. He turns to bite my earlobe and slowly reaches down to grasp my oozing crown. There are a thousand tongues of fire chanting around us as we meld into a singular pulse. We are African shamans beating our drums on a desert slope.

We are sex magicians practicing ancient body alchemy. We are tangled in the thornless rose garden blankets. We throw back our heads and shoot our wet seeds over this cool, eternal dust.

Autumn Equinox

Derek is leading me up a mountain trail in the Northern Colorado Rockies. He is meshing with the birch trees and buttercups. He is reflecting the rabbitbrush and soapweed plants. He is vanishing into the pale green shadows that linger on the edges of this treacherous footpath. "At some point, " Derek says to me, "you are no longer a tourist here." He puts away the guidebook and tells me to go on ahead of him, to pioneer the journey, to grow into the geography. I am letting my body follow the inclination of the September breeze. I am gathering a harvest of sumac leaves that have fallen to the ground. I am imagining what the branches are dreaming of as they creak in the afternoon air. I am forecasting the weather and the purple storm clouds overhead seem to dissipate. As we wend our way up the steep incline, I am merging with all the unseen creatures of the forest. I am flying with the eagles and hawks. My breath is in syncopation with the cougars and the coyote. I am one with the mule deer and bighorn sheep. I am kindred to the black bear and wandering elk.

We arrive at an open vista. I see the wild flowering hills around me as fragmented parts of myself I have yet to reckon with. Derek leads me to a tiny cave where a stream of fresh water runs down. We are naked in the pour of the warm waterfall. We are washing each other's backs with tongue kisses. We are dancing in the rush of the stream. We are losing ourselves in the froth and the lather. For a moment, it feels as though we are slipping into the basin, curling down to the bottom of a red-walled ravine. We are being swept away by the rush of currents. We are headed for the pulsing fists of the river, for the place in the canyon where the rain gathers, for the mystery's locus that cradles the secret as to why this forest remains fertile and alive and wet with life.

Samhain

Derek is writing poems on oak leaves. He is rubbing tiger balm on his balls. He is lying naked in a heap of mulch and fallen branches. He tells me to call him "Cloud Runner." He is making a bonfire out of shards of rotting tree bark, slash pine needles, and old journals. He throws in the poem leaves and whirls his sweaty body in widening concentric circles. He is wailing out a series of psalmlike chords. He falls to his knees and tells me that he is at the still point of desire. He compels me to bend over in front of the sparks and the curling tendrils of smoke. He prods me from behind with his tongue. He makes me rub my face into the ground. My moans lace around the shuddering blue flames. His skin smells like forest rainwater and musk as he takes me from behind. A snake rattles in the bushes and shoves his ebony hammerhead through the tall grass. I want to throw a stick at its slaking body, but I'm frozen. Cloud Runner thrusts harder. The serpent darts his tongue out just inches from my face. "You are safe," his voice gently rolls over my fear. The snake hisses and wends itself around my torso. "World without end."

Cloud moves into me seamlessly. The mottled snakeskin is smooth and earth-damp as it grazes over me. "Safe." The word hinges inside of me. "Safe," I say out loud. And we are.

Yule

Derek is fumbling with a folded map. We are walking on top of floating barges at the famous Flower Market on the Singel in Amsterdam and it is beginning to snow hard. I am tranced out on the metal buckets of Van Gogh's sunflowers on display. I am pointing out the red and yellow Dutch tulips to Derek. I am touching the petals of a pink geranium and inhaling the fragrance of the nearby cypresses and manobole plants. Derek is caught up in the bonsai trees. He is filling brown shopping bags with amaryllis bulbs, Delft tile fridge magnets, miniature windmills, and tiny herb pots.

We walk to the end of the moored barge where there are rows and rows of Christmas trees. White and red poinsettia plants are set around the unadorned evergreens stacked against each other in an open area. Effigies of Sinterklaas and tiny nativity sets carved from wood are set aside the I LOVE AMSTERDAM keychains and souvenir wooden shoes. Nearby, there is a trio of teenaged girls, bundled in thick flannel and scarves, singing carols in Dutch. One of the girls is wearing a tiny wreath on her head made of green silk ribbons and dried red berries. *"Vrolijk Kerstfeest,"* I pronounce carefully to her. "That means, happy Yule to you," I smile as I press a handful of euros into her cup.

Derek and I walk to our hotel room. I pour a cup of hot cider. I am breathing very close to Derek; both of us huddled in a blanket, looking out our hotel window at the lights on the canal. I am turning to cinnamon and nutmeg. I am the holly hung around shop windows. The silver lights and evergreen boughs wrapped around snowcovered street lamps. Derek lights a tall votive candle and the atmosphere goes mute. He is burning an incense urn filled with dried cedar and ivy, slippery elm and sage. The room is filling up with a winter silence. We can see our breath come out as ice mist and hashish vapor. We are watching the flicker of shadows as they move across the walls and ceilings. I am entering a field of snow and evergreens. I am a trail left by two snowshoes on the frozen white plains. I am a windmill on a *Welcome to Holland* postcard, turning in the far-off distance. I am the break of ice under skates. I am the frost and ice and cold slush of this December solstice.

Derek's warm breath begins to fill the concave of my ear. His whiskers lightly abrade my cheek. I am nibbling on his chapped lower lip. We are far away from what feels like home to us. The blizzard seems relentless outside, but we hold each other tightly, certain that our deep kisses will be what compel the spring to return. Our united tongues will thaw the chill that seems to have settled into Amsterdam. Our body heat will chart a course into places we've yet to discover.

Arcana

Prince of Cups

You always said you wanted a beautiful funeral, just like the one at the ending of that classic Lana Turner movie, *Imitation of Life,* with Mahalia Jackson leading a gospel choir in low cherubic tones, and a clutch of mourners weeping at your rose-covered casket. You always went for those tacky sentimental clichés, it seemed. The local florist unloaded hundreds of those out-of-season tiger lilies and dove wings around your silver-plated cremation urn. And when everyone had finished eulogizing you, everyone sang "Wind Beneath My Wings" to a karaoke cassette. It was what you asked for.

Your friend Dugan, who tended bar during your magic show acts, called the service "a paean to Chicago's most beloved 'Magic Man.'" The Indian sandalwood incense that pervaded the air that night mingled with the imported black China roses you requested, making even your stone-faced mother sniffle, although no one was quite sure if it was a result of her grieving or simply that her allergies were acting up.

Perhaps it was a bit over the top to play Olivia Newton-John's "I Honestly Love You" right after Maria Callas's "Norma," but, after all, it was what you had requested in your will, along with a presentation of a looping video highlighting your gigs as a novice magician at the Broadway Limited Bar in Chicago. You were going to be the next Uri Geller, you insisted. "I know I can make myself vanish into thin air," you'd always say. "Just watch me."

Instead of holy cards at your service, there was a collage of photographs laid out at the front of the reception area illustrating some of your jaunts around Colorado's open range and the Rocky Mountains.

Postcards from Heartthrob Town: A Gay Man's Travel Tales
Published by The Haworth Press, Inc., 2006. All rights reserved.
doi:10.1300/5732_11

I remember how small clusters of your acquaintances lingered around them to reflect on your life and the bucolic images of your last days.

"He looks just like a young Sal Mineo in *Rebel Without a Cause,* doesn't he?" Dugan remarked, holding up a creased photo of you sitting near a steep overlook.

"Actually, he looks like he's already jumped over the edge," your mother's voice cracked the way the carcass of a hollowed-out locust breaks when you step on it.

As if to mollify the observation, Dugan intervened, "But look how you can tell in this picture, he still had those gorgeous thick eyelashes, right up to the end."

I remembered your eyelashes. The way snowflakes would crust over them when we were standing outside in a Chicago winter waiting for the bus. The way they would brush against my cheek when you would kiss me hello on the cheek. How they framed your hazel-brown eyes, making your limpid gaze even more hypnotic, even more compelling when you fixed your stare onto some handsome stranger at a cruise bar.

Last night, I pulled the Prince of Cups from the deck of tarot cards you gave me. Swarthy and brazenly idealistic, the Prince is the archetype of masculine cunning and sensual bravado. In the illustration, he holds out his empty chalice as though a lightning bolt would explode inside of it, or a hailstorm of violets and comets might suddenly rain down and he could gather them up and just drink them in.

For a moment, I saw your face overlaid on his and I wanted to forget. I wanted to erase the memory of you sneering at those cynical physicians, the way you'd empty out your cocktail pill bottles into the toilet and go on insisting you would outlive everyone. I wanted to forget your fey belief in immutability, the defiance of an illness that finally overcame you. I wanted to forget that naive part of you that somehow convinced me too that you would regain your weight, get your healthy color back, and live on.

Fifteen years and it seems your life was preempted. In the post-plague era, survivors have appeared to be looking athletic and rosy in the airbrushed ads for the pharmaceuticals that inhibit the virus from overtaking them. By most accounts, it seemed the party went on without my best friend. The bug-chasing orgies and furtive lovemaking in the dank steam rooms, the crouching in the back rooms, the fast body frisks; the carefree revelers kept right on roaring, right through the quilt hangings and obituary announcements. Right through the collective amnesia and my own quiet shudders at night.

I stole a picture from your funeral. One of the pictures set out at the reception table. It wasn't mine to take, but I took it anyway. It's the one your hospice buddy took of you at your secret mountain grotto in Colorado. There you were, almost indistinguishable from the flowering brush, kneeling reverently near a steep overlook, looking like a bodhisattva or a fasting monk. Your hands were cupped as though you were receiving a host of holies. In the photograph you might almost resemble a saint or a desert mystic with your unbuttoned work shirt exposing your massive brown curly chest hairs, your eyes darting wildly around the rugged horizon.

There you were. Looking at the photo, I could almost smell the distinct odor of dew-laden Clarabelle's in the wet spring air. I could almost hear you calling me from that rocky incline, your urgent prayer of inextinguishable life still burning on those sanctified lips of yours.

You have always been my Prince of Cups. I remembered the last phone call from you from Colorado. You told me that you spoke to Zeus there in those woody slopes and heard his melodic voice singing through the prairie coneflowers and black-eyed Susan's. I set that stolen photograph next to the mighty Prince of Cups card and shifted my eyes back and forth between them. You merged and separated with the royal heir. Looking closer at your eyes, I could see how you must have felt some great, inexplicable force knew your name and was coming straight for you. I have tried to convince myself that you must have been ready for it.

The Two of Swords

Beneath a placid surface of calm, there was always a state of near dread tension and morbid anxiety in your visage. It seemed to be coming through the caricature of your pencil-drawn face, the portrait of you I kept from our Mardi Gras vacation together. I held onto that cartoon image of you as a souvenir of our first road trip down to New Orleans. It was our first stop on our trek to "someday visit the world together with each other." We said, even though we would bicker sometimes, that we would be good traveling souls, good partners on the journey. Somewhere along the way, though, I let go of your hand.

You were always dancing to the zydeco music that played in the French Quarter that February, making up your own dance steps, inventing your own inimitable style. You wore a crooked tiara the entire weekend, fifteen strands of Fat Tuesday monkey-headed beads and a zebra thong under your magician's cape. As you posed for the chap who drew you, you made drunken attempts at singing the lyrics to an old Evelyn "Champagne" King song: "Burning, you keep my whole body yearning; you got me so confused it's a shame."

The artist was steady with his colored chalk as he deftly captured your daffy persona onto paper. When you were presented with the souvenir drawing, you gasped out loud, "This isn't me; the person in this drawing here is an imposter!"

"Who is it, darling?" my inquiry was solemn.

"Why, it's none other than Blanche." Your voice pierced the carnival air. "Blanche fucking DuBois. Long live the stereotypical N'awlins' queens of the night!"

If you looked carefully, the artist had done his job. There was a lost wren in that simple but nearly accurate rendering that seemed to linger over your midnight party attire. You were captured as a conflagration of a tipsy martini drinker, a brooding, somewhat withdrawn and introspective intellectual, as well as a cross-eyed sea hag. Your souvenir portrait might have been mistaken as just another gawking tourist at Mardi Gras with a bad case of the hiccups. Another horny, loopy gay guy on the prowl. But there were more obscure forces inside of you that no one could discern, least of all me, your best friend.

You wanted to linger at the party. The entire trip, your eyes were always somehow expectant, as if an answer to some unspoken question was about to present itself. As if you were about to turn into one of the many assorted objects you would pull out of your magician's hat. As if the king of the New Orleans parade would invite you onto his float and become your savior.

We got a table with a view at the all-night Clover Grill to laugh at all the drag queens coming in at three in the morning, and you somehow fell into an insular state of paralysis. I lifted the plastic menu out of your torpid hands and ordered your Louisiana crabcakes for you and you drifted into some impenetrable foreign state; an inescapable ennui that seemed to disable you, as though you had no energy left to even breathe.

Back then, I didn't get it. Someone passed out party favors during the Mardi Gras weekend and I just followed the cue to dance. I licked every swizzle stick, shuffled mindlessly to a stream of Madonna videos on some gay bar's big screen, and watched you pull chocolate eggs out of the ears of handsome strangers.

"Wanna see me pull one out of my ass or would you settle for a hamster?" A sour cliché nonetheless and yet you had the Louisiana bar in stitches. After the circuit party had ended and they were sopping up the residue of spilled amyl nitrate from the floor, I looked into your face, the laugh lines gently creased about your eyes that seemed to be completely dead inside. In that moment, I barely recognized you. I kept looking at you then, with confetti stuck on your eyelashes and one nearly broken strand of beads left around your neck. You squeezed my hand so tightly my fingers went numb.

"No matter what tonight, we can't leave each other," you said. "Please. No matter what,"

In the years after your death, I have tried to convince myself that we're still together. That your ghost hangs around me, prompting me with advice, pointing me toward some elucidation about my life. I have tried to reassemble you, parts of you, into something that might have actually been you. But last night, pulling the Two of Swords card from the tarot deck reminded me that we were always a little at odds. Always clashing against each other a bit. Always a little pointy, a little sharp with each other. Never quite the way I have wanted us to be.

Last night the memories of you were urgent and haphazard. I remembered how our car broke down on the way to New Orleans, how you held out your leg to hitch a ride in from the highway. How you never wanted to sleep once the festivities began. We stood together on Bourbon Street, and I put some beads from my own neck around yours.

"We've made it at last," I said to you back then. But it seemed you always wanted to go a little farther away than I did.

In one of your inebriated moments you slurred, "I want to follow the parade to the other side of the Gulf. I just want to keep traveling on and on and never look back."

Last night, with the card of the drawn swords, I thought that, at last, you did just that.

Temperance

On this card, the rainbow moves between two chalice cups and, as e.e. cummings pointed out in one of his poems, "feeling comes first." It has been what I refused to bear that I can't forgive. All my stagnant, buried emotion won't raise you from the dead, all my forced macho bravado, stifled tears, the turning away from your bird-frail frame. You died alone in a hospice in Denver and the Temperance card, the insignia of instinct and emotion, won't provide a salve for me, will hardly save me. It only serves as a reminder that I didn't let the water flow, that I didn't cry at your passing. I didn't comfort you at your bedside. I didn't come when you asked me to. "You know, it would be better to see you now. Even if you can just take off from teaching for a few days, it would be better now." Your voice was weak then, when I last heard you speak over the phone.

Iris is the goddess that presides over the Temperance card. The ancient meaning for the word "Iris" means to announce. And there were all those words I wanted to say to you, but that benevolent rainbow goddess was not accessible to me in those days before you imploded. Before you reached that catatonic state where caretakers could only whisper to your hollow presence, or check to see that your windpipe was clear, your catheter in place.

I couldn't tell you then what I felt. Those two realms, the unconscious and conscious, always seemed to be at war in me. I wanted to be the one to hold the two chalices in my hand, just like the goddess on this card does. I wanted to be the one to mediate the feelings into some sort of logic. To tell you how my heart raged for you. How I wanted to be thought of as more than simply your friend.

"I don't think there is a word for what we are to each other." The deliberateness in your voice still resounds in me. "Maybe we'll never figure it out?" I looked away from you whenever you would confront the subject of our affection for each other. "Maybe it's enough that we take these little trips together, hang out and talk. Why try to put all that in the confines of a simple word?"

Then you'd rest the weight of your body on mine and I'd let us sink into each other for a moment, feeling the heat melding between us, and think of all the little deaths in life we endure. All the little shreds of time we let go by when all we can do is bear witness to each other. All the moments, the recognitions harbored in each other's eyes, that we couldn't begin to name or capture in language.

We'd fold into each other, body to body, and before I'd pull away, before I'd turn to solid rock, I'd kiss your shoulder, then move back into my separateness, my cavernous self, and become, once again, your friend.

I pulled another card in this deck several weeks ago that depicts a young man walking off a mountaintop. The archetypal Fool that moves forward without consequence. It didn't come up tonight in the tarot spread, but it has been my card, and I have known and recognized the certain implications of it. The Fool travels the spectrum of the tarot deck. He is met with different challenges along the way. He is called to be compassionate and to love throughout his passage. The truth be told, I stepped away from my ghost brother. I ultimately recoiled from our great alliance.

I wasn't there to witness the quiet agonies. The way your skin sagged and your muscles began to atrophy. I wasn't there to hand you the medication for the fungus in your throat, the bleeding in your belly, to assist with the electric monitor and plastic tubes bored into your neck and arms. I wasn't there to testify to the bleary, spinning confusion that presented itself as the hospice workers bundled you in morphine and tried to contact your next of kin.

Your next of kin had written you off. Your next of kin had clammed up in some small Midwestern town and sold you down the river as a "worthless faggot." Your next of kin was me too, and where was I?

"I abandoned you, my love." I said it out loud last night, as though you could hear me, as though admitting my culpability could raise you from the dead. "Go ahead, beloved one. Whatever we were to each other, whatever we can call it now. Go on—haunt me forever. Go ahead and try."

The Hanged Man

Your invisible hand reached over me to pull another tarot card last night, as I laid out the old Celtic spread you taught me. I was tired and I promised to finish it out tomorrow but before I pulled the bed-sheets back, I touched my face. Your mustache seemed to tickle my brow where you used to kiss me. I smelled your musk on my pillow, saw your striped mustard-and-red crepe shirt hanging in my closet; the frayed collar was still warm to the touch.

I stared at the card and all at once my blood seemed to be rushing to my head. My foot went numb as if it were tight in a noose and I began to slip out of consciousness. There we were, calling after holly-hocks. There we were, tumbling down a Tennessee knoll. There we were, getting tattooed with matching yin and yang symbols. There we were, getting our eyebrows pierced together, and you began passing out from the trickle of blood in your ear. There we were, singing a chorus from an old Donna Summer song at the top of our lungs. There we were, with a view of Short Mountain; you had lit up the camper with one hundred tealights.

"Make one hundred wishes tonight and they'll all come true," you said as though saying it could make it so. You had a way of convincing the people around you of your immunity to anything that might harm you. Even I was taken in for a long while.

You never missed an appearance at the Broadway Limited. Your magic show was celebrated around Chicago's Boystown, and there were moments on stage when the audience believed you could do almost anything.

"For my next trick—" you'd pause looking out at the first row, carefully eyeing the guests, "ah, he'll do." Everyone would chuckle and suddenly there was a fluttering pigeon flying out of someone's knapsack, or you'd walk through a mirror and leave everyone gaping, scratching their heads for the secret to your scam.

The magic shows ended, however, and there you were, suddenly leaving on a bus for Colorado. There you were, handing me your favorite top hat from your old act. "There you were," I said to myself, repeating it as if I was still trying to convince myself of your absence. "There you were. You were there. You were. You were."

I have been hanging upside down like the medieval serf on this tarot card. The prophecy connected to this card insisted that I must relinquish the past. Studying the face of the victim on the card reminded me somehow of Harry Houdini's final act. How the greatest magician in the world was hung upside down in a glass coffin of water. How he promised everyone that he would escape and return to the stage to perform more magic that night.

Like Houdini, it seemed you kept a secret key on your tongue, always holding your breath and hoping someone would come to break the thick glass pane around you, before it was too late.

The Tower

Lightning has cracked the castellated top of the ominous tower. In the illustration on this card, everything seems to be dismantling, coming apart in a state of irreversible upheaval, and by the looks of it, everything will soon be in rubble. A falling human figure wearing a small crown tumbles from his lookout perch to the hard ground below.

I remember that night at the faerie camp. You asked me, "Do you know your magical name?"

I laughed at you defiantly, defending that I didn't need one. "Why change when everyone knows me by this name?" I protested, scoffing a little at the notion that it even mattered. "But tell me then, magic man—what's yours?"

"It's something I'm trying to live up to." You always knew how to end a remark like that with a definitive silence.

The whole trip, I was nearly spellbound by your certitude. The way you embraced the heart circle with such open candor, speaking of your illness as a great teacher, a powerful force to partner and ultimately study with. How you called to the forces in the four corners to keep your spirit intact, how you wailed into the driving wind with your wild incantations to find your soul twin. With your worry beads dangling from your brittle wrist, you talked of animal spirits and sweat lodges, as you whittled away at a piece of bark, becoming what you deemed to be a sovereign amulet to keep away your night sweats.

You might have lingered around that storytelling campfire with the enchanted fey ones your whole life. But you didn't. When you returned from the Short Mountain retreat, you were triumphantly energized. "I'm going to be regular from now on with my hatha yoga postures," you announced. "I'm going to follow through with my aryurvedic herb remedies too." It seemed you had resolved something within yourself, you had tried to "live better," as you put it. And for a while, it all held together.

I have examined the Tower card carefully and I still don't know what the masonry of this crumbling castle is supposed to imply. I don't know why lightning bolts arrived to challenge this structure, "our false personas" as you once philosophized, or why stoic towers must be built in the first place. I remember the night you showed me this tarot deck and we went through the major arcana together. You reckoned that the edifice in this portentous-looking card was enclosing some kind of impulse—incest fantasies, a fascination perhaps with excretions and bodily functions. The tower, you believed, held back a bestial secret connected with the body, "something untamed and repressed," you conjectured, "that eventually must be let out, reckoned with somehow, or the tower utterly will fall."

I have wondered if any of us have ever reached that point of careful examination within ourselves in order to discover what we are ultimately living for.

"I need to take a trip and get away." As you began to become frail and birdboned, that seemed to be your new mantra. You surrounded yourself with brochures from spa resorts in Bali and Thailand, a nature sanctuary in Hawaii, a string of islands off the western coast of Canada. As if arriving at a foreign locale could lend you a new persona. As if being somewhere where no one knew you could make you over into someone who could live forever. As if stealing those perfect postcard sunsets and whitecapped beaches could make you into some kind of unassailable god.

After you moved to Colorado, you wrote me letters detailing your pseudoshamanic mushroom journeys in the Rocky Mountains, the severe fruit-and-tea fastings and sleep-deprived vision quests. The sweat purges you'd endure for hours in the steam room at the bathhouses and then afterward, a renunciation of the flesh, going without even so much as a jerkoff for over two months. What were you trying to open up to? What was it within you that needed to escape?

I've tried to write my own magical name many times since our journey together to Short Mountain. Tried to adapt to the namesakes of different mythological heroes: Orpheus, Pan, and Apollo. Nothing ever stuck. I have been searching for your name, my phantom friend. I remember that you wrote it down the night before we left. You were going to show it to me, but somehow we never got around to it. What was the name you gave yourself? What force did you want to covet so that you could go on wandering forever?

The High Priestess

That lyric from an old Psychedelic Furs' song still rests upon a tiny brain synapse: "Inside you the time moves and she don't fade, the ghost in you, she don't fade." Isn't that what we danced to the first night we did drag together? And I imagined last night that it was you I saw on this tarot card, seated at the bar as a high priestess that Halloween we drank Persephone's blood, a lethal combination of Rasputin vodka and unfiltered pomegranate juice. You looked like Glinda going through detox with your tin crown slightly askew and your spiked heel constantly catching on the fallen hem of your taffeta gown.

"Where are you taking us?" I remember shouting at you as you waltzed ahead of me down the sidewalk of Halsted Street. You were all cakey blush and crumbly wads of mascara when you opened the door to the Ram, a notorious leather back room complete with take-home souvenir paddles and pumpkin suede cock rings. And as you gently lifted your hoopskirt to reveal your engorged genitals in front of a body-packed video booth, your hungry minions knelt down before you to be grazed by your towering scepter.

"Pearls, pearls," you would deliver in your regal accent as you cupped the growing bulge in your saliva-slippery palm. "Pearls to anoint my liege with."

Watching you shift personas, your macabre transformations, always left me a bit unsettled. You'd move into them so seamlessly: hustler, prima donna, belligerent queen, aloof stud. I wondered if you'd ever be able to retrieve who you were when you were alone. But then, you hated the absence of people. You'd call me sometimes three times in the middle of the night, to say you safely got home. You'd go on relentlessly about the news headlines, the absence of peace and justice in the world, your growing fatigue. Anything to fill up the solitary moment.

I slipped into that old jack-off palace you'd frequent, just over a year ago, and found your restless spirit there, still mournful at the glory hole, still tortured in the throes of another faceless lover. I kept walking that dark labyrinth, feeling your breath quaking inside of me, your fidgety ghost still writhing at my pulse points. I kept seeing you tossing down quarters in that porno arcade, my martyred queen, my invincible conjurer. I spied you through a peephole and saw you make love to some insatiable Latin guy. I watched your spirit tongue linger in his ears and your hands gently fondle his balls. Then you stooped down, with your hungry mouth on those shaved beauties, as if they were the coveted pomegranate seeds you'd been waiting for all your life. And you were swallowing them without pausing, heading deeper and deeper into your own imagined Hades, without any promise of return.

The Wheel of Fortune

"I don't believe in luck," you told me once at a roulette wheel in Las Vegas. "It's all written out for us beforehand. We just show up and react as though it's all an accident."

"So you actually do buy into the notion of predestination?" I inquired of you, baffled at how you went on betting on the same numbers over and over, even though you were losing at each round.

"I know things happen for a reason." The dealer kept eyeing you strangely. I wasn't sure if he suspected that you were a diversion set up in the crowd or if there was some remote chance of a sexual encounter later on. It was only after you came back to our hotel room early the next morning that you divulged that he had slipped you his calling card and you had entered Sin City's back door together. I guess you had won your prize somehow after all.

"Don't you love the idea of being on vacation?" you would muse. "To never be bound by any of those workaday suffocating routines. To always be a happy little tourist, to always be scrounging for postcards and souvenirs to bring home?"

"That's if you ever did come home."

The rest of our trip you gave yourself over to a kind of encapsulating languor. You baked yourself into those staccato hours, sitting rigidly at the noisy slot machines. "Cash in this traveler's check, will you?" You'd plead with me to get more coins for you despite your dwindling cash reserves.

"How about nickel bingo cards at the Flamingo or a dip in the pool?" I'd proffer to buy the first round of cocktails. But you kept on cranking the handle of every quarter machine in the casino.

"I know the next one will pay off." Your zeal was almost convincing. "Just one more."

It has always been a challenge to see any divine plan in any of this. How things were all supposed to match up somehow in that synchronicity that you claimed must exist. For me, everything seemed to rest on a kind of randomness. Still you would insist that there was a mysterious pattern at work. You'd reference the daughters of Nyx, the goddes of night, the three Fates in mythology who were gifted with the task of choosing the length of life and the time of one's death. You spoke of how once the Moirai chose the destiny of a human being, it was unalterable.

"Nothing can be done." Your voice hung in the air, a torpedo icicle, when you announced the doctor's prognosis.

"You can fight this," I insisted. "You can change things. You don't have to give up."

"I'm not giving anything up." You were resolute as you opened up the bottle of freshly prescribed pill capsules. "I'm going to ask that time grant me the ability to use my days wisely. It's really the best that I can hope for."

There you were. Hunched over at the end of a long bank of slot machines. You were wearing your souvenir Vegas visor cap and cranking away, convinced that your payoff was destined to come in the next pull. What would you have done with your fortune? Would a win have provided you with a comfortable retirement stash? Would you have donated a small fortune to your favorite bird and endangered animal sanctuaries in Florida? Or would your cash legacy simply have been handed over to another table of roulette?

There you were, rooted to the stool with your eyes fixated on the spinning images: two dollar signs and a lemon; one clover, one harp, and one silver dollar; one apple and two horseshoes. In my mind, you just keep pulling that handle, waiting for your triple cherries, your predestined payout, to come through.

The Chariot

Scrutinizing the Chariot card, it's nearly impossible to discern whether or not the driver of this cart is able to see. He's covered in a mask that appears to have very narrow spaces cut out for his sight. The two horses pulling the chariot are moving in opposite directions, and it seems impossible for the driver to even advance, although there is an indication of dust rising from the hooves, and wind blowing through their ratted manes.

"I'm moving to Denver." There was humming electricity in your timbre the jittery afternoon you showed me the brochures for assisted living. "I've been corresponding with this fellow in my support group who's lived there for two years and it's really amazing. Horseback riding, nature retreats, gourmet cooking, even an alternative medicine health coach on site."

"A health coach?" I was impressed with the vigor with which you seemed to embrace the balmy vision. "So it's a retirement home for people living with the bug."

"Just say it." You pulled the leaflet out of my grasp and threw it across the davenport. "I have AIDS. You can at least admit it to me if not yourself. After all, I'm the one living with it."

But I wouldn't say it. I refused to let those four letters cross my tongue. Up until you sold your furniture and whittled your possessions down to a roll-away luggage cart and bought your one-way ticket on Greyhound, I was insistent that you were just fine. You were taking a holiday. You needed a rest. A long time out in the woods where you could chase after deer and follow freshwater streams and hiking trails. You just needed an alternate landscape to come back to your senses in.

I used to dream that someone had pulled a stocking cap over my face and thrown me into the backseat of a car. I knew I was moving but I couldn't see who was driving the vehicle and I couldn't even begin to imagine the landscapes that were passing me by. There was a part of me that was excited by this eerie wanderlust, by being held captive by individuals I couldn't see; then this strange relief that everything would simply take care of itself would pour over me.

The dream reminded me of being a child. On a long drive home at night, I'd lay down in the backseat of my parents' station wagon and look up at the vinyl-covered ceiling and drift off into the darkness, comforted by the fact that my father was alert at the steering wheel. As I child, I held onto that trusting notion, even though I could sometimes sense the car wheels were not properly aligned, and there were potholes in the road that could knock out the engine or jar the vehicle off the paved road. I remember thinking that sometimes it didn't matter where I was going, but that I was moving, and maybe just going somewhere, anywhere, was enough.

You sent me postcards from Denver. Every other week I'd view a different panorama. "It's like always being on vacation," you wrote. One picture was a gloved hand picking some bluebells that were jutting through a weathered fence railing. WELCOME TO DENVER was emblazed over the purplish petals and I imagined, in a strange way, that it was your hand reaching over that rustic boundary to hand me the souvenir bouquet.

It reminded me of that time you placed your two hands around my neck one birthday. "I bet you think I'm going to kiss you?" You spoke so softly I was completely disarmed and ready for your tongue to graze mine. "Surprise."

A necklace of dried dandelion heads was suddenly hanging down around my breastbone. How did you manage the sleight of hand? I felt your empty palms on my shoulder blades and blushed.

You always had something hidden, something to conjure from the thinnest air: the jack of clubs or the ten of spades from under your shirtsleeve perhaps. A silver dollar in someone's pina colada glass. Some confounding spell ready to rise up from your throat, ready to throw your gaping audience in your convincing world of illusions.

The Ace of Wands

Last night I drew the Ace of Wands. It came up in a Celtic cross spread and the position where this card showed up suggested a revelation about my hopes and fears. I'm remembering you from a sojourn up to Toronto, that summer it wouldn't stop storming.

We sat on the patio of some twink bar on Yonge Street and drank a pitcher of frozen daiquiris between us. You kept eyeing the husky fellow at the table next to us, his thumbtack nipples jutting through a T-shirt still damp from the August rain.

"If he's a Royal Canadian Mountie, he can mount me anytime," you said in your overreaching shrill voice, vying for a slice of his attention. And when you did finally secure his glance, you found yourself on a weekend lark: nude sunbathing at Hanlan's Point, open-mouth kissing while you strolled with your temporary beau through Kew Gardens, and then making a dither on a hydrofoil ferry near Niagara Falls.

You took me to that iconic attraction with you. "Ah, just think of when Joseph Cotton stalked Marilyn Monroe all the way up those stairs," you said from the side of the tour boat as you pointed to the Prospect Point Observation Tower. "He pursued her so vehemently and if he couldn't possess her," you paused abruptly to stare at the momentary rainbow rising from curling mist, "he'd have to kill her."

I used to like to remember you like that. In your waterproof rubber smock and a Greta Garbo-like, transcendent look in your eyes, as you took in all the sights the Maid of the Mist had to offer. "I want to enter the Niagara Gorge," you said. "I want to part that curtain of water and know what's behind that massive waterfall."

The Ace of Wands is said to be about creative energy and courage—the pursuit of one's unique vision. It was clear to me that you possessed that outpouring of raw force, but I don't think it had galvanized in your life completely. You were still held back by something. "Promise if no one hits on me at the bar tonight," you'd nudge me sometimes, "you'll come home and watch *Now, Voyager* again on the VCR with me?"

You gave your kisses away to spurious lovers strolling behind the parking lot of public parks. You let your dream of becoming a professional magician smash at the bottom of a gorge, shatter with the turbulent force of the river hitting those pointy rocks. You could never tear back the Bridal Falls to see the treasure waiting on the other side. But your memory has kept me hoping that I might do it for you someday. The fact of your life. That you were here. That we stood to share the same atmosphere. That has offered me purpose and a kind of solace.

It has been enough for me sometimes that I can still hold up my finger and trace your outline before closing my eyes before sleeping.

The Magician

You said you'd come back from the grave, just like Houdini. You promised me. You told me things like that on those long afternoons when I'd sit in your college dorm room watching you turn glass marbles into goose feathers. You'd touch my ear and an Indian-head penny would show up. From my shirt pocket you'd pull a bouquet of tiny papier-mâché daisies and somehow you could always tell what card I would secretly pull from the deck. I don't know how you did it but "a true magician never reveals his aims," you often warned.

To say you put a certain spell on me would be exaggerating the story. But for a long time, the truth be told, I had a genuine crush on you. You with your widow's peak and black goatee that made you look like Mephistopheles. How you always would brag about your family lineage to Scottish warlocks. You smoked clove cigarettes with gold-and-blue bands around them and you often quoted Carl Jung and Aristotle. You'd let me try on your red satin cloak, the one that made you look like Lance Burton, but we'd just roll on our sides with laughter because on me it looked like I was some sort of a wimpy Batman.

You loved anything to do with the paranormal and you surrounded yourself with literature on the Theosophical Society of Madame Blavatsky and Aleister Crowley. You would read Yeats out loud at toga parties during our college days, choosing rambling passages that confirmed his belief in "the little people." Once, you even attempted a séance party in your dorm room and one of the residents screamed because they thought they saw a floating head. "A glow-in-the-dark skull candle on a hanger," you secretly confessed to me later. "But I bet you were smart enough to figure that one out."

Last night I dreamt of you again. You were waving hoops of burning fire over my naked body as I levitated in the air. Then you placed me in a narrow box and drove steel spikes through it. Of course, in that dream I felt nothing. And when you opened the paneled coffin, I stepped out, still alive, still intact, and I walked over to you and there were fluttering doves pouring out of your Dr. Seuss hat. You wrapped a long rope of knotted rainbow scarves around us and we kissed to thunderous applause.

I pulled the Magician from the deck last night. It was always your card, my dearest friend; the second card in the major arcana, the one that comes after the Fool. It is the card of Hermes, the god of crossroads, the winged patron of thieves and travelers. The card you want to pull when you are taking a long journey, uncertain of your travel maps and not ready to commit to coming back to where you started out. On the card, Hermes waves his caduceus, his wand of magic entwined by two snakes, and the world of opposites suddenly unites: two becoming one.

A year after your death, the hospice where you stayed found my address and sent your personal belongings to me. They said in the letter that your parents had refused them. They were afraid they might be tainted, and they had no use for these meaningless trifles: a long row of colored scarves you'd pull from your top hat, an autographed picture of David Copperfield, a keychain from a discotheque in Chicago that had burned down, a ticket stub from your plane ride to Denver, a paperback copy of *Houdini on Magic,* a deck of soiled playing cards, a trophy you won in college at a variety night for "Best Entertainer," and something quite unusual—a small cardboard box filled with sand.

I opened the black-lidded carton, no bigger than a small container for teabags, and let my finger feel the coppery grains. There were small pebbles, pieces of wiry roots, and granules of damp red clay mixed into this sample of Colorado range. I rubbed a small piece of grit between my fingers, then touched my face, my lips, as if I could get a sense of where you stood, what you might have seen. What had possessed you to gather up this sandy soil and stow it away?

The folded edge of a small piece of paper stuck out, buried beneath the fine gravel. I hesitated, and then opened the note. One word in your scrawl:

Shape-shifter.

Your faerie name revealed at last? The remnants of some arcane ritual of which only you would understand? I buried the name back in its container and listened to myself quietly breathing.

There you were, the stutter on my tongue. There you were, the damp breath on my shoulder that would cause the hairs on my neck stiffen. The catch in my throat, the piercing banshee yelp stuck in my core. There you were, the song of alchemy that always bound us together. There you were.

"Now you see me, now you don't," you would always call from behind the curtain during the last hoax of your act. It became your signature sign-off slogan.

I always wanted to see you for who you really were. To see through to you and know you as, simply and utterly, my best friend. My comrade. My faithful companion of the road.

There were times I thought to myself, "I have him all figured out." But that was just a stupid trick I played on myself.

Brujo

The state of Oaxaca, bordering the Pacific on the Isthmus of Tehuantepec in southern Mexico, is a conflagration of ancient Aztec history and modern desire. Upon my arrival, I noted that the flaking billboards advertising Orange Crush set over the Xoxocotlan Airport clashed with the brooding mountain peaks reaching over a pink horizon. Its capital, the colonial city of Oaxaca, sits on a plateau a mile above sea level hugged by tall cliffs. The valley was settled as far back as 8000 BC, but it was the Zapotec Indians that dominated the region until the Mixtecs took over in the seventh century. Eventually the Aztecs conquered and ruled in the fifteenth century only to be overtaken later by the Spanish. Hernan Cortes founded the city of Oaxaca in 1529 and since then, its charm and warm congeniality has become renowned.

The capital, with its wrought-iron-fenced balconies and sparkling fountains, is heralded in tourist brochures as a place to savor, where stately women walk with stacks of roses on their heads and fruit vendors push carts laden with the most amazing tropical gems anyone is likely to ever see. Since arriving last week, my favorite pastime was to simply sit near the Portal de Flores in the zocalo, sucking on a melon ice wand or sipping some summery rum punch, handing over my spare pesos to the overtly friendly children who come up to me or watching the locals meander about, reading the newspaper, conversing in the open plaza, or getting their shoes shined.

Before I left Chicago, my travel agent put together a very comprehensive tour package that included a trip to a chocolate factory, a meander through an artisans' village, an interface with a cactus plantation, and even an all-day seminar on the preparation of Oaxacan cuisine including a rare demonstration on the making of homemade ice cream mixed with dried rose petals. He even planned an overnight

Postcards from Heartthrob Town: A Gay Man's Travel Tales
Published by The Haworth Press, Inc., 2006. All rights reserved.
doi:10.1300/5732_12

trip out to a coastal town called Zipolite, "just in case I wanted to get lucky." But I was swept up in the atmosphere of the city itself, content to sun in the open plazas and mingle with local merchants, with no desire for a lengthy bus ride to a notorious cruise area.

I applauded myself for avoiding the regime of tour buses and structured group outings in favor of feeding my whimsy. As a history teacher just graduated from a master's program and currently teaching at an inner-city college prep school, I had found my limit for conservative curriculum meetings and the monotony of class schedules. For an entire week I simply blended into the pastel architecture in the old town and wandered about the historical district, nodding to the marimba music from street bands and eyeing the effigies of Catholic saints carved from tree trunks and the rows of inexpensive indigo pottery that gleamed in the open-air markets in July.

I stayed at the Hotel Antequera, and my room, with its red-and-black velvet bedspread and well-worn leather reading chair, had the most amazing views of the town square. I took my early breakfast, strong coffee and coddled eggs covered with a spicy mole sauce, right on my micro balcony, and watched the tourists snap photographs in the purple-flowered gazebo in the center of the zocalo. The mornings had a tropical edge to them and the air was heady with the perfume from wildflowers. A local street vendor played salsa music, and even during the workweek, people were seen lightly stepping, shifting hips and throwing their heads back to the hypnotic rhythm of the beat.

On the day before I was to leave, I sojourned out to peek into the Basilica of Our Lady of Solitudes, the church honoring the patron saint of the entire state of Oaxaca. Known simply as "Soledad," she had become a special devotion of local fishermen who still offered her effigy gifts of pearls from their catch. According to the hotel clerk, who took pride in showing off his English-speaking skills, these pearls were often sewn next to the diamonds that lined her black velvet robes.

I took an unhurried stroll toward the church, leisurely passing a small protest group just outside the tall edifice. Even in a seemingly sleepy town like Oaxaca, there were militants demanding more benefits from a government that left nearly the entire state at the bottom of the financial heap. Inside the seventeenth-century complex, devout worshippers were praying silently, kneeling before the stoic Virgin or offering up their few pesos in order to burn their devotional tapers. An old woman reached into her purse and kissed a holy card, then clasped it between her two palms and began to weep.

I walked out past the rows of pews to an outdoor garden in the center of the buildings. I nestled into a corner of the botanicals where I was surrounded by all kinds of roses: black roses, tea roses on thornless stems, seashell roses. The most exquisite orange roses were nodding in the late morning sun and something compelled me to reach over and inhale the aroma of an open bud. It's not the familiar rose scent I had come to associate in my memory with the stereotypical red blooms one receives on Valentine's Day or the tumble of American Beauties heaped on a casket during a funeral procession. I noted that there was something puzzling in the perfume, as if I had stumbled onto a rare specimen containing a fragrance so dizzying I was unable to fully articulate its power.

Astonished by the unnameable bouquet circulating within the dewy petals, I inhaled another fiery open bloom in an attempt to interpret the mystery. The delicate scent trailed up my nose and before I could pull away I was met with the most piercing shock. A bumblebee nestled in the core node of the rose had emerged with its released stinger now firmly planted precariously close to my left eye. I let out a wail that caused a priest to drop his Bible and sent echoes across the tan walls of the stone churchyard.

With my hand holding onto the bridge of nose, I scrambled out of the garden, past the candlelit pews and out into the front plaza. I zigzagged through a cluster of lounging teenagers, stumbling over a tossed backpack and knocking over a small chair where a woman was selling handmade rosaries and statures of the Virgin. Apologizing in half-English and half-Spanish, I revealed to the woman my now swelling nose and pointed to the bruised area. I stuttered, "Doctor, medic, hospital . . . *donde?*"

Sweeping up the disheveled artifacts, the woman wiped her brow and pointed to an alley just past the church. But the shadowy thruway appeared to be a just another long parade of vendors selling everything from textiles and pottery to dead chickens. *"Medicina alli,"* she said and pointed to the dodgy marketplace, her head bent down in order to scoop up her rosaries. I moved away from her, wavering toward some unclear destination, hoping that another American tourist might assist me or that someone would speak enough English and direct me toward a medical facility, or at the very least, some ice cubes wrapped in a towel.

The entire left side of my face was now tingling as I shifted through a crowded space filled with locals and tourists bargaining for miniature bottles of local spices and carved wooden animals. Toward the back of the closed-in street, a larger stall was host to everything from silver belt buckles and cheap radios to baskets of mangos and woven rugs. Someone was bidding on a brown leather satchel as I stopped to get the attention of a young vendor polishing a paperweight fashioned from a polished stone.

"Ayuda," I half-whispered to the man with the multicolored bandanna around his forehead. *"Medicina, por favor?"* I revealed to him my sore and puffy skin.

My rescuer set down the carved onyx and removed his sweat-damp scarf. Without even a pause, he drew close to me and began to dab my swollen face. Wordlessly, he took me behind the tent to a makeshift kitchen consisting of a hot plate, a tub of water serving as a sink, and a mini fridge plugged into a tiny generator. He opened a metal handyman's box that looked as if it would hold fishing tackle and quickly sifted through an assortment of bandages and ointment tubes. Without speaking, he rubbed an oily salve over my throbbing bee sting.

"Lay down here." He pointed to a woven mat on the ground.

The balm had suddenly and effectively cooled my injured facial area, so I quickly decided to obey my stealthy medicine man.

"Close your eyes," he instructed in perfect English. "Don't open them until I tell you to."

As soon as I dropped my head to the ground, I felt the prickly edges of a sharp set of tweezers and, quite thankfully, the release of the stinger. I sat up, startled by the expediency of my stumbled-upon healer, and attempted to lift myself back up.

"Closed, I said!" The tone of his voice was serious and comforting at the same time. I laid back down and half-squinted to get a peek at his hands as they worked the sap out of what appeared to be a shaved cactus ear. The cool gel was then dabbed onto the patch where the bee's arrow was lodged. He offered me a wet rag and a small cup of clear alcohol.

"Pure Oaxacan mescal," my handsome physician announced. "Not like the cheap tequila you get back in the States. This is distilled on my uncle's ranch, made strictly from the agave plant."

I took slow sips of the potent fuel. *"Gracias."* I felt the brew burn as it went down. My breathing had normalized and I began to feel calmer. "I can't believe you knew exactly what to do. I'm completely indebted to you."

He took the tweezers and held up the tiny thorn that had been plunged below my left eye. "Another couple of inches and we might have been looking for a pirate's patch for you." He took the towel from my hand then held up a small cracked mirror to my face.

"My God!" I looked to see where the stinger had lodged but my face seemed perfectly normal except for a few traces of the gooey layer of cactus sap. "How can it be so?"

"Take another sip of the mescal, my friend," he said as he helped me to raise the cup to my lips. "Living here teaches you how to respect the land. The old ways insist that for every harm there is also a cure."

"You are a practitioner in these old ways of healing, then?"

"They called my grandfather 'El Brujo' and like him I seem to have the intuition." He began to pour a cup of spirits for himself, and then offered me a bit more. "The *brujos* are wizards or shamans who know how to mediate. We are the priests who carry the messages of the Great Spirit."

"I thought those stories were myths or legends," I said, realizing suddenly that my tone must have seemed overly dismissive and somewhat wrought with cynicism.

"You don't have to believe," he looked intently into my eyes. "You simply have to listen, be present and bear witness."

After a moment of strained silence my doctor had closed his medicine chest and helped me to my feet.

"My name is Carroll," I said. "It's androgynous. You know, one that could be for both a man or a woman."

"I know androgynous well," he smiled knowingly. "My name is Cruz, born here in Mexico, schooled at UCLA, and replanted back in my hometown of Oaxaca for the past three years. Are you visiting my city for long?"

"I've been here on holiday for over a week but this is my last day. I came here because I didn't want to swim inside of a frozen margarita while watching my skin burn on a crowded beach in Acapulco." I handed the empty cup back and reached for my wallet. "Please let me offer you something for your kindness."

"It was my honor," he said, refusing my folded bills. "In honor of Guelaguetza, however, you can accompany me to the lantern-lighting part of the festival for your last night here."

"Guelaguetza?"

"The city's carnival honoring Centeotl, the goddess of corn." Cruz had gently placed his arm around my shoulder as he guided me back to the market. "Guelaguetza is a Zapotec word meaning to cooperate in the flow of things. It simply demands that people become aware of reciprocity."

"Give-and-take?" I felt my skin beginning to burn and tingle again, but it was coming from the rush of blood to my head, the spirit of the mescal as it plowed through my veins.

"For every action, a loving and gracious reaction," Cruz winked as he stuffed a card in my pocket with his address and number, along with his striped bandanna. "A souvenir for a stung but now immortal tourist."

"Immortal?"

"Bees are messengers from the gods, symbols of such an immortality," Cruz said in a matter-of-fact tone. "Now you've been gifted with the poison to see through to forever with."

For a moment, I was stuck at how to imagine time going on into infinity. How could I, even as a bodiless spirit, simply exist through an eternity, living out beyond the parameters of what humans have named time? "Who wants to live forever?" I shouted back at my hospitable wizard.

"See you at the Hotel Camino Real, tonight around seven."

I walked back to my hotel in a storm of heat. Wrapping the bandanna around my neck, I made my way back to my room, where I collapsed in a feverish pitch onto the cool afternoon bedsheets. All I kept seeing were his hands touching my face. His wide, dark eyes steady on my lips and my neck. His knees resting quietly on my thighs as he sat cross-legged next to me quietly unraveling himself.

I looked over the table next to my bed, strewn with sightseeing brochures and tourist maps of the city. I noted the two books on Mesoamerican history that I intended on reading, with every hope of piecing together a classroom lecture on the background of Oaxaca. I wanted to detail the influence resulting from the Spanish invasion and the revolution that later occurred in the 1920s. I wanted to discuss the friendly nature of the indigenous people, their customs chafing against the city's slow move toward modernization. I wanted to talk about the spiritual nature of the country, the mystery held within the tombs at the tall pyramids at Monte Albán located just outside the capital.

But the idea of merely lecturing on history suddenly left me cold. Where was the great adventure of my own life? Had I simply become a mere mouthpiece detailing the dried-up remnants of passing cultural traditions? How was I myself a part of real history and where was my own path that allowed me to shape and interact with life? I rested on my hotel bed thinking about the academy where I taught and about all the things I needed to still learn myself.

When the hour of my meeting with Cruz finally arrived, I was dressed in a white crepe shirt and tight blue jeans. His bandanna was tied onto one of my belt loops as I made my way through the hoards of people standing around a raised stage. Women with ribbons braided into their hair were twirling their multicolored skirts around baskets of bright flowers and cornhusks. Onlookers huddled around the guitar players and dancers and clapped loudly between the musical pieces.

From the corner of my eye, I noted a slowly moving procession of large oval lanterns swirling down a side street near the hotel. A woman wearing a lavishly embroidered blouse and a wide necklace made of tiny ears of corn whirled in front of the brightly lit shades. Could it be the fertility goddess herself? The long march of lantern bearers seemed endless as I waited for Cruz to arrive.

"For you." My sorcerer had materialized out of nowhere and handed me a stick with a tiny round cup at the end of it. "You place the candle here, and the shade over it like this, then you simply surrender and allow Centeotl to guide you."

"It's my name!" I exclaimed as I noted that Cruz had artfully carved "Carroll" onto the side of the thick white votive. Handing me a match, I lit the wick and watched as Cruz lifted the shaded flame into the buzzing night air.

"Now, the procession of the lanterns can really begin," Cruz laughed. "Just follow me."

My sinewy companion led me down curving streets festooned with brightly colored banners. People were singing and thrashing about to music that seemed to be seeping out of the old walls of the city. There was a strange choreography to the movement of the crowd, as though everyone was happily parting in order to make room for Cruz and me to easily pass through them.

After several long blocks, we arrived at a small storefront with its awnings bearing down over the shop windows. "This is where I apprentice," Cruz whispered in low tones. "Come in and see some of the work I've created."

We entered the small shop, which turned out to be something resembling a working artist's studio. The walls were lined with shelves filled with a multitude of hand-poured candles ranging in various sizes and shapes; most were cast in a pale white tone but some took on a range of colors.

Cruz took the lantern from my hand and began to light several tall pillar candles next to a table stacked with metal and rubber moulds, empty jars and large chunks of tan wax. I noted the tapers decorated with wax roses, the tiny skeleton figures that are common around Mexico's Day of the Dead, and other candles that had been shaped into sunflowers and lilies that were floating in wide glass jars filled with water.

"You're a candle-maker?" I noted a somewhat superior tone in my intake of breath. "You studied that in California?"

"I studied archaeology at university, actually." Cruz's grave whisper barely escaped from his throat. "My family makes the best candles in the entire region. I'm helping them out because I want to." The dimly lit room began to reveal some of the most exquisitely crafted candles I had ever seen. "On my off days you'll find me out at Monte Albán interning with a professional excavation team, digging around the Aztec ruins, sifting through the subterranean tombs and putting together a historical time frame through a cache of uncovered relics."

"I'm not underestimating the art of fashioning candles," I half-apologized. "I just didn't expect it."

"Isn't that the best part of life?" Cruz had set afire a row of votives using the lit wick of my namesake candle. "When you encounter something that is a bit of a mystery, you know, unexpected."

Cruz sat me on a stool next to a large vat of softened wax. "It's still warm," I said taking a small portion of the lightly scented beeswax into my hands and pressing it between my fingers.

"I used that to make your namesake candle," Cruz said, cupping his hands around mine and instructing me to shape the ball into a long conical shape. "I'll show you how I inscribe now."

Taking a thin-tipped stylus, Cruz began to slowly write the word *Deseo* in a cursive script onto the side of the candle. He then took a small bottle filled with oil, and gently rubbed the sides with its contents. "Once it's fully cooled and set, you can light it." Cruz's warm breath filled the concave of my ear and I could feel the light stubble of his chin next to my skin.

"What is that strange humming sound?" I asked quietly, not wishing to disturb the somewhat soothing monotony of the muffled drone. "It's coming from behind that wall?"

"Be careful," Cruz whispered, opening the blue painted door in the back of the shop. "Step in and crouch down. Don't breathe if you can help it."

I entered what appeared to be a narrow passage with the back wall seemingly made from mesh wire. Inside the small, cool room were crudely made wood boxes filled with wet honeycombs pulsing with tiny, droning bees. I muffled my sudden reflexive gasp.

"I watch over their loving procreation." Cruz seemed to be talking from the hollow at the center of his chest. "They make their orange honey for *mi familia*'s table and the coveted wax I use to fashion all of my candles with. I owe a special debt to these creatures."

I hunched over a lidless box, watching the worker bees spinning and climbing over one another in their hexagon-shaped cells. All of the tiny combs were interlocked with one another, independent, yet interdependent upon the alchemy occurring within them.

"Why don't they fly out at us?" I could hardly get the words to shape on my lips. "How can you trust them not to sting you?"

"The word for trust in Spanish is 'confianza.' I can teach you the word, but life itself will have to teach you the meaning."

We reentered the studio space and the glow from the candles seemed to reconfigure the walls to the room. The flickering seemed to elongate the space and at times I felt in fact there were no walls, but that we were lightly anchored, moored in some vast pulsing, unnameable galaxy.

For a long time Cruz sat next to me on the apprentice stool. After a while, it seemed natural to simply allow my hands to fall into his lap and for my head to rest on his thick shoulder. We listened to each other quietly breathe and then I glanced up at the flickering shadows wavering on the tin ceiling of the shop. "Look at the little stars," I said.

"*Estrellas pequenos,*" Cruz murmured back. "That's what we are. Do you know your own fire? Do you make a habit of following it? Do you keep it as your quest, your mission in life? Do you know how to divine its message?"

As Cruz spoke, I felt my own breathing sync in unison with his. He led me to a wide velvet divan, where we both laid down. I watched the ceiling disappear and become a large indigo canopy dotted with constellations. My body rested quietly against his and I began to doze, the scent of his skin and the warm candlewax wafting around me.

In a dream, I imagined Cruz and I were climbing the stairs to a large structure on top of Monte Albán. He kept calling it "the hill of

Sacred Stones," and though I kept stumbling on the scarred incline, Cruz would find a way to reach down and pull me up. We entered a tomb where Cruz opened a sarcophagus filled with the most exquisite humming tones I had ever heard. The sound produced a kind of enchantment. Peering into the jar, I noted that it was a hive filled with bees. The opened lid dripped with honey, and I reached in to taste the raw nectar, unafraid of being harmed.

In one part of the dream we were passing a frieze with some sort of hieroglyphic writing. It was Cruz's voice that came from out of the carved stone, telling me how the trees were listening to my thoughts. His disembodied voice kept reminding me that the ground is sending vibrations through my body all the time. Informing me that the sky is always telling me where to go, how to act, when I should speak and listen and move.

Toward the end of the night vision, I remembered wondering what it might be like to kiss the master. What it might be like to touch the tip of my tongue to his skin. To place my hand in his hair and gently stroke his temples. I remembered wondering if this was indeed a dream, an apparition. If it was, then I didn't wish to wake up. I only wanted to walk through the pyramids, past the Aztec ceremonial altars and the ancient stone carvings. I only wanted to wander the crumbling ruins with my handsome *brujo*.

If there had been a prayer to say to halt the morning from coming, then I would have said it. If there had been an incantation to recite, a spell to mix, a mystic's dance to mimic, I would have given myself over to the charm that would prevent me from leaving Oaxaca. I embraced Cruz in front of the Hotel Antequera for as long as it was socially feasible. There were fragments of ribbons on the streets and the burned-out ends of candles that had glowed in last night's festival lanterns.

Cruz bent down and placed a blue baby corn in the palm of my hand.

"You can write me the next time you plan to come back," he said, offering me the unlit candle with DESEO inscribed on it. "I'd like to show you the relics I've found."

"Mi brujo." I lifted my head toward the sun sparkle dancing in a nearby fountain in the zocalo and after a long parting handshake, Cruz turned down a side street and vanished. "We walked the ley lines together and found where the gods sleep." I spoke aloud, although I was certain no one within earshot could understand me. "Now can I take the secret home with me?"

The taxi ride to the airport in Oaxaca was rather lackluster despite the momentary panic at my driver's taking the wrong exit. I eventually arrived at the airport and hunkered down in a waiting area that was colorless and somewhat shabby. The seats were narrow and unyielding and a mother's baby was screaming relentlessly.

Going back to teaching in August seemed to hold little romance for me and the notion of lecturing on the wooden "History of the Americas" suddenly paled next to the notion of archaeological digs with Cruz.

I rolled the baby corn back and forth between my fingers. The gate door opened to the plane and a tempestuous breeze filled the stuffy terminal with the smell of approaching rain. Outside the plate-glass window near the waiting area, I noted the silver wing of the jet nearly obscuring the mountain range in the distance. Without warning, a rather large bumblebee floated in from the open boarding passage and landed squarely on my carry-on luggage. I didn't breathe.

I watched as it settled on my nametag, fluttering its translucent wings and turning about as if it were trying to read the inky lettering on the label. It hovered slowly in midair for a moment, eye-level with me, and seemed to circle around me, making little halos about my head. Then, the buzzing, winged creature moved away from me, out past the information desks and rows of seats, beyond the electronic checkpoints and X-ray screens, and further beyond the baggage claim and the taxi stands.

"Of course," I laughed out loud, suddenly quelling the screams from the fidgety baby. "Who can leave Mexico without tasting its best honey?"

I gathered my roll-away luggage, discarded my boarding pass for home, and followed the bee's invisible path through the balmy and welcoming air. In a way, it felt like entering a kind of immortality.

François at the Toilette

I know he'll be here. Every Thursday afternoon at four, for the past three weeks, I have come to this metro latrine in the Gare de l'Est station to meet my new lover, François.

It's always the same routine. I arrive to greet his uncut cock standing straight up at the urinal. I take my own out and begin to gently stroke my lengthening shaft. Then we move quietly to a stall to finish off our compulsion for each other's skin: the soft biting and gentle nibbles of earlobes and lips, and our fetish for sucking each other's dirty fingers that have been riding steadily up our asses.

After four months of living in Paris, I have yet to visit the *Mona Lisa* at the Louvre or make a pilgrimage to the top of the Eiffel Tower. But I know the section in Pere Lachaise Cemetery where half-clothed men linger in mausoleums to get quickie blow jobs. I know the promenade of horny strangers in the Tuilleries Garden just like the back of my *Plan du Paris*. I'm all too acquainted with the cruisy park at the east of the Ile St. Louis by the Seine, where you can kiss another guy amid the festive-colored lights of the Bateau-Mouche. I even know the little bridge at the Rue de la Mare where you can hook a trick in a matter of minutes, even when it's raining.

But it's François I breathe for now. His soft brown eyes and full lips framed by a well-trimmed goatee. The tufts of brown chest hair that curl out from over the top of his thick Shetland wool sweaters. The tiny blue star tattooed on his wrist that moves gently over his hanging balls.

At exactly four o'clock, I hand my centimes over to the white-haired attendant sitting at a little booth. She is fumbling with a cas-

This chapter appeared originally under the same title in *Velvet Mafia* 14 (2005). Copyright 2005 Gerard Wozek. Reprinted with permission of the author.

 doi:10.1300/5732_13

sette of old Jane Birkin tunes. She snaps the antique plastic into a small player and when the slow music begins I become invisible to her. The turnstile cranks and I walk up to a row of men, mostly middle-aged mustaches, all standing with their zippers down at the latrine. Their eyes scrape my painted leather jacket, the flag patch on my worn jeans, my Marine crew cut.

"*Allemange,*" someone whispers and leers toward my direction, my soft dick barely out past the edge of my buttonhole crotch.

I move toward the stalls in the back of the latrine but there is a herd waiting to get inside an empty one. So I stand with my hand on my cock at the urinal, covering my rising shaft, while everyone becomes somewhat agitated. There are craning necks and mutual hand jobs resuming all around me, but I remain focused on François.

He has just arrived and stepped up to the row of jerking Frenchmen. His foreskin is the color of burnt copper. Around his swelling shaft is a yellow suede cock ring with spindly metal studs. The acrid smell of amyl nitrate emanates from the other side of the latrine and meshes with the odor of stale piss and cum. I watch my cohort as his nostrils flare and we both begin to grin.

"I hoped you would come." His accent is thick and for a moment it drowns out the chanteuse on the tinny boom box.

"I haven't come yet, but I'm planning on it," I whisper delicately across the corroded urinals. "*Mon cher.*"

His eyes roll back for a moment as he rolls the tip of his thumb across the giant head of his uncut cock. I can smell the sweat and stale urine at the tip and I feel my knees beginning to give. The crowd has finally dispersed from around the toilets and I follow him into an open pen. The scarred metal door closes behind us and I watch as he drops his dark corduroy trousers and sits down on the toilet seat.

I have quickly straddled myself over his dark, hairless legs. His lips are thick and rough and the color of freshly iced salmon. He wears a knotted kerchief around his neck, which smells like lemony vervain, and he takes it off and wraps it around the back of my head and pulls me up to his wet tongue as though his parted mouth were an oxygen mask. Breathing him in, I can almost forget that I am in a dank toilet near the metro.

The mournful chords of *"Ne Me Quitte Pas"* float over the stench and our rhythmic jostle. Jane Birkin keeps mixing in American words with her French and as François begins to thrust, I can't help but focus on a page in his open journal. There is a tightly knit ceiling of cursive French words and tornado scribbles surrounding the elegant swirls of a trained artist's hand: profiles of young men, the curves of an ancient street lamp, then, a perfectly drawn angel, something you would see pestering a nativity scene or the mantel of a cathedral altar, writhing in ecstatic terror. The body is placid but the head is askew, the mouth agape as though a horrific scream were passing through it.

I am bouncing on the legs of my lover. I am reaching for a coat hanger to balance myself. The turnstile is cranking and Jane Birkin begins to sound more and more like Marlene Dietrich. If I close my eyes I can imagine a cabaret, just like the one in *Blonde Venus,* and there are swooning legionaries and a stream of smoke from my clove cigarette billowing through my nostrils and I am the vision of love, just like the key lit icon, in a sequined gown with blue star earrings in the shape of François's tattoo. No one can take their eyes off my neon skin, my smoky eyes, the perfect points of my fingernails. I keep my eyes shut, my lover keeps thrusting, and the film just keeps rolling on.

In one scene I'm Ingrid Bergman in *Casablanca,* spilling champagne glasses across a café table and clutching the shoulder of Humphrey Bogart. In the next frame, I'm Gene Kelly in a tight striped T-shirt, whirling under the sanitized bridges near the Seine. If I keep my eyes shut tightly I can see the invented Paris of my childhood, the Paris fed by Saturday afternoon movies, and encyclopedia articles, and collected travel guides. The Paris that is fully alive and in the moment, the city that actually breathes and exists somewhere out beyond this train station piss palace.

But where I am situated right now is a scene I have never imagined. François licks cooling *riz au lait* off my chest hair and lets his tongue wander down from my armpit to my pelvis. He's sipping on a chilled Orangina, then resumes gently nudging his nose down to my groin and balls. Eyes peer through screw holes pierced through the sides of the stall as my French lover opens a second condom, preparing to make another entry into my anxious body.

He rides me, softly at first, then we crescendo into a sweaty fever. In the space between ecstasy and wiping the spilled cum from our rolled-down pants and the concrete floor, I think to manage another rendezvous by exchanging phone numbers. As he pulls his sticky sweater over his head I motion with my hand as though writing with a pen: "Number . . . telephone?"

François shrugs with a soft roll of his eyes, opens the stall door, and, with a tilt of his head, exits the toilette.

With a determined charge in my pulse, I buckle my jeans and make off toward the metro, where I can see that my estranged lover has bolted through the gate toward the destination point, La Courneuve. I pass my ticket through the entrance and keep several paces behind François. When the crowded subway pulls in, I jump on the car behind the one he is in and keep my head staring between the glass car doors so I can view him.

Chateau Landon. Stalingrad. Riquet. The train stops at each metro station, and still he doesn't leave his seat. I'm imagining the pulsing world aboveground. I'm imagining the tourists taking snapshots of the sun going down behind the Conciergerie, or the last hints of twilight off the glass pyramid entrance to the Louvre, the children taking their boats out of the fountain at the Luxembourg Gardens, or the gray stones mute against the flashing neon of the Champs-Elysées. Crimée. Corentin Cariou. I'm riveted to his body and still he doesn't move.

Porte de la Villette. Finally he moves toward the door. I step off the car and follow him down a narrow artery. Drunken beggars singing some strangely familiar American pop tune and the faint smell of cherry-infused tobacco from the trail of François's lit cigarette tip. Stairs and more narrow tubular passageways. Again, I'm paces behind him and shadowed behind the heft of a backpacker's overstuffed sack.

How do you make love to someone as though you were traversing a great city? How do you fornicate without inhibition as though you were encountering the foreign smells of an urban market for the first time? I can think only of my lover's gentle thrusting, his thick lips on my eyelids, the smell of his sweet breath, the long trail of sweat running from his temples down his neck. I think of his insatiable kisses, the sucking of his lower lip, the electric pulse that seems to run through us, the humming connecting current, as I take all of him inside of me.

Finally, we reach the upper terminal. François pauses to rub out his cigarette with the tip of his brown boot. He tosses some euros into a vending machine, which dispenses a small tin of some sort of candy, then enters what appears to be another latrine.

I stand outside the toilette, brooding over whether I should enter. My groin is still on fire from the stubble of his beard against my own chafed foreskin. I pass some coins onto the matron's plate and enter the white-tiled public restroom. There are three stalls. Two of them with closed doors. I gingerly enter the unoccupied one and situate myself upon the porcelain bowl.

Peering through a wide bolt hole the size of a quarter, I begin to recognize François's unshaven chin in the next stall. His full lips are moving up and around another man's firm buttocks. I watch as he pushes open the dark hairy ass crack with his fingers and begins to pleasure the man's hole with his extended tongue. A deep sigh permeates the warm enclosure next to me and François's cohort begins to bend over more completely.

I open the buttons of my fly and my hardening cock pops out. I am the voyeur now, the blinking eye at the stained peephole, the stroking onlooker. I can hear inaudible words, moaning, a guttural laughter. François tears open a condom and begins to wrap on his second skin. Then I take it all in: the slow mount, the straddle around the toilet bowl, the athletic thrusting and pumping, torso to torso. I peer up to see the animal-like flaring of François's nostrils. I imagine his breath again, his slow drool dripping down my own neck, and in a matter of minutes, the three of us collapse into a storm of moans.

I try to swallow my gasps of breath. There is a sudden silence that takes over the latrine. I listen for the untangling of dropped trousers and belts. The wiping of sweat from brows with toilet paper. The shuffling apart.

I slowly open the stall door and watch the dark stranger emerge—a Moroccan gentlemen, I think for a moment, though I'm not entirely sure. Then François steps out, emerging like a Napoleonic swordsman, a stealthy warrior after meeting the challenge of his quest.

I somehow find the core within me to call out, "François, *mon cher.*"

He turns for a moment, as though startled by the shrill echo wending through the stark restroom. In the fluorescent light, his skin looks somewhat sallow, his sunken eyes less familiar, world-weary even.

I'm still gushing, "François, *mon ami.*" I know there are still pearls of drying cum on my hand as I extend it toward his frozen stance. *"S'il vous plait."*

I suddenly recall a moment in Jean-Luc Godard's classic film *Pierrot Le Fou,* where the protagonist looks back for a moment at the fading background of Paris. It all seems to be washing away, crumpling in torn shreds behind his stony face. That is the moment that comes to mind as I watch the now-familiar tilting of François's head as he makes his way toward the exit.

I gather my things up and run out to see my Frenchman popping a small lozenge into his mouth as he turns the corner of a narrow walkway. I stand for a moment, unable to make sense of the last hour's chase scene. From the corner of my eye I see a giant poster advertising a McDonald's Happy Meal and the discombobulating continues.

I head back toward the betro station, but I don't return to the subway. I walk up the stairs where my imagined city has been waiting for me like a distant lover for so long. It's a colorless neighborhood in the nineteenth arrondissement. I gaze around, still disoriented, and face a small fenced-in park with a dog drinking out of a low fountain situated next to a low-budget brasserie with two small tables in front.

It isn't the Paris of old movie stars, or even the one fabricated in my childhood's eye. But it's the stop I got off at. There are men casually leaning on a railing, some who almost resemble the profiles of the guys caricatured in François's journal. One of them draws me in with an almost half-smile, an almost sneer.

"Bonsoir," the chap whispers under his breath to catch the rim of my silver earring.

I turn around for a moment and he's suddenly gazing at some boy emerging from the escalator coming up from the metro. I near the street corner and, far in the distance, if I stand on my toes a bit, I can almost manage to see what appears to be the top of the Eiffel Tower.

So I take a deep breath, dislodge my *Plan du Paris* from my shoulder bag, and go toward something. Maybe it's Paris, maybe it's just a myth in my head; but it lingers in the air like a ponderous, unanswerable question.

He Said Those Roses Would Be Sanguine

"We'll both die here of heatstroke," he said as he fanned himself at the rusted gate to Alhambra's Garden.

I'm staring into the fire swirls located at the center of the flaming-red amaryllis, the one that's coiled like a garden snake around the iron frame of the gate. The one that wants me to get lost in its dewy petals and its narrowing and sticky dark center. The one that keeps me riveted in my path, rendered speechless by its indefinite fragrance, unable to look up at him. Unable to say what I've wanted to say since last week, when we first arrived in Spain.

Our overnight stop in Granada has been precipitated by my desire to roam the lush gardens of the Alhambra. I have this notion that everything between myself and my partner Cameron will be resolved once I see the roses that are purported to be the color of dark red blood.

"Look—it says right here," Cameron points out to me as I rummage through my backpack looking for a tissue to wipe my forehead with. "'The rare black-red blooms that grace Alhambra's Garden near the Court of the Lions seem to originate from a fairy-tale world where anything is possible. Legend has it that a sultan killed an unsuitable suitor who tried to win his daughter's hand in marriage.'"

"So the color derives from the blood of a slain lover?"

"So it would seem," he muses. "Another one of love's casualties."

Cameron and I have flown three thousand miles from our house in Ohio just to make tracings of the ornamental reliefs that are found throughout the landmark palace and gardens. I have brought with me several soft crayon pencils and onionskin paper in my carryall, in order to capture the latticing and raised tile decorations based on stylized quotes from the Koran that are located throughout this historic stronghold.

Postcards from Heartthrob Town: A Gay Man's Travel Tales
Published by The Haworth Press, Inc., 2006. All rights reserved.
doi:10.1300/5732_14

The air is morbidly still at the base of the bastion, dense with humidity, smelling of mildew as a result of the standing water in small stone pools that are rife with mosquitoes and rotting lily pads. I catch a glimpse of the snowcapped Sierra Nevada mountains from beyond Cameron's shoulder and think about how in ancient times that melted frost provided the conquerors with fresh water for the fountains. I try to take a breath and nearly choke on the stench.

"We have to move along, Cameron." I'm gasping for a clear breath.

I want to regain my composure and blow cool air on my partner. I want to send for a bucket of ice cubes so that he can set his feet down in something frosty. I want to take a napkin from my pack and wipe the streaming sweat off his wet face. Tell him that once we get back to the hotel room we can order sangria. That he can take a fresh shower. That I'll rub his feet just like I used to when we were new lovers just four years ago.

"Cameron, how do we get to the Court of the Lions?" I call out for directions from him but his face is expressionless. "I think if the fountain there is working we can both rest and cool off there. Doesn't a spray of water on your neck sound good right about now?"

Pearls of sweat have formed around his unshaven upper lip and he is motionless in the relentless sun. His black hair is glued down around his forehead and ears and his lips are cracked and nearly white from dehydration. I point to a glint of sunlight reflecting off of a distant temple dome inlaid with gold.

"I wish the clouds would roll over this damn sun," he spits back.

I step back to form a postcard of this moment in my mind. My partner Cameron is leaning against an ancient castle wall with a look of exasperation on his face. He is fumbling with his travel guide, oblivious to the blue dragonfly that has landed on his sleeve and the shower of genie dust that has shaken from off of a nearby almond tree branch to form a kind of nimbus of finely powdered sugar around his tilted head. The Alhambra, a square, towered product of the wars between Christianity and Islam, is brooding over him in the distance, but he is unable to glean its kingly, almost mystical presence.

This Islamic palace complex built in the ninth century sits on a plateau in the Sierra Nevada mountains. The name Alhambra derives from an Arabic root that means "crimson castle," perhaps because of the particular reddish hue of the crenellated towers. Muslim history, however, suggests that this unique color is derived from the reflections of the torches that surrounded the fortress during its initial construction, somehow leaving the walls transformed with these uneven pink and terra-cotta tones.

I have come here to examine the terraces of ornate gardens, interspersed with sun-splashed pools of clear water. I have come to take in the vistas of the old Moorish quarter and the Sacromonte, the old gypsy quarter where some gypsies still live in hillside caves. I have come to wander through the Royal Palace and find the blood-tinged roses that I believe will offer me a piece of Koranic paradise.

"Why don't you go on ahead?" He seems to be gesturing me toward some vague future and so I pass through the gate by myself into the steep incline of the palace garden. Alone in the viney alcove, I want to take off my clothes in order to bathe in the thousands of black rose petals I know must be waiting for me. I want to follow the ancient arteries of the barefoot sultan. I want to get lost in the furnace heat pouring out of the exotic garden flowers and mossy vines. I want to forget everything that has transpired before this moment, everything that has conspired to forge this crumbling fortress, this stony Alhambra I've come to know as Cameron and me.

True enough, I came to his arms prematurely perhaps, instead of reconciling with my own feelings of inadequacy. How was it, I tried to rationalize with myself back then, that as I neared forty I had not secured a stable relationship? I came to his arms with all my self-recrimination and fears of growing older alone. I came wanting to trade my cycle of online dating for the simplicity of a daily routine with one person, the slow lather of a monogamous arrangement, and the comforts of a suburban home that reflected back like the pages of a brand-new Pottery Barn catalog.

"Do we have to have the oak-trimmed modular wine bar?" I remember Cameron asking me the day we chose our dining-room set. "We hardly have any time for ourselves let alone for entertaining friends."

"Everyone has to have a place to set up their prized champagne and imported vodkas." I rolled my eyes back at him then. I was building a life in my imagination and I believed that by purchasing the Italian soup tureen and the etched wineglasses, the initialized champagne bucket and the matching silver candleholders, I could create some sort of a legitimate future.

I am the one who wanted to paint the walls of our bungalow the color of mute Midwestern wheat fields. I chose the stone-colored suede fabric for the sofa. The sage-colored pillows. The lichen-colored floor rug. The framed pictures of ferns and willow rods to remind me of how I grew up surrounded by grassy fields and a farmer's pond. I am the one who ordered these benign furnishings hoping that I could find my own life amid these linen slipcovers and artfully arranged bookshelves.

But by the time we were finished decorating our newly purchased suburban cottage, the paint had darkened in every room, leaving everything oddly tinted and somewhat morosely overcast, as though a photographer had redone everything in sepia tones, or painted maudlin shadows over the wood cabinets and furniture. I breathed in the new paint fumes that seemed to linger for nearly a year, before realizing that I had set up a house, created a life, I no longer wanted any part of.

"I'm going to run over to the tourist stand and see if I can get a new battery for my camera." His words hit my back from behind the rusty gate. "I'll catch up with you later if I can."

Cameron was still marking a passage in the guidebook as he turned to go. I watched his familiar, predictable gait as he marched off in the distance, inattentive to the sights around him, sighing heavily in the afternoon blaze. I wondered what it was in me, what character flaw, what deficiency I possessed, that would not allow me to continue on in my conventional relationship with him.

"You get bored so easily," Cameron once accused me of as I opened a fresh set of Amish quilts and bedsheets. "We've barely used the five sheet sets that we have."

"First of all, you need to change your sheets seasonally," I defended, smoothing the yarn-dyed stripes into each corner of the California bed. "And what's wrong with having something fresh to sleep on? After all, it might make things a little more interesting for us at night."

"Sheets don't make intimacy happen," Cameron shuddered. "Lovers do."

I am the one who wants to sleep with blue monarchs now. I am the one who wants to fly kites in a sandstorm off the coast of Algeria. The who wants to walk blindfolded on an empty, rainy beach in Australia. I am the one who wants to meet a stranger on a fishing pier in Amsterdam. The one who wants to dance sock-footed in some blues dive in New Orleans or flirt lasciviously with a group of drunken Greek sailors in some all-night taverna. I am the one.

I used to think of us as an impenetrable palace or an unassailable fortress. But now I find myself imagining ways to disinherit this stoic structure we have built up over the past several years. Should I simply engage in an affair and allow myself to be discovered? Should I write Cameron a letter explaining how discouraged I've become with my inability to maintain a sincere and conscientious bond with him? Should I write to the *Dr. Phil* show requesting to be considered for a guest spot on a program dealing with individuals who cannot follow a prescribed path of monogamy and trust?

On the train ride to Granada, Cameron pointed out that during the eighteenth century, the Alhambra descended into disrepair as a result of its salons being converted into taverns and dung heaps. Thieves and beggars inhabited the vast series of connected ornate rooms and the faerie palace of the Moors became a cavern for stray bats and Spanish criminals. Later on, Napoleon's troops marched into Granada and tried to convert the palace rooms into barracks. Soldiers set up mines in one of the towers and destroyed a good part of the citadel. Our relationship now, I'm thinking, is just like this palace, fallen to ruin and set up for onlookers to walk through and ponder. Our sullen fights have become more frequent, and my insular stance has become a natural reflex.

"Just wait until you see the blood roses," Cameron assured me as the plane landed in Madrid. "They'll change your mind about romance. I've seen pictures."

"You don't think I'm romantic enough?" I spoke to the wing of the jet from outside my airplane window. "I'm not fulfilling you enough, is that it?"

Cameron rested his head on the foam pillow set behind his neck. The plane touched down and neither of us spoke another word until we picked up our suitcases at the baggage claim. I realized that my defensiveness had overtly revealed my own desire to wander away. I am the one who wants to wake up every morning, either alone or beside another lover. I am the one who now wants to be a hunter again. I am the one who wants to be solitary with my thoughts at night. I am the one.

I think of Cameron now as I walk through this royal relic. There are reminders from history's heroic days within these walls, but the swashbuckling past has collapsed within this fortress, and though it still retains its grandeur, it is merely a tourist site now. History buffs line up to take the usual photographs and casual gapers purchase cheap souvenirs outside the gate at various shops and boutiques. The torch fires that reddened these ramparts, the legendary kings that once ruled these towers, are all gone now.

I pass the charred stone walls and walk past remnants of fountains and broken water ducts that lay in ruins. Smoke drifts above untrimmed purple hedges. I brush the tips of oozing honeysuckles and lilacs and each leaf sends a pulsing electric current through me. The labyrinthine path lets me meditate awhile and the warm smell of fresh mulch and Spanish earth helps me to lose the stoic chill I've nursed since our arrival in Madrid eight days ago.

I move forward a bit more and suddenly the garden collapses and a sudden turn reveals a grove of oversized stone columns circling around the oasis of the twelve-sided marble fountain resting upon the backs of twelve regal felines. I have finally arrived at the majestic Court of the Lions. Churning water ascends and spills from the gold-and-green basin to the open jaws of the carved lions to where it is distributed throughout the expansive courtyard. I dip my hand in the rush of chilly water and nearly expire.

"Cameron!" I call out to one of the flesh-eating cats spewing a stream of bubbles at me. "You really need to see this. You need to feel this."

For a moment, I'm surprised that I am actually missing my partner's heft. It occurs to me that I should turn back and run after him. That he has probably become frustrated and maybe even worried, that he has misplaced his guidebook and gone down the wrong path. I imagine that he is probably furious with me for running off without him even though he was the one to suggest it.

Instead, I squelch the thought by entering a small alcove in order to stare at the intricate carvings around the graceful stone portico. I bend over to touch the tile mosaics inlaid along the walls. I reach down in my backpack and take out the crayons and paper I've carried with me.

The stone relief contains various geometric patterns and as I pass my crayon over the engravings, a pattern begins to emerge. My eye follows the slowly forming pathways of the Islamic design and I imagine I am just small enough to be a miniature pilgrim following its narrow paths. I am just like that ancient Christian warrior, I think to myself, that *reconquista,* who drove out the royal armies, conquering this vast fortress, only to leave it behind for something else.

I keep tracing, following the curving braid of the elaborate detailing, pressing my crayon harder and harder against the paper, and then I stop.

I begin to write the words *Dear Cameron.* I pause to reflect on his name, then halt myself again.

I am remembering how I refused a makeup kiss from my lover yesterday on the train ride from Madrid. How I insisted on sulking through the entire excursion, my arms folded, offering up only a sullen posture and the hard silence that fell between us.

I am recalling how months before we left for Spain, I would often pretend I was asleep when Cameron would come to bed in order to resist any ardent initiation from him. How even this morning, I pictured someone else looking across from me at the breakfast table, imagined a conversation I might be having with someone else, someone I believed I could reveal myself to, someone, I told myself through sips of espresso, I have yet to meet.

My crayon breaks in two and I am suddenly accosted by the rich, heady fragrance of blooming roses, a deep penetrating aroma that seems to inhabit every pulse of my being. As I look up through the portico, I see exactly what I have been promised. The anticipated garden of those perfectly sanguine roses.

"Aha!" I call out to the sprawling garden. "You blood beauties have found me at last."

I would swear that the gazebos and lattice arches in this walled terrace are all in flames. I breathe in the aromatic scent of the dark burgundy roses and nearly swoon in the ardor of these indomitable ebony buds.

Here they are, just like he said they would be. A compass of petals tinted in a mix of voodoo red and heat-flash lightning. Colored with a rare concoction of pure scarlet and the essence of nighttime. Flower petals painted off a palate derived from a lover's legendary quest to consummate his passion hundreds of years ago, only to meet with his untimely death.

For a moment I flash on our cherrywood bedroom furniture in Ohio. The tall Puritan-inspired headboard is crumbling into an inferno and the tufted mattress has become a jumble of hot coals and exposed wire bedsprings. Our dresser is now a furnace and the nightstand has been devoured by a tongue lick of sparks. A part of me wants to grab for my journal, which I left in the drawer of the bedside bureau. A part of me wants to dash in and save the photographs from our past trips together. But I stand, motionless in the encapsulating waves of heat, watching the whole bedroom transform into an overwhelming bonfire.

"I thought I'd never find you!" Cameron calls from beyond the lion-guarded fountain. "You can't believe how lost I got just now looking for you."

I take another breath of the sanguine roses broiling in the Spanish sun and, looking up at my companion, I manage to finally extinguish any hope for the two of us.

Vienna Waits for You

Last year I taught a humanities course at the Institute for European Studies, but my real purpose for securing the job was to make my long-awaited pilgrimage to Austria. Since my college days, that melancholy Billy Joel chorus had haunted me: "When will you realize, Vienna waits for you?" That question always seemed to hang over my head as I'd read travelogues detailing the architecture that spun out of the Hapsburg empire and the sprawling palaces and cathedrals that were laced throughout the old city. I always pictured myself roaming the Vienna of my imagination, sampling a mug of hot chocolate and a slice of the infamous Sacher torte at Demel's Café, or strolling through the Stadtpark, admiring the statues of famous artists placed amid the lush greenery.

When I received notice that I would be teaching in our college's teacher exchange program, I made my list of to-do's: visit the State Opera House, dine on smoked sausages and schnitzels, drink Viennese coffee, write in the strudel-filled cafés, bow at Mozart's grave site, and roam through the dark catacombs of St. Stephen's Cathedral. But it was the opportunity to ogle Gustav Klimt's paintings and see firsthand the genius worked into his masterpiece friezes that ultimately brought me to the elegant European capital.

At the Belvedere Palace one colorless afternoon in November, I witnessed Klimt's magnum opus *The Kiss* with its magnetic erotic pang still held intact. I stood in the gallery of the converted palace, transfixed by the painting's luminous power, the shimmering robe of the dark male figure as he embraced his submissive female counterpart. As I leaned closer to view the detailing in the geometric patterns, I tipped one of the metal posts holding up the velvet ropes that blocked off direct access to the canvas. One of the guards called out sternly to me in German and hastened me on to another gallery. But I

Postcards from Heartthrob Town: A Gay Man's Travel Tales
Published by The Haworth Press, Inc., 2006. All rights reserved.
doi:10.1300/5732_15

found myself thinking about that sensuous embrace captured in glittering gold and oils long after I arrived back at my rented room.

Klimt came to prominence in Vienna during the late 1800s by painting murals and decorative flourishes around theaters and most notably, the Kunsthistorisches Museum. At thirty he had his own studio where he focused on easel paintings and only five years later he founded the Vienna Secession, a movement with a design aesthetic that railed against commercialism and sought to make art an integral part of life. Klimt himself was preoccupied with the dazzling world of Vienna's intellectual, turning his attention to the darkly erotic and themes focusing on the search for happiness and the meaning of death. Like the artist, I found myself overwhelmingly attracted to the myth of a sensual and decadent life in Vienna.

But even after living and teaching in the capital for three weeks, I could write all that I knew about Vienna on the back of a postcard. I knew how to get to and from my temporary neighborhood digs to the Institute. I knew of an arty gay meeting place called the Berg Café just north of the inner Ringstrasse, but only visited there once after browsing the adjacent Lowenherz bookstore. I knew where to find the paintings of Caravaggio and Vermeer at the Kunsthistorisches Museum. But I wanted a more profound knowledge of the city and a chance to discover experiences that would justify my long love affair with the destination.

I lived above a brothel for the entire duration of my academic post. Sometimes when I would arrive home late from a field trip with students or a night out at the opera, the prostitutes that lined the entrance leading out from the U-Bahn would proposition me. One buxom and wigged brunette who always wore burgundy-tinted heart-shaped sunglasses and silver-threaded fishnet stockings would follow me to my front door, begging for me to try to negotiate an intimate session with her.

"Forty euros for you and anything you want," she'd say through a heavy German accent. "Thirty-five and you can be sure you won't forget me. Let's say thirty then."

I'd shut the door to the staircase leading up to my studio firmly on her and quietly listen at the window, hoping she wouldn't ring the doorbell and disturb my often-surly landlady. Then I'd peek from be-hind the curtain, and watch her join the rest of the young women. Sometimes they would stroll up to parked vehicles in the street. Sometimes they'd get in beside a patron and sometimes they'd simply open their palms for cash and unzip their leather jackets to expose their silicone-laden breasts. I'd fall asleep to the sound of opening and closing car doors on the street below and the laughter and catcalls from the high-pitched voices of Viennese hookers.

In the mornings, I would commute to the Institute where I would teach a course in theater arts to both exchange students from my own college in Chicago and regular undergraduates from the Institute. My syllabus requirements mostly covered the dramaturgy of early Vien-nese playwrights. When our deconstruction of Austrian scripts would end in the early afternoon, I would wander about the city looking for a café to write in or a restaurant where I could get a good plate of Wiener schnitzel.

Figlmuellers, a popular wine tavern located just blocks away from the school, offered a generously sized schnitzel that would overhang the plate. Served with their own local wine and a side of German pota-toes, it quickly became one of my staples. I often took myself there for a solitary table where I would watch and listen to members of the Vi-ennese Residenzorchester perform Strauss waltzes and polkas or sing operettas in original Biedermeier costumes.

One night at the restaurant, after a rather intense discussion of Vi-ennese playwrights with my students, I discovered that I had drank too much Heuriger wine. It seemed my overly friendly waiter had de-cided to provide me with an extra carafe of the prize-winning vino on the house. By the end of my meal, I realized that my fork had become too heavy to lift my apple torte off the dessert plate. I sat, bemused by the other tables of customers who were slouched over their breaded meats and potato salads. One of the costumed performers started up a bar song and as I made my way to the cashier, I stumbled into my waiter, knocking over his tray of lemon-garnished schnitzels.

"*Bist du verletzt?*" He seemed to be holding me up by the extended sleeves of my wool pullover. "Okay? Are you well?"

"Excuse me, please." I tried to regain my footing as I made note of my server's twisted name tag. "I didn't mean to run into you like that, Otto. I'm so sorry. Let me help you clean this up."

"So you know my name?" His demeanor suddenly softened. "It is I who shall be helping you then."

By the time I bent over to pick up an overturned plate, the serving tray had already been reassembled and the carpet swept. I paid my bill and watched as Otto said something in German to a busboy who quickly dashed into the kitchen to take over Otto's serving duties. As he approached me I placed an extra ten euros in his hand for the tip.

"It isn't necessary to pay me," he said in almost a whisper. "Perhaps it was a happy accident, yes?"

"Happy?" I saw that his thick eyebrows were raised as I repeated the word. "I'm happy that you speak such perfect English."

"Let me walk you to the taxi stand." The tall, fair-skinned young man with wide hazel eyes and thick lips seemed to be in his late twenties. He steadied me as he reached over and firmly held my arm. "Don't worry because I'll wait with you."

"Really, I'm fine." As I began to walk toward the front entrance, he grabbed my hand, replacing the tip money back into my open palm and forcing my fingers to close around the bills.

"Don't take the bus or walk home tonight." He left his warm hand on my left shoulder blade for a long while as patrons lined up for seating. "You need to be safe."

As I limped down the sidewalk, I kept turning around. I could see him lingering in the alcove entrance to the restaurant. I waved and called out, "Thank you so much for all your help, Otto."

"Call me soon and let me know how you're doing." The handsome waiter waved back.

I shrugged my shoulders, thinking it must be my slight intoxication from the new wine or that his English was poor and he had misspoke as I made my way to the taxi stand. But it wasn't until I had unfolded the bills in the back of the cab that I realized Otto had written his telephone number on a bill receipt and lodged it into the wad of folded euros.

Three days later we were on a tour bus together and Otto was showing me the sights of Vienna. We huddled close together on a Cityrama motor vehicle and I sat gaping at the architectural sights the tour guide pointed out: the Anchor Clock with its curvy art nouveau design, the Burgtheater, which was once an unused dance hall, the Hofburg Imperial Palace where the Hapsburg family ruled, and the Karlskirche, the largest baroque cathedral north of the Alps.

But it was Otto's witty ad-libs to the tour guide's historical data that interested me more than anything.

"And here please note Vienna's famous Ring Boulevard, built by Emperor Franz Joseph in 1857." Otto cupped his hands around his mouth and slightly mimicked the nasal tone of the English tour guide. "It was the emperor's gay brother Ludwig, the archduke also known as Luzi Wuzi, quite fond of drag by the way, who convinced Franz Joseph to wrap the city in circular roads after all. He said it would be like dressing Vienna in a ballroom dress that would crescendo outward when she curtsies."

"Really?" I nodded noting the authority in Otto's educated tenor. "The emperor had a gay brother?" I had no reason to doubt his expertise since Otto had explained to me how he was studying architecture at the university and working his way through school as a part-time waiter.

"Why, but of course!" Otto pointed out the tour-bus window. "And did you know that the State Opera House was designed by a gay architect couple as well?"

"No kidding?"

"Sadly the Opera House was constructed before the street level of the Ringstrasse had been completed and the final result was that the State Opera sagged a bit too low, with ramps that were a bit too short." Otto instructed me to look as we passed the monumental building. "Eduard van der Null, one of the architects, took his own life as a result of the foolish mistake."

I gasped. "And his partner?"

"Not even three months later, von Sicardsburg, his longtime lover, died from a paralyzing grief."

We sat silent for a long while; letting our shoulders jostle together as the tour guide continued on with more dry historical data regarding the old royalty's imprint upon Vienna. At one point, I grabbed for Otto's gloved hand and he quickly pulled off his wool scarf and covered our locked fingers.

"Vienna is still a bit conservative," he winked. "But there are places waiting for us where we can totally be ourselves."

The bus tour ended in front of the famous Spanish Riding School located in the center of Vienna near the Hofberg Palace. We were instructed to enter for an ongoing performance of the famous stallions being led through an elaborate ballroom. But as the tourists exited the bus and quickly huddled around the spectacle of the show horses below, Otto guided me into a small empty room down a hallway where hay bales and buckets of feed were kept for these trained animals. Otto quickly locked the door and began unbuttoning my coat.

"What if someone catches us?" I felt my pulse racing wildly as he reached for the zipper on my jeans.

"They're too busy with that garish equestrian spectacle," he said quickly. "Kiss me and don't worry about being quiet. The clomping hooves will drum out your moaning. Trust me."

It was the first in a series of erotic encounters with Otto that I would engage in throughout the city of Vienna. Since my landlady would not allow me to have any guests, and since Otto lived with a straight roommate who forbade any visitors as well, we were forced to be inventive in choosing covert locales for our lovemaking. We'd meet for a clandestine fondle at the Imperial Chapel during a Sunday Vienna Boys' Choir performance, then head down Michaelerplatz to consummate our desire in the aristocratic Church of the Augustinian Friars.

"See how these unlocked confessionals are a perfect spot for us?" Otto would giggle, as he'd dab his forehead with water from the baptismal font at the entrance to the church.

"Not so loud," I'd warn my companion. "Someone will hear us."

"Only the pickled hearts of the Hapsburgs preserved in the silver urns behind the altar will mind." Within moments we'd be undressed behind the priest's confessional screen and drooling over each other's exposed chests and torsos.

On my days off from teaching, we would rendezvous at the Schönbrunn Palace, where we'd sneak baby kisses in various chambers of Empress Maria Theresia's summer cottage or later outdoors in the adjacent Alpine Garden, behind a viney alcove or a marble statue, or sometimes within the walls of the Orangerie.

Above my bed, I'd keep a record of all the places we'd make love by highlighting the locations with a little pushpin on a taped-up tourist map of the city. In the basement latrine of the Sigmund Freud Museum. Behind a potted fern at the Palmery. In a closed upper gallery of the State Opera House during a matinee performance of Lucia di Lammermoor. During a puppet show at the Urania Observatory. In a swaying cabin on the giant Ferris wheel in Vienna's Prater district. Behind a display case at the Johann Strauss flat while a piped-in "Blue Danube" muffled our heavy sighs.

In my mind at night, I would play over the inscrutable images that would fill my head, souvenirs of my furtive escapades with Otto. It was a scattershot travelogue. A barrage of disjointed locations and items, as though I were a set designer bringing in all sorts of mismatched props for a surrealistic play. The pearl crane heads ringing the toes of Isis as Otto's whiskers rubbed against my belly fur. Kaiser Elizabeth's circular fan made from marabou feathers noted as Otto tweaked my nipples. Black soot embedded on my pulled-down white briefs in a sacristy pew in St. Stephen's. Chinese tea spilled on a tabletop at the Hawelka Kaffee Haus while we reached underneath for each other's engorged genitalia.

"Do you like Gustav Klimt?" I inquired of Otto one afternoon as we were passing one of his public murals on the staircase of the Burgtheater.

"I like his painting of the kissing couple," he mused. "There's something rapturous in the way he's holding her dreaming head, the way he's melting so close onto her cheek."

"I'm mad about the picture too. Sometimes I think I've spent my entire time here in Vienna trying to replicate the ecstasy divined in that work of art."

"And have you found it?" Otto's question seemed to hang uncomfortably in the icy Austrian air.

"I wonder if that's really why Klimt made his painting after all. Because finding spurious bliss in real life is one thing, but holding onto it is another."

"You can crush a bird if you grab its wings too tightly." My lover confirmed what I already knew. "Better to just sleep with your prey and then let them fly away the next day."

"It's the same dilemma in Arthur Schnitzel's plays." I realized I was beginning my familiar course lecture in Austrian theater. "His dramaturgy was always concerned with the idea of maintaining a fresh, spontaneous sexual intimacy with someone. I believe his works were banned by the Nazis as being indecent."

"And how do these Austrian plays end up?"

"Often with the bewildered protagonist going on to satisfy another craving for closeness."

"So only the artist seems able to preserve that gesture toward rapture?" Otto seemed somehow distracted, removed from his very own dialogue. "Everything connected to desire in real life just fades, you know."

"Otto, I want to believe that any human being can hold on to that intense level of sensuality laced through Klimt's *Kiss*. Even me."

"Perhaps Vienna will teach you otherwise."

It was then that I began to examine the boundaries I had placed between Vienna and myself. The European capital that I knew was not on any tourist map that I could locate. My students would bring back mundane details from a walking tour of the Roman ruins underneath the Hoher Market, or speak of how they visited the graves of Schubert and Brahms at the Central Cemetery, or drew pictures of plant specimens at the Botanical Garden at the University of Vienna.

But the Vienna I was seeing and experiencing for myself was only glimpsed around the broad shoulders of my casual lover. Examined only as I was passing through a gallery on my way to a bleach-infused janitor's closet to disrobe with Otto. The Vienna I had imagined in college, the swirling mornings walking on ancient cobblestones listening to the bells overhead on Stephansplatz, the meditations on all the great masters in all the art galleries of the Kunsthistorisches, the pilgrimage to where Gustav Klimt had lived and painted and shown his work, all of that seemed to still be waiting for me, vastly elusive and vaguely taunting me from the pages of my unopened travel guides.

On the last Sunday before I was to leave for home, I decided to spend the day alone with myself. I obtained a ticket to the Secession Museum where a special lecture and exhibit of Klimt's *Beethoven Frieze* was taking place. I arrived mid-afternoon and waited until I could get up close to the monumental art nouveau fresco.

Klimt had created his famous *Beethoven Frieze* in the early 1900s using casein and gold paints, black and multicolored crayons, graphite, and stucco, along with different appliqué materials such as mirrors and mother-of-pearl. The theme of the wall painting was taken from Richard Wagner's interpretation of Beethoven's *Ninth Symphony*. Comprised of several painted sections displayed on three gallery walls, I was overtaken by the artist's vision of redemption in the final panel.

In this section of the fresco, a female figure with a lyre is followed by a "heavenly choir" of idealized women surrounding an eroticized couple embracing in a shroud of shimmering gold that recalls a tradition of Byzantine art flourishes. The ecstatically intertwined bodies are iconically set in gold, forging the lovers into a kind of timelessness.

All around them, the world erupts with hostility and rabid beauty, but they are blind to it, sensing only what can be experienced within the yoke of their union. The tremor of each other's pulse. The waft of perfume from each other's skin. The desperate clutch and tug at each other's back while their windblown locks of hair are set aflame, the appearance of phantom masks emerging from the blaze.

I thought of Otto and myself over the past months. How in my violent desire for him, my rampant hunger for his flesh, I had somehow managed to keep myself completely insular from any authentic inner spark. Our lovemaking had become something of a mechanical feeding. But my overzealous appetite for sex, my hunger for body heat, had all but blocked out my own passions that lay inert within me. I realized I missed my coveted dreams of sightseeing in Vienna and that I was left now with only memories of Otto as my erotic tour guide.

I thought again of that old Billy Joel song that nearly brought me to this city, and the album from which it came, *The Stranger.* I used to have the album cover of that record taped up on the wall of my college dorm room. I recall that Joel was positioned in this black-and-white photograph, crunched up on a pulled-down bedspread, pensively gazing at a theater mask positioned beside him on a bed pillow.

For a moment, I imagined myself kissing Otto with that same harlequin mask on. I thought of lying alone at night in my studio, falling asleep to the sound of masked prostitutes calling after their trade. In my mind, I imagined Vienna was waiting for me at a splashy ball, as a masked debutante, anticipating her waltz with me at this massive gala of suitors. But it was as though I had misplaced my invitation and snuck off with the doorman.

After a long while, I stepped away from the preserved fresco. Downstairs was a little souvenir shop with a plethora of Klimt's images plastered onto everything from T-shirts and coffee mugs to neckties and calendars. All of his famous paintings were represented, replicated and accurately reproduced for sale and mostly manufactured in China.

I fingered several postcards and address books before deciding on a small pillbox with a close-up of the two faces depicted in *The Kiss.* I convinced myself that with this souvenir in tow I could at least take away a small facsimile of the soulful elation I had sought out for so many years. Maybe it was the best I could do, I told myself as I made my purchase. Maybe this is as close as I'll ever get.

I walked from the Secession toward the Institute, then wandered through Stephansplatz toward a shopping district where I was hoping to find some memento chocolates to take back. Since my arrival in Vienna, I had developed a serious addiction to the candy confections known as Mozart Kugels. Made from pistachio marzipan and a hazelnut nougat center, each individual piece was dipped in the most sumptuous light and dark chocolate. Eating them had become the next best thing to having sex with Otto.

I was making my way into an open discount store to purchase a tin of them when I spied my amorous cohort walking rapidly across the square.

"Otto!" I called across the wide expanse of the cobblestone plaza. "Wait up!"

My breath formed a heavy vapor cloud that seemed to linger in the chilly air. I attempted to shout out again but Otto seemed focused and intent on reaching his destination and didn't turn around to address my exclamations. I hurried across the open square and attempted to snag the back of this long wool coat. I called out again but then something seized me and I became compelled to follow him silently through the winding streets of the old city like a kind of spy.

Walking behind the man I had been intimate with for the past several months gave me pause. As I scrutinized his trailing overcoat, I thought of all the things I knew about Otto. I knew he was enamored with the Baroque architecture executed by his Viennese hero Gottfried Semper. I knew he was born in Vienna and planned on touring the world before he was thirty. I knew he hated the smell of boiling sauerkraut and disliked most classical music before the nineteenth century.

I knew he liked to have his neck gently licked while being masturbated. I knew he liked my tongue in his ear when he was undressing. But, for as intimate as we were for the past several months, there were so many things about Otto that remained unreachable and muddy.

I trailed behind him through a jumble of crooked streets to a large painted wooden door. He paused for a moment to withdraw his billfold from his front coat pocket, then stepped quickly inside, the door closing behind him with a heavy thud. As I approached the windowless establishment, I looked up to see the name KAISERBRUNDEL in large gold letters above the front entrance. I halted in my steps.

Otto had once told me about this gay sauna that was built in the 1870s at the height of the Austro-Hungarian empire. He told of the Moorish influence in its architecture, its dewy cathedral of Islamic arches, mosaic pools, and marble slabs. In fact, it was at this very spot that Franz Joseph's gay brother had caused a scandal because he had been assaulted as a result of the undesired advances he made upon a naked solider in the swimming pool.

I stood for a few moments listening to the steady throb of trance music coming through the door. I thought of entering the gay sauna and following my lover through the maze of sweaty orgy rooms and porno arcades. I thought of being a voyeur to his exploits in the wet steam room and whirlpool. Of watching him kiss and embrace other men, seeing him fan that flame, the way I would stand and watch the clutching figures in a Klimt painting.

Instead I turned around and headed toward the U-Bahn. Like a character actor at the end of a play, I had taken my cue from one of the minor characters who had just exited stage left. As the antiheroic protagonist in this drama carved from the Theater of the Absurd, I knew I had to carry out the plot and end the drawn-out tale here.

I flashed for a moment on the last conversation I had attempted with Otto. We were pulling up our jeans from behind a stall stacked with homemade fruit spreads and raw honey at an open market near the Prater. As Otto turned to leave, I grabbed his shoulder and turned him around.

"Wait for one more minute," I whispered so close to his face I could feel my lips softly brush against his cheek. His eyes were tightly shut. Then I slowly pulled back. "I just want to look at you for a minute. I just want to see your face."

"What does my face have to do with any of this?"

It was the last full sentence I can recall hearing from Otto's mouth. The rest of it is just a played-back echo of jumbled foreign languages. A cacophony of screeching trolley cars and buses and the nearly inaudible piped-in subway stops delivered in German on the U-Bahn. Everything Otto had said to me all seemed to have evaporated like the flutelike notes held by Cio-Cio San at the end of *Madame Butterfly,* that terrible gargle of blood rising in her throat as the lovesick geisha slowly expires.

I arrived at the street on which my studio was located as the street lamps were being turned on. I walked past the all-night pharmacy, then farther past the little porno shop with its liquid neon sign depicting the outline of a dancing female figure. Once again, the full-figured hooker with Valentine sunglasses came up from behind me.

"How about it?" Her voice was like the trickle of water pouring from a rusty fountainhead. "Are you ready to try the best Vienna has to offer, Mister Tourist?"

I abruptly turned around to face her. She smiled and took off her dark glasses and folded them into her shiny plastic purse. Her eyes were deep-set, the color of a postcard sunset with tiny flecks of amber in them. Her crudely drawn-on eyebrows gave her the appearance of a badly aging Maria Callas.

"This is for you," I said, unwrapping the exquisitely tiny porcelain box with the ubiquitous Klimt figures embossed on the lid. "I've been wanting to give you a gift. I hope you like it."

"*Abschiedskuss,*" she pronounced the word slowly. "A good-bye kiss for me?"

"Yes, a sort of parting kiss." I nodded a bit nervously. "Or at least, a replica of one."

"*Danke.*" She cradled the duplicated image of the famous painting in her palm and the lights overhead seemed to dance upon the gold coloring on the lid of the tiny souvenir.

I shook her hand and left her there in the street and walked alone the rest of the way to my studio door. For a long time I laid in bed, thinking about kisses. There were so many ways one could place one's lips upon another human being, so many intentions and desires that could be carried through the pressing of one's mouth onto another's. I began to wonder if perhaps the brooding male figure in the Klimt painting was in actuality saying good-bye to his lover. That the thrust of his kiss was laden with utter remorse for having to pull away, for recognizing that as enveloping as this dancing rapture was with her, it was all ephemeral, momentary, and impossible to fully sustain.

I was kissing Vienna good-bye, I thought. Hoping she would wait for me to return to the ball someday. Hoping she would reveal to me one day all the vistas and pathways I had imagined since college.

I was kissing all the gold flecks of paint in the Klimt frieze good-bye, blowing farewell pecks at the twisted migration patterns of birds appearing suddenly over St. Stephen's Church. I was offering a good-bye kiss now to the burned smell from the sausage stands I would pass on my way to the classroom, to the endless subway stops I would count on my commute to the Institute, to the tall rooftops and spires and domes that shot up toward the sky, leaving me so acutely aware of the ground I was standing on and how earthbound I was.

I was kissing good-bye to all the secret places I discovered with Otto as well, the crouched-over positions held behind the louvered doors of old telephone booths and in church confessionals vaguely smelling of frankincense, the embraces we both lingered in within the closed stalls of subway lavatories and behind the cluttered racks in museum coatrooms. I was saying goodbye to the secret holding of hands under folded overcoats until our palms sweated profusely while the stodgy Rubens and Durers and Rembrandts went on brooding in their respective galleries at the Museum of Fine Arts.

Then I thought of the last time I really kissed Otto good-bye, my mouth clamped onto his. I could barely remember the manner in which I had pasted my lips onto his, or how I would often try to memorize the soft features of his face in the neon-twisted half-light falling behind some reeking market lean-to.

Once, out of the corner of my eye, I stole a glimpse of our reflection embracing flagrantly in front of a gilt-edged mirror at the Schönbrunn Palace. It was near closing time and the blue-smocked matrons had begun to dust the roped-off Baroque ornaments in the various apartments.

Otto and I stood together in a small reception area for guests of the empress. We looked around and quickly hugged near the grand fireplace surrounded by painted dove wings on the walls and ceilings. I noted that the heads of the quietly ascending birds were edged in gold wreaths and nearly translucent pink and yellow clouds.

Anyone looking into that ornately framed mirror over the fireplace might have mistaken that reflected embrace for a painting, two lovers who were locked in a passionate yoke, unable to tear away from each other's spinning heat, motionless, barely breathing, and nearly oblivious to the pulsing world that was completely escaping them.

Ephebus

A form of Sufism involves prolonged contemplation of a beautiful young man—an ephebus—in order to ascend to mystical states.

Ferris seems to be on an ecstasy crash. His head is splayed over the steering wheel of his 1981 Mercury as a plastic effigy of Shiva dangles from the rearview mirror. He holds up a silver Buddha on a chain in the light of the open glove compartment and places it around his breastbone. His car engine is still rumbling and the hum seems to move into mine as he fumbles over outdated highway maps and sweat-damp tissues for a box of gold-wrapped condoms. His emerald nose stud reflects a flinty moon.

Ferris leaves his clothes in a heap on the floor of his car. His oak-brown skin seems glazed with flecks of ice as he steps onto the gravelly parking lot. "I'll meet you at my tepee." He looks at me grinning with a cottonwood twig falling between the gap in his teeth.

From the front seat of my station wagon, I watch his lithe naked body become a hazy streak as he merges with the dew-laced evergreen trees and bushes. As he edges his way into the thicket, I imagine Ferris grazing the tips of blackberry bushes, their purple crowns breaking onto his smooth shoulder blades. I think of his cloudy breath in the damp night air mingling with the sound of crickets and owl screeches. I see him wiping the gritty sweat from his forehead, his cock jostling to the rhythms of his half-trot through the woods, his nipples erect in the thick Southern twilight air.

This chapter appeared originally under the same title in *Rebel Yell 2* (Binghamton, NY: Harrington Park Press, 2002, pp. 171-179). Copyright 2002 Gerard Wozek. Reprinted with permission of the author.

Postcards from Heartthrob Town: A Gay Man's Travel Tales
Published by The Haworth Press, Inc., 2006. All rights reserved.
doi:10.1300/5732_16

I shift backward in the front seat of my car and listen to the sound of men drumming in the field that falls just beyond the wooded campground. I hear their banshee wailing and sudden dog yelps. I count their gravelly shouts. I hear their rattles and tom-toms from across the Radical Faerie sanctuary, this place where men come to gather and camp out on the land and celebrate the turning seasons. There is merrymaking in the bowl of this Tennessee valley and soul churning, as the faeries like to call it, going on everywhere in this secluded park. Even from this distant vantage point, I can smell their musky sweat, feel their pulses jangle and merge with their crooked yodels and rising heat.

I move my hand across my Yankee crotch and feel a tingle that moves up into my belly. I glance across my dashboard, at crushed Styrofoam cups, a used-up evergreen air freshener and assorted chewing gum wrappers. On the seat next to me is an old *Gay Times* with a muscle-bound stud in a leather harness on the cover and I look right through his stare. I'm almost indifferent to this squat pose, the model's oiled biceps, this overtly masculine jut. For a moment I think back to my old porno film collection at home, my ten thousand downloads of uncut cocks from off the Internet, my towering stacks of *Torsos* and *Honchos* that are meaningless to me now. I hold my breath for one instant on the edge of the woods, then decide to make my way toward the tepee.

There are bonfires burning all around the camp area tonight. This is not Chicago and I am no longer a city dweller. I have traveled here to drown out the incessant ambulance sirens. The scrawl of the graffiti on subway signs and pedestrians who are willing to topple me for a seat on a bus. I have become as rigid as the concrete I walk on every day. I have forgotten what it is like to smell air that has been scented with lavender and wet field grass. I have lost my sense of walking on ground that is simply soft dirt. I have lost my sense of the earth.

I inhale a sooty fog as I open my car door and follow the circuitous footpath into the brush. The ringed moon sifts through branches of trees, illuminating cigarette butts and used condoms left on the muddy trail. I step over prints left from animals and I try to forget the city where I live, the concrete and Plexiglas, the rush of the cars outside my loft window, the stifling pace of Chicagoans. I want to forget my job as a part-time freelance writer. I want to forget the incessant ring of my cell phone. I want to lose my paranoia of looking over my shoulder when it is dark on my street. I want to fall into a natural state of being. I want to wake up to feel own heart racing with anticipation for the day. I want to fall into a state of grace.

I glance at the map handed to me at the sign-up post and note the references to unmarked graves of Civil War soldiers buried under my feet. I become more conscious of my own pulse thinking of handsome young Southern boys, barely men, who have turned into mulch and gravel underneath these woods.

I approach a clearing and notice a palpable shudder behind a thin cluster of pine limbs where Ferris fumbles with a wool army blanket spread out at the entrance of his roomy tent. He is prone on his hands and knees, tucking the edge of this dark cloth into a rock cluster. The slick sweat on his freckled back throws back a soft glow. I rub my palms over the rough folds of birch bark and wait for my heavy breathing to calm.

He is wearing a long skirt constructed from willows and supple grapevines and a mishmash tiara fashioned from scrap tin and painted acorns. He prances about the open bluff that overlooks the Tennessee pasture. He sings a few lines of "Don't Cry for Me Argentina" in a deliberately exaggerated Southern drawl, while throwing crumpled daisy petals into the nocturnal spring air.

"He can call me Ferris or he can call me Dewballs," his voice seems to quake then bounce off of the gutted rock formations of the nearby caverns. "I'm bursting with juice for you."

His mottled hair seems to be animated all on its own, like Medusa's serpents writhing and hissing into the airless pitch. The last flecks of twilight linger inside the recesses of his deep-set eyes. There is something about his smile that suggests genuine warmth, something that I could never find in the urban rancor of Chicago. He slowly lifts the beaded flap of a stand-alone tepee made from animal skins and old Confederate flags and, with a gentle turn of his head, he motions me inside.

"First, he must genuflect at the altar." There is a hint of whimsy in his voice, as though a casual tourist could almost believe in the fey kind of world he is attempting to bring into being. He lights a kerosene lamp and my head scrapes the needle edges of an inverted antler mobile. On top of a shaved tree stump he has placed several polished river stones, an effigy of a goddess with a lion's head, assorted bronze deities, a feathered kachina doll, a cracked Mexican Mother Mary night-light, and a tall white taper melting over an empty beer bottle.

We both kneel at the makeshift altar and Ferris lifts a string of amber beads from around his neck and places it next to the smooth, dark rocks. He gently touches my thigh with the furry end of a wheat stalk. Goosebumps quiver up my spine. "I knew when I saw you at the welcome post, we'd become fast friends," he says, rubbing sandalwood oil on his wrists. The tent air is damp and the thick deerskin walls hold in the heady essence of incense and musk.

"I'm still covered with city dust, so you'll have to forgive me but I'm not used to such sincere openness. Do you camp out here often?" My hand grazes over the fur tarp on the floor of the lean-to and I accidentally knock over a tall stack of magazines that have been set next to the fat log.

"I am the essence of camp, my dear," he laughs as he opens a locket swinging from around his neck with a picture of Bette Davis in it. "I never did get over that dress she wore in *Jezebel!*"

As I attempt to straighten the pile of *Gentleman's Quarterlies* and *Esquires,* I notice that the issues are dated from several years back. "Why are you saving these old style magazines?"

Ferris searches out a fading picture from *L'uomo Vogue Magazine.* "Don'tcha recognize the stud on this cover?" The boy in the photograph is handsome, dressed in a tailored blue Armani suit with eyes that hold in a kind of sophisticated aloofness. He seems to radiate a soft glow as though he were a haloed apostle.

"Debonair." My response seems to hang awkwardly in the pagan atmosphere.

"Are you ready for your mystery date?" He hands me an advertisement for a designer's cologne featuring the same striking lad, now standing knee-deep in a swirling body of water. The model's taupe linen pants are soaked, revealing the seductive outline of his crotch.

"It's you." My words almost form a question. I closely scrutinize his unshaven face in the dim lantern light. His pale blue eyes are unmistakable. The same sexy teenager that had posed in these foreign glamour magazines is dressed in semi-drag in this cockeyed tent tonight.

"There was this guy I met in Belgium once," he begins to speak very deliberately, keeping a lit match hovering over the wicks of several small candles. "He'd collect all of my fashion spreads then cover his bedroom walls with them. He even sent me a picture of his shrine to me. The guy claimed he would just float through those images, as though he were levitating or something. He said it made his everyday jerking off kind of spiritual."

"What was it like to be someone's fantasy?" I touch the full lips on one of his photographs.

"It did nothing for me." His voice seems to suddenly halt the persistent drumming that pervades the air. "I mean, the Navajos have this belief that if you take a picture of someone, you are stealing their spirit. I became this pornographic dream for a herd of strangers I never even knew and, I'm telling you, it never brought anything truly fulfilling back to me."

"And so you've come here."

"I came out here to live as authentically as I could." Ferris closes his eyes and starts to drift into reverie. "There is a circle of men, very Southern, mostly from the recesses of Georgia and Tennessee, who really make an attempt at channeling each other's erotic energy. They bond in an attempt to heal what has been damaged or to rekindle those natural loving instincts that have been submerged. I wanted to join together in a faerie circle with those blazing companions."

"But I'm just a tourist here, so I don't understand what you mean by very Southern?"

"Oh, you probably have this image of icy mint juleps and Paul Newman playing the role of Brick in *Cat on a Hot Tin Roof* or something." Ferris throws his head back and his eyes appear larger.

"Well, I remember very clearly that the characters in that Tennessee Williams' play had this image of Brick as someone he really wasn't."

"You've got it, love." Ferris looks down at an image of himself hawking designer cologne. "I suppose you could say that I was Brick. Well, at least I was when I was much younger. My family had these stark expectations for me. And I played along, always very gracious, always well mannered with my obligatory 'yes, sir' at the end of each sentence. But there was a wilder spirit growing in me. I suppose I took the very best of my docile Southern boy and tempered him—well, came to terms with him anyway."

"You mean you'd fix a mean fried catfish and corn bread, line your black-eyed peas up perfectly on a fork, and wipe your lips with a napkin after every bite."

"Stereotypes aside, my sweet Yankee," Ferris begins to mimic a tipsy Vivien Leigh, "I bake a fierce pecan pie, I always hold open a door for a lady, and yes, I do wipe up after my voracious little nibbles and bites."

"I have this idea of chivalry being linked to what is uniquely Southern."

"Chivalrous in the sense that I believe in nobility and courage," Ferris continued with his exaggerated pose then paused to open the flap of his tepee and point in the direction of a sprawling field nearby. "Southern men have always felt the need to light passionate fires for whatever cause they were obliged to. Our own General Braxton Bragg led his brigade over Lookout Mountain in the 'Battle Above the Clouds.'"

"Sounds romantic."

"Yes, we Southerners have a peculiar way of romanticizing the past, but you know that hundreds of zealous boys were killed during the Civil War. If you meditate on the land here for a period of time you can almost hear the deafening gunshots that riddled the air once. I often listen for their wailing ghost stories buried out in those fields, those adolescent desires that were never quite consummated."

"So you believe in ghosts as well?" I inquire with a half-smile.

"How could you not?" There is seriousness in his eyes that I haven't yet seen. "All around us you can feel the spirit of the land. The heroes went to their graves too soon. You ask me what it means to be Southern and I tell you that it is having a sense of loyalty or faithfulness. The word of a Southern gentleman is linked to a time when all agreements, even implied ones, were binding. This is what our ancestry is made up of and this is what defines the authentic Southern character."

Eight candles blaze and Ferris seems more handsome in this light than even in his expensive soft-focus photographs. He carefully lifts a delicate piece of yellowed paper from his altar and begins to read. "Not even losing this battle, not even death will keep us separate."

"What is this?"

"Part of a letter written by the son of my great great grandmother. He died while fighting in the war between the North and South."

"It's so tragic that there were countless casualties." I glance at the intricate, almost calligraphic, handwriting on the paper. "He was writing to his mother then?"

"He was writing to another Confederate soldier, another young man serving in the war. My family kept this locked away until my sister came across it in an old trunk and she gave it to me." He places the note back and puts a river stone over it. "I know this soldier kept his word. I know that not even death separates him from his true heart."

Ferris locks his thumbs together and his hands form the image of wings. He listens for something I'm not quite sure of, maybe it is the wind or the sound of singing in the basin, but the stillness is almost unsettling.

"I know that especially in the South it is difficult to be a softer man, but you seem to have somehow managed to dismantle the revered macho image."

"Dismantle is a good word." Ferris curtsies with his willow skirt. "Brick by brick, if you will!"

"Quite a feat, considering that everything in our culture calls for us to conform to some exaggerated image of the hypermasculine male. But somehow you've reclaimed yourself as a being who is more androgynous and . . ." I pause for a moment.

"Humane?"

"Yes, humane; with a gentle, unassuming disposition."

"Why, thank he for the compliment, sir." Ferris reaches over and pats my hand. "Vacation Baptist bible school taught me to never be too proud to know that we're all linked to one another. We're all part of the same fabric, honey lamb, though I'll never get used to that hideous Yankee flag of yours."

Ferris giggles delightfully then places four lit votive candles in a semicircle around the tepee. He gently tosses dried foxglove and eucalyptus petals around the circumference of the tent and sets several burning incense sticks of jasmine and bloodroot around an outstretched blanket in front of the tepee. The night air seems to carry an electric charge with it and the resumed drumming outside seems to lend a hypnotic edge to the collage. Ferris, motionless and poised in the axis of the blanket, seems to have momentarily suspended his breathing. He hands me a small bottle of oil and lies down on his stomach. "How about a rub, sexy sir?"

Kneeling above his sweaty back, I massage clover oil warmed from the heat of my palms over his skin. The heady aroma coils up through my nostrils and I can hear Ferris begin to moan as he falls into the motion of my hands grazing his body. The sinewy ligaments and muscles along his spine and vertebrae begin to ease. I pour out the syrupy unguent over his thighs and legs and work the pungent salve into his buttocks. He lets me undo the supple willow laces that are strewn around his torso and I fall into an almost hypnotic rhythmic motion.

"Let's bay at the moon," I whisper. Clasping the furry blanket, he moves toward a clearing near the back of the tent where a fire pit is still aglow with afternoon embers. Ferris lies down on his back and for a long time we are cupped in the silence. He keeps his hands open and extended, then slowly begins to speak.

"And what did you come here for, Yankee tourist?"

The words give me an opening. "I feel stifled by the urban rush, the pretense and disconnection I feel in Chicago. I want to slow down. I want to feel like myself again, like the boy I once was. I want to remember the spark."

"Look at me." Ferris speaks in a hush. "I mean, really look at me, and enjoy what you see. When I was a kid, I was punished for staring at people. It was considered impolite. But I want you to look deeply and don't be ashamed of whatever you're feeling. Let it be a kind of enduring devotion."

So I stare lovingly at my newfound friend and feel my body begin to spiral and ascend. My pulse becomes rapid. I don't take his engorged cock into my mouth, but I can taste its oozing crown. I don't encircle his nipples with my tongue, but they rise and become pinpoints for my desire. I don't wedge my hand at his scrotum but, staring down at it, I can sense the sap churning and rising, the tiny muscles clenching. I don't smell the heavy musk scent of his crotch, or lick the beads of perspiration at his underarms and belly. I don't stroke his face, bite his earlobes, kiss his full mouth or wedge his thick, dark-tipped manhood inside of me. But I can taste him, sense his rabid desire, and in this moment, I absorb the pure pulse of his wanting.

Outside, a rowdy group of men passes by with a sound blaster turned up on The Smashing Pumpkins singing "Landslide." The half-drunken imps are singing along with the tune and seem oblivious to our spontaneous bonding. The drums they are carrying aren't timpani from the Civil War. The long wooden sticks they're holding are just fishing poles, not Confederate rifles. I touch my lips to my companion's shoulder and I can feel all of the unrequited longing of the forgotten soldiers surging underneath us. It is as though I can feel their pulses laced into the land and they seem to urge me on.

A thousand voices seem to be singing around me, resonating through me as I move my hand over my own shaft. My raised organ shoots a hot stream of white balm over Ferris's chest. He rubs the warm, wet pearls over his own hand then down to his foreskin and he comes instantly. Watching this, the ground underneath my feet appears to tilt.

Ferris opens his eyes and kisses the spunk. "Love medicine." His voice is steady and assured. "So good for us."

I reach down and offer my hands to help him stand up. We embrace and his slow, even breath fills the concave of my ear. My skin prickles and the thin hairs on the back of my neck stand erect. The heat of his body is absorbed into my own as we mesh into one pure throb of light.

"Y'all should spend the night, you know," he half-whispers in his overly dramatic, breathless fashion. "I mean, it would simply be un-Southern to leave now."

"Will you make me grits and chicory coffee in the morning, sir?" I tug at the blanket he holds around himself.

"You have my word."

Ferris moves away from the tepee and into the stirred-up night air, into the black holes that are forest shadows. I follow him, tripping over fallen oak branches. He takes in a deep breath then turns to look back at me, a compass of honey shimmer on his face. The faerie revelers have all gone to bed and the crickets have quieted.

"Feel the heat rising?" Ferris holds his hands over a raised mound of earth as though he were warming himself over a bonfire. "All the lost soldiers go on dreaming of a new world." He pauses for a moment and looks through the tangle of trees overhead.

He lets the blanket wrapping his skin drop and I take a snapshot in my mind, a secret momentary postcard, then let it go, allowing all of his curvy, boundless, pixie energy to return back to him. I look at Ferris and for a moment I flash on the young face he had as a boy model, then almost a dead ringer for Paul Newman.

I am a tourist here and I want to take something back with me. Some kind of keepsake to remind me of my Southern adventure. I wonder for a moment if I can simply hold onto this feeling, not take anything off the land or from my companion, but simply let this sense impression press deeply into my memory. Could that be enough for this urban Yankee?

Tonight a lilac bush rests as a diadem in his auburn hair and flecks of lightning bugs orbit in a golden nimbus around his frame. For a moment, it appears as though he is dancing inside of a wheel with tiny tongues of flame flickering in a hoop around him. I follow him over spindly fir needles and whispering graves back to his makeshift tepee. He holds the flap open for me and waits as I enter the place where we can sleep skin-to-skin, man-to-man. In dreams I locate that brave, untrammeled spirit that still breathes fire inside of me. I decide I can take that back to the city with me as a souvenir.

Then Ferris and I wake up again to feel our pulses pounding in unison, a kind of electric humming that goes on and on.

Pulse Points

I cut through this crowded cruise park like a scalpel through a splayed cadaver. Even though I've been in Sitges less than a week, I already know the best posing section of the boardwalk promenade where I can seduce the neighborhood trade. I know how to follow the spark of well-heeled gentlemen who stroll down the palm-tree-lined Passeig de la Riberia. I know the best hour to arrive at the hip beachfront disco Mediterraneo, in order to gain a free drink pass and effortlessly fall into the arms of a half-drunk local. I also know which secret arteries of the park behind Dead Man's Beach to negotiate, so that at the edge of twilight, I can blend into the darkness seamlessly and navigate toward my current conquest.

I tell myself that, in a way, Sitges is like any other place where men come to lose themselves. I could be behind the stone mausoleums in Pere Lachaise Cemetery in Paris. Or kneeling down in the lagoon gutter off Lincoln Park in Chicago. In a bathroom stall at the Picasso Museum in Barcelona, or in the middle of dripping trench coats and briefcases on the London metro at rush hour.

Dead Man's Beach doesn't have much sand to speak of. I brush the fine pebble dust off my oily legs and arms for the past twenty minutes, trying to decipher the little signposts written in both the Castilian and Catalan languages. Underneath one phrase is a crudely drawn skull and crossbones, so I can only guess that this area must hold some modicum of danger, but I go farther into the dark brush anyway.

I follow several dark-eyed, swimsuited men who are rapidly whispering to one another in Spanish. I pass by honey-brown boy limbs wedged between garden trellises, shaved torsos curled around scarred

This chapter appeared originally under the same title in *Off the Rocks* 8 (Chicago, IL: New Town Writers, 1996). Copyright 1996 Gerard Wozek. Reprinted with permission of the author.

Postcards from Heartthrob Town: A Gay Man's Travel Tales
Published by The Haworth Press, Inc., 2006. All rights reserved.
doi:10.1300/5732_17

tree bark, and the stomped-down wire fences in back of the dune bridge near the nude wading beach. I watch the half-clothed bodies of three *guapos,* hunched over in the hollowed-out hub of a bush. Other shirtless strollers are embracing in the trench of a sloping gully and crouching behind a jimmied rain duct.

I step softly on the sandy clay path and keep forgetting where I am. I tell myself this could be a near a garden grotto in a park in Berlin where businessmen gather to circle jerk. Or in a remote pond area at a cemetery in Budapest where male hustlers frequently barter. Or under the fishing piers off the coast of Amsterdam where kef-blooded tourists pull down their pants for another toke of an offered pipe.

I have been in those places. I have sought out a man's heat there without having to speak another foreign language. I have mapped out those destinations and taken home detailed souvenir photographs in my mind. I have relived those memories before giving into sleep. I have returned to this cruise park because I want to initiate new ones.

I step farther into the woods and notice a slight tremor on my upper lip. I have to keep reminding myself that I am here, in Sitges, Spain. Once primarily a fishing village, the area became a haven for artists in the late nineteenth century thanks to a painter by the name of Santiago Rusiol. He opened up his art studio for lovers of poetry and paintings, and the town developed a reputation for harboring bohemians and those who would experiment with their lives. I am making my third pilgrimage to this mecca, I tell myself, to trace the footsteps of some of those early initiates and to rekindle my connection with those vanguard deviants and early artists.

I remind myself that seven days ago I got on a train in Barcelona in order to arrive at this Catalan coastal resort just thirty-five kilometers south of the capital. I walked from the train station through the mazelike streets, unpacked my bags, changed into my torn jeans shorts, and began to roam the Platja del Home Mort, this remote pebbly beach with a quiet, wooded area beyond the train tracks, complete with infamously circuitous trails that lead off to a panoply of covert alcoves and hollowed-out bushes.

It is almost evening and the air is nearly cooling and I am compelled to follow what appears to be the cigarette smoke trails emanating from other men's gravelly breathing. I seize upon the outline of one perfect chest—his smooth upper body licking the brambles and mist among my other Don Juans of the Hidden Forest. I have joined the Mavericks of the Middle Kingdom, the Rapt Bodhisattvas of Ecstasy. I tell myself that there is a part me that could stalk this hidden nebula forever, for one clandestine embrace, one singular moment to be sunk into the sweet musk of his underarms or to feel the bite of his stubble kisses like a burning coal against my cheek.

Wet palm leaves and gentle fingertips graze over my slightly sunburned skin. I stumble over green oranges and the branches sticking out of the red-brown clay, but that deeper part of myself goes untouched.

I am thinking in this moment that I simply want to evaporate, leaving only my erotic pulse intact. I don't want to think about my ex-lover's repeated admonishment, "a man only resorts to habitual fucking when he feels impotent." I don't want to retread the pseudo-psychology doled out by Dr. Phil and Oprah about how sex addiction is the world's biggest secret or that the cliché of promiscuity is still rampant among both gay and straight married men.

I don't want to dance with my memories about being humiliated in grade school for being soft-spoken or how when I was a child, my father abandoned me and I turned to sexual experimentation as a quick remedy. I don't want to mourn the string of unsuccessful trysts that led me from continent to continent, trying to convince myself that all that mattered was being desired in the moment. I really don't want to think.

I tell myself that all my sticky demons will go convulsing out of me eventually. All my submerged devils will go pouring out onto the unyielding dirt or, perhaps better, into the open mouth of a kneeling Castilian god.

I am trying to locate the remedy in this park that will help me to escape for another three hours. I can roam this sexual playground, this junglelike park where men come to retreat from their mundane lives. Where men come to unlatch their inhibitions and feel that holy spark of what animates them. Where men come to interface with the life instinct, to engage in their zeal for another's organs, to be overtaken by their holy and insatiable libido.

I glance around me here and see that there are a few unlatexed foreskins being fondled around me, but most of the men are pushing and pounding in between the safety of a second skin. The lingering scent of amyl nitrate merges with the balm and the fragrance of dewy palm leaves and mulch. Occasionally a man is startled by the flapping of a gull's wings in the branches above his head, but then he's carried off by the throb of the earth, the heart rhythm that has drawn all of us here in the first place.

The guidebooks have warned me to be careful. However, I assure myself that this is not Playa el Espigon, where I have read that sometimes the unseasoned cruiser can lose his wallet. I tell myself I am careful. I have left my money belt in the safe at the hotel. I drank only bottled water at the disco earlier and I have my sharper wits about me. My mini flashlight and my tourist map are in my back pocket and I know the path that leads back to the main roads in town. I have my adrenaline coursing through my veins right now and I'm assured that this rising energy will carry me out of this park in case of a police raid or an attack by local thugs.

From across a wet gully, someone is sighing, *"Chupa me vega,"* and a symphony of refraining moans counterpoint like a surge of heat rays rising off of steaming desert sands. Everyone jockeys to find the right spot in this cruise park. Everyone wants to find that certain pulse point, that power spot where he can align with the procreating energy of the forest.

I stand naked and ready to be taken in. The dark stranger before me begins to tie oblivion onto my hair and carves out my secret name in the wind with kisses that seem to say: *"My son, my lost one, wild child of the turning spheres, prophet of my becoming, prince of my peace, snake charmer, mercurial sex sultan, dragon dakini, priest of tantra, kundalini lightning bolt, consort of Shiva, mushroom-headed, wet-lipped, man pussy, fuck slave, slick prick pleaser. . . ."*

Then with one hand on his shoulder blade, my eyes raked with the blur of dead stars above me, I float, weightless, toward some uncharted territory, a dreamscape where I spin in amniotic fluid and vibrate with an ancient serpentlike energy.

I become the primordial throb, the glint of the first sun ray over a pregnant ocean, the first flush of pink on the pomegranate peel, the swirling pattern of flight taken by kiwi bird or crow, the minion of Kali, the messenger of the Rapture, the supplicant at my father's black boot heel, my father's jizm genie, my father's baddest boy, my father, who art in me, let me whisper thy name.

"Father, my found father at last, make a resurrection of me."

All over the world, I can hear men whispering and moaning in the still night air. From within a zippered beach cabana on the oceanfront near Mykonos. Wedged up against a tree in the Bois de Vincennes near Paris. From the edge of a jungle cliff in Puerto Vallarta, Mexico. From behind a tavern Dumpster in an alley off Church Street in Toronto.

Dawn baptizes this abandoned zone in dew, its footpaths heavy with cigarette butts and used condoms. I remind myself that just beyond these hidden ventricles is the city of Sitges itself. That I can shower back at my hotel and linger at an outdoor café table all day, drink strong coffee and gape at the tourists taking pictures of the landmark parish church. I can go for a stroll along the boardwalk, have a plate of fresh seafood paella at a storefront restaurant or pause to listen to the day's Europop or watch vintage porn at my favorite bar, El Candil.

But after the hard house music has lost its hypnotic spell, and the taverns have turned up their unyielding house lights, I'll return to those secret vortices of fire at the park behind Dead Man's Beach. I'll come back because I want to keep forgetting.

My biological father's face the day he said good-bye. The look in my best friend's eye when I told him in high school that I was gay and he walked away, never speaking to me again. The hollow chill I felt inside when I ended my first "serious" relationship and slipped into an underworld of anonymous encounters, half-recalled mouths, and arms, and bodies.

I know why I've come to Sitges.

I'll go back to Dead Man's Beach because I want to feel like I'm alive again. I want to inhale the musk of the Spanish men. Listen for my name accented on their tongues. I want to be as close as I can be for as long as I can be to the sparking, libidinous rhythm. I want to be part of that perpetual journey where instinct and trust marry the uncertain night.

Urge for Going

He got the urge for going
when the meadow grass was turning brown.
Summertime was falling down and winter was closing in.

Joni Mitchell

"Bury me in the real Ireland," Seamus said when he and I first arrived in Dingle some thirteen years ago. "Scatter my ashes in the west, along this mountainous rim of the Atlantic, where there were never any traces of Cromwellian armies or the Anglo influence of the Pale. Wave what remains of me over the sands of Brandon Bay, in the heft of a remorseless western wind. I want my dust to float near the Gaeltachts where the old culture is still intact. When I go, I want to be united with the real Celts."

I have come back to the Dingle Peninsula in Ireland to honor his wishes. In my backpack is a metal container with my former partner's sandy remains, which I will scatter off the top of Mount Brandon, one of the highest points in all of the country. I still have the first photographs we snapped of that cloud-capped, black giant when we were first falling in love. In one snapshot he is holding out his arms as if he's trying to emulate the girth of the mound. In another, he is pointing toward the tallest peak, as if to say, "I will get there one day. I will reach the summit and be free."

The last time we were in Dingle, well over three years ago, we took a bus from Dublin to the little town of Tralee, then hitchhiked into Dingle. We walked around Dingletown, then had a picnic on the southwest coast near the castle ruins that look out over the Blasket Islands. The peninsula itself extends nearly ten miles wide from the

Postcards from Heartthrob Town: A Gay Man's Travel Tales
Published by The Haworth Press, Inc., 2006. All rights reserved.
doi:10.1300/5732_18

southeast of the island of Ireland and it is the point in Europe that is closest to North America.

"Do you feel like you're in the film *Far and Away* with Tom Cruise?" I asked Seamus back then.

"It does look like we're in a film," he nodded. "But as long as I'm with you, who needs Tom Cruise?"

Apparently, it was his in his genes to pour out the Irish blarney. But even after so many years together, I still had a crush on my constant companion. We met in college in a required geometry class. The theorems were impossible for me to decode, and it was Seamus's tutelage that helped me to not only pass the course, but to locate the map into his idiosyncratic world, inextricably linked to his overbearing family. One full year of dating and we were on our way to an apartment and a passionate, long-term partnership.

"How can you choose someone like that over us?" his mother said in front of me the day Seamus told her he was moving out. "The Pope says it isn't right and you know it. Your home is with your father and me until you marry."

But in our own way, Seamus and I were married. And the home we shared together was the most welcoming I ever knew. The house we purchased together no longer feels like a home now. Weeks, then months, passed after his death. One day I sat down in the kitchen and realized the table I was sitting at was entirely foreign to me. The entire structure I was standing in was merely varnished floorboards and plaster walls. Nothing but carpenters' nails holding this bricked structure up. Nothing there now to call me back to the smell of his warm skin on the fern-colored bedsheets, or to his habit of forgetting to turn the lights off in the office, or to the Sunday breakfast tray he'd arrange for me every weekend, with *The New York Times* arts section all ready for me to peruse.

I have decided to be his legs for this journey. I recall how we climbed this Irish mountain when we were first in love. The incline was easily traversed. Every rock on the trail, every barricade seemed to melt before the power of our blushing ardor. "I want to see what the holy saints did when they marched up that three thousand-foot-high mountain," he declared emphatically. "I want to be canonized by actually witnessing their ancient visions. Then I want to be called Saint Seamus."

I have come to scale Mount Brandon, to make this pilgrimage with his spirit and ashes in tow. I am walking up a purple-shaded boreen, through a crooked gate that is waiting to fall off its creaky hinges. I am tracing the steps of ancient Celtic heroes and legendary Christian saints. There are signs warning that the gentle winds at the base of the mountain can be dangerous gales once I reach the summit. Undaunted, I pull my backpack tighter around my shoulder, and breathe deeply, leaning forward.

"Hold steady," I think I hear Seamus whisper in my ear, but it's just the local sheepherder calling for his flock. Just the bleat of wooly field animals as they saunter at the base of the mountain, edging together against one another almost seamlessly. I wait in a kind of stoop, nearly genuflecting on the little trail, as they shuffle past me.

A little ways up this wending footpath is a makeshift shrine to the Virgin. "This might have been a pagan memorial to Bridget," I remark out loud to the gusts of cool air moving around me. Out of respect for Seamus, however, I make the sign of the cross and whisper softly under my breath, "Hail Mary, full of grace."

If my deceased lover were with me, I'm certain he would have begged that I take a photograph of him next to this five-foot grotto made from sea stones and krill. He would have lingered at the stature of the Holy Mother, reciting his memorized Catholic prayers from childhood, making a garland of mossy clover and daisies for her chipped plaster neck. He might have even told me to go on ahead of him, to allow him some privacy. I remember how he relished his moments of talking into the wind, or praying quietly in the evening before coming to bed.

After a long while, I might have called to him "Seamus, I'm not taking this trip alone!" I might have known, though, that in the moment I would turn around, he'd be running up the hill toward me with his arms wide open. I can almost imagine it, though it's all invented. Just my made-up memories. Projections of things that will never be. His red hair tussled in this Irish wind. His two freckled cheeks ruddy. His eyes a quick flash in the sunlight. I want to imagine it as something that really did happen somehow and if I linger with this thought, perhaps I can convince myself of it by the time I reach the summit.

Seamus, my Seamus. He was baptized and named after his uncle who moved back to Galway in the late sixties as soon as he made a little money in the States. Seamus vowed he would return to Ireland too one day, "to live among the open fields of shamrocks and the howling of the storm weary mermaids." Seamus had his uncle's innate talent for turning every statement about Ireland into a kind of poem. He loved the country's history and spirit so much that he devoted several hours a week to reading James Joyce or Seamus Heaney, often quoting one of the authors randomly.

Sometimes I called my lover Seamus. And sometimes I called him "my sea mist." His eyes were light green mixed with flecks of shimmery gold. The color of a green ocean when the sun peeks through a substantial cloud and throws sparkles of light onto the surface of the deep water. I'd fall into his sleepy deep-set eyes back then. "I want to go swimming now," I'd say to him every time I wanted to linger in a kiss. "I want to get drenched and shipwrecked and lost in you, my sea misty one. Come on and let me."

I would anchor there, half-delirious in his Celtic gaze for years, while we lived in a modest apartment near his parents' home. He taught at the same Catholic high school his father did. Following his dad's legacy, he instructed his students in geography and social studies with a distinctive passion. Despite the meager pay, he took his summers off to travel to Europe with his family, spending his free time tracing his genealogy, divining the paths of his colorful Irish ancestors. Though he made pilgrimages throughout the western half of Ireland, he never made it up to Mount Brandon.

"That path up to dear old Brandon keeps eluding me," he'd always tell me on his return. "Let's try and make it up there together one day, just us."

I would spend most of my summers without him. His family wasn't fond of seeing him with "the boy he lived with," as I was so often referred to. We spent holidays apart as well, so that his family could have their "private hours." Climbing up this mountain today, for a moment, I vehemently want all that time he spent away from me back.

We fought over the repressive climate that pervaded the atmosphere in the household he grew up in. We fought over his refusal to come out and acknowledge our relationship to members of his extended family. I wouldn't make him give up his faith in Catholicism, but I shudder even today thinking how he would pray that "our fornication would not condemn us to hell," as his mother so often reminded him.

"Screw the Pope!" I screamed at him one day, flinging his church bulletin across the kitchen. "No one can dare denounce what we share between us. No Catholic church, no priest, no holy book can interpret what I share with you as anything but sacred and blessed."

"I pray to the saints that what you say is true."

"You don't have to supplicate to your hollow statues of Saint Joseph." I grabbed his arm, knocking him off balance for a moment. "You don't have to recite your pithy Act of Contrition or make the sign of the cross at your mother's built-in holy water font or rub the Sacred Heart medallion you refuse to take off. You only have to acknowledge that what you feel for me is real. Just trust that."

I kissed him then. Kissed him so hard I knocked my front teeth against his own, my tongue almost blocking out his air passage, forcing him to pull back for a moment. But he returned the stark impulse with his own passionate embrace, breathing with all his force into my lungs, taking me down to the floor, to his arms, where I always knew we were sanctified.

Now it is this relentless Irish wind whirring inside of my lungs as I lunge forward up this steep path. The violets are bent down all around me. The white clover is woven through the grassy plains like the lace rendered from stars and the clouds are hung on a pale scrim, almost daring to descend on top of me and cover me in their gray bulbous fog.

Hikers are moving past me in pairs and small groups. They are laughing out loud and stomping quickly up the path. Someone calls out from a tightly knit pack, "On to Bran's head! On to the top of Ireland!" I cannot keep pace with their vigorous gait, so I fall back a bit and begin a reflective saunter through the rough fields. Along the shoulder of this mountain ridge, I notice a photo opportunity with the glacier-molded valley of the Owenmore River. But I don't pause to take out my Nikon.

Instead I walk steadily, slowly up the increasing slope of the mountain. It is here I locate a pre-Christian Celtic sanctuary known as Binn na Port. It is a plateau promontory that juts out of the side of Mount Brandon, protected by two thick stone walls. A man asks me to snap a photo of him and his wife, standing against the ancient fortification. I oblige his request, then lean for a moment on one of the iron-age walls and reflect on the tribes that might have stood here, huddled against the ambush of their enemies.

"Seamus," I whisper to the cracked, moss-covered stone. "We were each other's fortresses. Each other's stronghold. Weren't we, sea mist?"

The name Binn na Port translates as "Peak of the Fort." But my guidebook also suggests that an alternate name adheres: "Peak of the Music." I listen for the far-off sound of winsome Norns or faerie harps. I listen for something that might remind me of the Irish band Clannad. Or even Enya or Loreena McKennitt. But I am met with the unceasing whoosh of the wind rushing against the edges of the craggy rocks and cliffs that envelop me.

Seamus used to crave Celtic music. He haunted Irish bars, swallowing down glasses of dark Guinness and tapping his feet to the fiddles and pipes and accordions of traditional Irish tunes. "I want to come back from the dead one day, reincarnated as a modern Van Morrison," he'd say. "I'll make my recordings with The Chieftains and lament the passing of the old ways."

"But you don't believe in reincarnation," I pointed out to him sharply that day. "You're meeting me in purgatory, aren't you?"

"I believe in Irish ghosts, however," he winked back. "And if you're not careful with your casual blasphemy, I'll come back with heavy chains to firmly bind you with."

Since he has passed away, I have come to believe that those chains he once eluded to are real.

Sometimes at night, he would play "Carrickfergus" and sing softly along with Van Morrison's voice playing on the stereo. I'm listening now in the wind, for that low breathy mournfulness that used to fill his chest cavity and rise up through his vocal chords. I am listening now for his phantom. I am knotted within this rain-lashed defense shelter, longing to follow his voice up the side of this mountain. Aching to hear my departed lover call me to his side one more time.

But I cannot divine his voice out here. I am zigzagging up the summit now, through ancient, scratched bedrock, through fossils and broken snail shells. I pass through uneven ridges of scattered stone debris called moraine, loops of layered rock and passageways that wend through split-open boulders and the remnants of calcified ice glaciers.

I am climbing through millions of years of sedimentation, geologic history, and Irish myth. I am grazing the edges of rock where continents once collided. I am trekking upward, hundreds and hundreds of miles above sea level, to where the tips of matchless ice glaciers once covered the world.

This pilgrim's path I am on now opens up to an expanse of land that is inhabited by forceful winds and grand vistas. I lean into a makeshift railing that overlooks the Dingle Peninsula and a scattering of islands that float on the surface of seawater. I can't help wondering if legend prevails and this mountain takes its name from Saint Brendan.

Dubbed by his contemporaries as "The Navigator," he was born near the present city of Tralee and became a highly educated monk during the dark ages. Myth has it that Brendan, along with sixty other monks, sailed out to locate the Isles of the Blest in an ox-skin boat launched from a cove at the base of this mountain. A seven-year voyage took him to the coast of what is known as America, long before Columbus was ever born. The saint and his followers went in search to find the place where God resides, although there is scant evidence that the journey ever took place.

I am breathing hard and nearly sweating in my pullover. I look up and see that I have arrived at the top of Mount Brandon at last. I can't help but kneel down next to a half-collapsed stone structure at the summit of this mountain. Did Saint Brendan rest at this unmortared oratory himself, gazing out to embody his vision of eternity?

I open my backpack at last and take out the bound container. I open my Swiss Army knife and cut the plastic bindings holding the contents intact. I set the box on the edge of the remnants of a stone wall and carefully unlatch the metal lid. The fierce tendril of a southern wind gust scoops the powdery dust into the air and in a flash, the container empties and my lover's ashes are suddenly mixed with the untamed field grass and the edges of a brooding fog that seems to threaten to swallow the open plain entirely.

For a moment, the air seems electrified and the wind switches directions, blowing at first from the south, then from the west, then back again to the south. I take in a few deep breaths as I patiently wait for the last convoy of hill walkers to finally exit the summit overlook before I shout out my beloved's name.

"Seamus, my sweet sea mist!" I shout over the edge of the precipice. "If I could fall into the deep green vapor of your eyes again."

The condensed air from the clouds has mixed with the impending haze.

For a moment, I stumble on a broken stone and catch myself on a clutch of sod before nearly toppling over the cliff edge onto the stony beach below.

But I'm safe and I begin to recognize the outline of that beach below me as the shores Seamus and I once sauntered on together. We were looking for washed-up crystals back then. The tide was out and everywhere we looked, there were perfect specimens of those coveted, see-through gemstones.

He laid down on the sandy beach back then, too tired to make any attempts to climb the mountain he wanted so desperately to conquer. He quietly instructed me to lay the newfound crystals over the places in his body where the cancer had invaded him. I followed his wishes and carefully placed two wet crystals upon his throat, and another three over his fragile breastbone. He took off his Sacred Heart medal for the first time since it was given to him by his mother and placed it in the middle of his rib cage.

"Are you praying right now?" I asked after a long while of listening to the sea wash against jutting stones.

He turned his head to look out at the constant churn of the Atlantic, then back toward the mountain, shielding his eyes as he gazed at the summit of Mount Brandon. "Of course I am praying. What do you think a good Irish Catholic boy does when he doesn't have enough strength to climb up his dream?"

"To whom are you praying?"

He didn't answer me then, but he is answering me today. He was praying to the fish-tailed mermen guiding the boatmen safely into harbor. He was praying to the sea Norns and water sprites that swirled in the legends told to him by his uncle and other Irish relatives. He was praying to the Virgin Mary and to Saint Bridget and to the Goddess Dana. He was praying to the lily of the valley sprouting just off shore, and the flotsam and old wreckage left over from decaying fishing boats. He was praying to the ferns bent down in the sudden gusts, and the sun that warmed his forehead, and to my hand that gently rested on his wrist that sunny day, as if together we could summon a stronger pulse.

I remember that during his last few days at the hospital, I asked him if he could still somehow find it in him to fight the cells that were overtaking his weakened lungs and throat. He told me that he was done with chemotherapy and that he had the "urge for going now," and that he simply wanted to be that suffocating hush that falls over the great fields of Ireland at twilight.

He wanted to be the lightning flash over the ring forts and medieval castles that line the gravelly Connor Pass. He wanted to be the electrified air that lingers within the Gallarus Oratory, that miniature church made of blocks of stone that resembles an overturned boat. He wanted to be the creak of the flaking boats moored at Dingle Harbor and the smell of twisted cord and twine in the drying nets of the fishermen. He wanted to be the sunset at the harbor and the sound of footsteps making their way home in Dingletown, in the cooling twilight air.

I am unsteady as I stand up and turn around in order to locate the trail that will lead me back down to the base of the mountain. The fog has developed into a thick green pea soup and I have to put my hands out in front of me in order to find my bearings. I scrape against the side of a pebbly wall and cut my hand. As I suck the blood from the edge of my finger, I think I can hear my Seamus singing from behind me, back from the summit of the mountain, those half-remembered lyrics to "Carrickfergus" coming back to me again: "I would swim over the deepest ocean, for my love to be with me."

By the time I make it back to town, the pubs and shops are all lit up and the fishing boats are all tied down in the harbor for the night. I stare out at the water, at the gray-green fog that still hovers just over the surface of the inlet. It is the same color of Seamus's eyes, the same inexplicable vapor. So I blow a saved-up kiss out over the lapping water, happy to know that he has come home at last.

Time Capsule

Sherman keeps forgetting the camera. Every time his partner Lucas asks him to go on a short road trip or to wander the bird sanctuary, they end up turning back, halfway down the sandy beach road. Last weekend, the batteries were mysteriously absent in the digital Nikon. Then just last night, when they went to search though the red coral coves under the causeway, Sherman dropped the lens kit into a tide pool.

"I like to take pictures in my head anyway," Sherman would insist.

Lucas tried to ignore his companion's forgetfulness and be soft with him. He knew that Sherman had been complaining of exhaustion, and losing himself in reruns of old *Hollywood Squares* episodes on the Game Show Network, or lounging for hours on the divan with his knitting bag and Carly Simon cassettes playing.

"Can't we just be like a normal couple and go shopping in town for some salmon and Merlot for dinner tonight?" Lucas had a slight nasal whine to his inquiry.

"I'm fine with avocado dip on celery sticks, sweetheart, but if you want fish, then just go get some."

Lucas kept thinking that Sherman was falling into a kind of entropy. After nine years of living together in their vacation home, he wondered if the two of them had fallen into a kind of somnambulism. While Lucas still maintains his antique warehouse through the Internet, Sherman gave up his financial consulting business after September eleventh and the two of them retreated to their summer beach house in Florida permanently. For the last several years, they have

---

This chapter appeared originally under the same title in the *Blithe House Quarterly* (http://www.blithe.com/), 8(3), 2004. Copyright 2004 Gerard Wozek. Reprinted with permission of the author.

Postcards from Heartthrob Town: A Gay Man's Travel Tales
Published by The Haworth Press, Inc., 2006. All rights reserved.
doi:10.1300/5732_19

found themselves wrapped in madras and sunscreen, looking for shells and pirate coins in the morning surf. But of late it was only Lucas who dug for the sand dollars and dried starfish, while Sherman slept through sunrise breakfast and well past *Oprah*.

"Do we have to keep that bucket of bleaching shells by the front door?" Sherman moaned.

"Last time I had it on the lanai you kicked it over when you sat on the folding chaise, so where would you like me to put it?"

"It's not like we need another goddamn shell in this house." Sherman motioned to the overcrowded white ledges next to the bay windows. "I mean, not even Martha Stewart wants to house a nature museum in her living room."

Lucas was silent, shaking his head. Then, after Sherman had crumpled onto the sofa, he folded his arms in a defiant posture. "You used to love collecting them because they reminded you of our long walks together. Telling each other stories and losing ourselves in the morning hours with the foamy rush of the Gulf and the morning fog burning off the palms."

Sherman punched on Carly singing "Boys in the Trees" and returned a blank stare. Lucas backed into a gilded bamboo stool and carefully scrutinized his partner. It was as if Sherman's body had been suddenly drained of its life force, as if Lucas could break off one of his partner's arms as though he had become a mannequin or a brittle statue.

"I'm going into town to get some groceries. Do you want anything?" Lucas could not compete with Carly's voice, which now seemed to be braided onto the cottage walls and wicker furniture. He grabbed the car keys from the flamingo ashtray and headed for the Impala.

Even though he was a resident of the beach town, Lucas liked to wander through the gaudy malls and stare at the souvenir postcard racks. He liked to eavesdrop on the tourists and try to capture for himself some of their virginal excitement with being in a foreign place. He liked to try on faux alligator sandals and Hawaiian shirts and sample the citrus aftershave balm and key lime cologne. Even though they had a fully stacked linen closet, he bought a new beach towel with a mermaid on it. He thought Sherman would like it because it might remind his partner of when they met at a piano bar on karaoke night and Sherman was singing "Under the Sea" from Disney's *The Little Mermaid* and the whole crowd was riveted.

Sherman was exuberant when they met. He collected almost everything: souvenir snow globes, match covers from restaurants, vinyl records of lounge singers from the forties and fifties, *National Geographic* magazines. He was an avid photographer and often wrote mini essays on the back of the photos, which documented where he was when he took the picture. He liked to go to the cinema in Chicago at least three times a week and he kept up with all the trendy gallery openings near the river district. His address book was crowded with acquaintances and friends from places all over the world where he had traveled and he was famous for his overnight parties that began with cocktails and supper and ended with a Bloody Mary brunch the following day. But when they moved from their loft in Printer's Row to Sanibel, Sherman gave everything away.

"I'm saturated," he stated the day the Paulist missions truck pulled up to take away his collectibles. "I don't need to keep looking back, memorializing the randy days of my youth."

Lucas interpreted the vast donation as either the onset of an early midlife crisis or a desire to begin afresh. Either way, they were heading for South Florida and all Lucas wanted to imagine for them were purple sunsets, spongy flip-flops, and barbecue shrimp parties under the soft glow of multicolored tiki lamps. For a while, all of that seemed to unfold, like a selection of slides seen through a child's vintage View-master. But when he thought of their life together now, he thought of a flurry of days hallmarked by separate meals and nostalgic television sitcoms and his partner's reclining body on the couch, motionless under a half-finished afghan.

When Lucas arrived back at the house, he noticed Sherman had gone to bed. He listened for a moment at the closed door to hear his partner's familiar snoring.

"It's only nine o'clock," Lucas remarked to himself, then shuffled back to the unkempt living room.

Lucas made himself a light salad of baby spinach and figs and poured himself a glass of Spanish sangria and added a few extra wedges of watermelon and oranges. He threw a plastic Hawaiian lei that had collected dust on a lamp shade around his neck and floated through the quiet rooms as though he were a newly arrived tourist anticipating the wet splash of an untried ocean.

He moved around some plants on the patio where his toe accidentally caught onto some loose tiles on the floor of the raised lanai. As he bent over to examine the disheveled terra-cotta, he noticed a deeper hole in the flooring. Underneath a layer of boards and gravel was a black metal box. The latched chest was about the size of a small coffin. "My gosh, you could put a four year old in here," Lucas said out loud as he unhooked the lid.

It was Sherman's treasure. Fragments from a lifetime crammed into what seemed like the kind of jumbo safety deposit box someone might rent out at a savings and loan. But there were no war bonds or rare coins or legal documents in the metal cavity. It was his partner's memory. Sherman had buried a sacred portion of his past life under the patio.

Lucas's fingers twitched for a moment. At first, he felt a powerful urge to slam the lid closed. How could he even begin to intrude on his partner's private history? But something made him lift out the bubble wrap anyway and examine the cherished bounty.

"What could provoke someone to save all this?" He spoke as though an observant stranger were watching. "And then to bury it here, no less."

Things seemed scattered and thrown in haphazardly. A map from the eighties to the metro system in Paris. A sample vial of Karl Lagerfeld cologne and an invitation to a Sunday tea dance at the Bistro dance palace in downtown Chicago. A skinny black leather necktie with a gold hoop earring stuck through it. A vinyl 45 of Gloria Gaynor singing "Honeybee." A champagne flute with a clove cigarette inside of it. A keychain from the Lucky Clover Motel with the number 131 on it.

These were items that could only hold sentimental value for the one who held them as keepsakes. Lucas felt like a voyeur but couldn't resist rummaging through the nostalgia, wondering what memory was inscribed on a toothbrush wrapped with orange dental floss. Or a tortoiseshell comb-and-brush set that seemed to still hold someone's hair strands. Or a nearly indecipherable ticket stub from a plane ride to Las Vegas.

For a long while, Lucas held in his hand a photograph of a man he'd never seen before. He set the picture down on the patio table, then held up his glass of melted ice and orange rinds. He went inside and came back with a bottle of Campari and poured himself a generous helping. He took in the cooling salt air and paused to listen to a gull's cry past a hedge of trees.

"Summer is over," he conceded. He looked at the stranger in the picture through his half-glass of liquor. He was handsome, perhaps no more than twenty-two, with a full head of strawberry blond hair and impossible broad shoulders. It certainly wasn't Sherman, but it looked like him in a way. Something in the eyes. Something captured in the click of the camera, something like poured honey reflecting out of those deep blue orbs, some kind of unearthly light that seemed to say, "Take me in. I want to hold him and be his. Be possessed by him and share this secret ecstasy."

Lucas felt his heart racing. After all these years, could it be a kind of jealousy? It was the only procured photograph in the box. Just scattered memorabilia filling the rest of the chest, cresting the dewy face of the young man in the photo: a Snoopy Christmas ornament with the famous beagle holding out a red heart, an envelope with no letter in it, addressed to Sherman when he lived by himself in a university apartment near Evanston, loose confetti and a cocktail napkin with NEW YEAR'S 1981 embossed on it, an old concert program from the Chicago Symphony.

Lucas took another long drink of his Campari. He imagined the lost love letter. The look in Sherman's eyes when he had caressed the young man's cheek. He imagined the stench and the disco music at the late nightclubs, the woozy stumble into each other's pulsing heat, then the tuft of the bedspread at the Lucky Clover Motel, where they remained tangled in each other's arms for hours.

Lucas wanted to remember his own secret entry into joy with Sherman. He wanted to remember their urgent wet kisses, the way they'd stare into each other for hours. But it seemed so distant from where he sat now, with urgent mosquitoes biting at his wrists and a wilted arbutus on the sill. He felt like Ariel, the sometimes voiceless little cartoon mermaid, submerged into a dark, inert Disney ocean.

As he scrutinized the photo, he tried to untangle the mystery behind the passionate glance that Sherman had captured in this photograph, but he knew he would always remain barred from that covert romance. It was someone else. Someone his partner had wooed and savored. Someone Sherman had perhaps loved; someone, not Lucas.

He held the photograph tenderly in his hands, and then placed it back into the memory chest. Delicately, he set the little relics like a halo around the sanctified Apostle of Love. The saint in this sarcophagus hadn't grown old; in fact, he would never age. He was still all stealth and bluster. An aura of potent sexuality seemed to radiate from him. His smile, his half-delirious, desirous grin, deified forever under this cottage patio.

Lucas sealed the box and placed it back in its grave. He walked back into the house and looked over the divan, which was layered with cracker crumbs and loose yarn scraps. He tiptoed up the stairs to the bedroom to his lover. His bare feet were chapped from walking over driftwood and rough stones and he scratched at the sunburned outline of a sandal strap. He ached to feel an urgent tide swelling over his ankles. For a warm wave to curl over him and pull him out to some remote island. For an undercurrent to sweep him into Neptune's arms. To be engulfed once again.

He knelt over his aging companion and stared at Sherman's mouth agape in the enveloping darkness. His companion was breathing steadily, the air rushing to fill his lungs, to fuel his dreaming. "Where are you now, my husband?" Lucas whispered to his half-wheezing lover. "Dugan's Bistro near Hubbard? Some old smoky casino on the Vegas strip? A cheap motel with your secret lover?"

Lucas moved his face so that it hovered closely over Sherman's. "Nine years and not a word about the man in the little box under the patio." Lucas spoke quietly above the blowing air conditioner. "Nine years and you never spoke of him."

He thought of how he and Sherman met. Moved in with each other so quickly. Took trips together collecting postcards of all the exotic gay meccas: Palm Springs, Puerto Vallarta, Mykonos. How together they talked of embarking on this early retirement and of antique hunting and shared reading lists. How Sherman would have time to take photographs of seascapes and Lucas would take up his old hobby of landscape painting, and replicate those ocean views onto canvas.

Lucas panned the room and saw that the walls were still empty. Only a frameless mirror reflecting back indigo shadows and his face, which at the moment seemed somewhat disheveled and barely recognizable.

"At last," Lucas whispered under his breath. "This is what it's like to move into our sought-after, perpetual vacation life."

He gently curled next to Sherman the way he always slept next to him, and placed his husband's hand into his own. He stared at the patterns of light that danced on the ceiling of their bedroom. Sherman's rhythmic snoring soothed him and he liked the way his partner always smelled like buttercream frosting on a cake. He thought that tomorrow he would try to coax Sherman to get up for breakfast. He would bring him a sliced pink grapefruit, cut into little sections and sprinkled with granulated sugar the way he liked it. He would set out Sherman's favorite safari hat and persuade him back to the beach. Back to the tidewaters and the soft haze and the careless mornings. Together, he anticipated, they would find the perfect shell specimen.

"And pictures." He spoke out loud, though Sherman continued to snooze. "Honey, you will have to take more pictures."

Lucas imagined that he could hear the sound of the ocean coming in through the whirring air vents, even though the house was closed up and they were miles from the beach. He nuzzled into Sherman's musky armpit. After a long while, he drifted off into his own dreams, and the hand that held onto his beloved's so tightly gently opened, though neither one moved.

ABOUT THE AUTHOR

Gerard Wozek is the author of *Dervish,* which won the Gival Press Poetry Award in 2000. His short fiction has appeared in the *Harrington Gay Men's Fiction Quarterly* (Haworth), *Erotic Travel Tales* 1 and 2, *Best Gay Erotica 1998, Blithe House Quarterly,* and *The Road Within: True Stories of Transformation.* His award-winning poetry videos have played at festivals and conferences around the world. He teaches creative writing at Robert Morris College in Chicago.

Order a copy of this book with this form or online at:
http://www.haworthpress.com/store/product.asp?sku=5732

POSTCARDS FROM HEARTTHROB TOWN
A Gay Man's Travel Tales

_____in softbound at $17.95 (ISBN-13: 978-1-56023-623-8; ISBN-10: 1-56023-623-X)

202 pages

Or order online and use special offer code HEC25 in the shopping cart.

COST OF BOOKS_____

☐ **BILL ME LATER:** (Bill-me option is good on US/Canada/Mexico orders only; not good to jobbers, wholesalers, or subscription agencies.)

☐ Check here if billing address is different from shipping address and attach purchase order and billing address information.

POSTAGE & HANDLING_____
(US: $4.00 for first book & $1.50 for each additional book)
(Outside US: $5.00 for first book & $2.00 for each additional book)

Signature_____

SUBTOTAL_____

☐ **PAYMENT ENCLOSED:** $_____

IN CANADA: ADD 6% GST_____

☐ **PLEASE CHARGE TO MY CREDIT CARD.**

STATE TAX_____
(NJ, NY, OH, MN, CA, IL, IN, PA, & SD residents, add appropriate local sales tax)

☐ Visa ☐ MasterCard ☐ AmEx ☐ Discover
☐ Diner's Club ☐ Eurocard ☐ JCB

Account # _____

FINAL TOTAL_____
(If paying in Canadian funds, convert using the current exchange rate, UNESCO coupons welcome)

Exp. Date_____

Signature_____

Prices in US dollars and subject to change without notice.

NAME_____

INSTITUTION_____

ADDRESS_____

CITY_____

STATE/ZIP_____

COUNTRY_____ COUNTY (NY residents only)_____

TEL_____ FAX_____

E-MAIL_____

May we use your e-mail address for confirmations and other types of information? ☐ Yes ☐ No
We appreciate receiving your e-mail address and fax number. Haworth would like to e-mail or fax special discount offers to you, as a preferred customer. **We will never share, rent, or exchange your e-mail address or fax number.** We regard such actions as an invasion of your privacy.

Order From Your Local Bookstore or Directly From
The Haworth Press, Inc.
10 Alice Street, Binghamton, New York 13904-1580 • USA
TELEPHONE: 1-800-HAWORTH (1-800-429-6784) / Outside US/Canada: (607) 722-5857
FAX: 1-800-895-0582 / Outside US/Canada: (607) 771-0012
E-mail to: orders@haworthpress.com

For orders outside US and Canada, you may wish to order through your local
sales representative, distributor, or bookseller.
For information, see http://haworthpress.com/distributors

(Discounts are available for individual orders in US and Canada only, not booksellers/distributors.)

PLEASE PHOTOCOPY THIS FORM FOR YOUR PERSONAL USE.

http://www.HaworthPress.com

BOF06